Awakened

A Seelie Court Chronicle
Part Two

J.B May

Dedication

One person has been invested in every part of this story. He told me when things were rubbish, offered me a unique perspective when I had none and helped me find my way back to the big picture when I was lost in the unimportant details.

For Michael,

You are only sixteen years old and already a better person then I could ever hope to be, this book is for you.

Acknowledgements

I want to thank all the fans who bought a copy of my first book. I had feared the only copies sold would have been the ten that were purchased by my family to be 'supportive', so seriously a huge thank you goes out to you. It warms my heart just thinking that someone somewhere is reading something that's so special to me, and I hope it's bringing you joy.

To the amazing Sue Kennedy, who is always keen for the next part of the story, your encouragement gives me the boost of confidence I need to finish.

A special thanks to my nanna Patrica and my grandma Margaret, both of whom were eager to read my stories, that are well and truly out of their comfort zones. I love you both and am grateful to have such strong and kind women to influence and motivate me.

To my best friend, Amanda, who has been by my side since I was four years old, I appreciate everything that makes you who you are and find so much inspiration in your exceptional qualities. Your courage, loyalty and ability to love wholeheartedly is infused into more than one of my characters, and they would be nothing without your spirit, thank you for everything.

To Ben, thank you for being my sounding board, even when you had no advice to give.

Table of Contents

Introduction

Sadness and LOSS don't stop the world from spinning, even when it feels like it should. The inevitable is still coming and it's time for Adaline to go home.

With her heart shattered and the world around her caving in, will she be able to embrace new LOVE or will she be lost in the darkness of her past?

When secrets and deception lie around every corner, LOYALTY has never been more important.

-1-

Adaline

I hate porridge. The consistency never feels right on my tongue and I cannot be swayed by the amount of sugar someone puts on it. Deklan forces another spoonful of the vile tasting sludge into my mouth and I swallow it, it's easier than facing the concerned look on his face when I decline. The last bowl of slop that I refused made him threaten hospital admittance and his face was too serious to be joking.

I can't remember how many days have passed since we left the island. All I know is it's been long enough that my clothes are loose around my waist and I forget how the sunlight feels when it touches my skin. Unfortunately, what I can't forget is the image of my uncles dismembered body or the hollowness that consumed Seth's once piercing brown eyes. I hate that I'm unable to block the images from my mind, but it would be worse to forget them, and after all, it's my fault they're gone. The constant reminders I see when I close my eyes are my punishment and I deserve it.

Another spoonful. It's worse the colder it gets, it tastes like glue between my dry lips. My face must reveal my disgust because Deklan lowers the next mouthful back into the bowl. He brings a hand to his forehead and tries to wipe the worry from his brow. He looks like he's aged years since I met him all those months ago, back then he could have passed as my older brother or a young uncle, but tonight he looks old enough to be my father. The battle seems to have taken something from each of us, something more than just our losses, it has stolen a piece of our souls and there's little hope for repair.

My friends have been taking turns babysitting me. A steady rotation of forced food, comfort checks and fretful faces. When my mother died, at least I had a piece of her that remained. The small fragments of her that lived on in my uncle gave me some comfort and I didn't realise how much I needed that glimmer of hope. They gave me something to cling to, and now there's nothing, only emptiness. No, not emptiness, emptiness would be a blessing. The unwavering stream of guilt and anger that washes over me isn't empty, it's vicious like rapids that try to sink an unmanned boat, the water hasn't realised that the captain is already dead and the battle pointless. I feel like I'm ready to give in and let the waves of sadness drown me. My abilities aren't helping either. I'm feeling everyone else's grief, every splinter of anger and guilt. Nothing compares to the agony I feel when I'm in Aedan's presence. He lost his brother and that's a kind of pain that can be unbearable to live with.

"I just want to sleep," I tell Deklan.

"You must eat Adaline. Please just have two more bites and some water. Then you can go back to sleep," he promises.

I swallow down the food as promised, but I can only stomach half a glass of water. I see the lines on Deklan's forehead deepen and it only adds to my despair. Deklan tucks me back into bed and I close my eyes to sleep. I feel myself drifting off, a willing victim to the blissful shadows of slumber.

It's still dark when I wake, or perhaps my eyes are just clinging to the darkness of sleep. I can hear the soft sounds of the others who are still slumbering. Deklan has fallen asleep in the chair by my bed, he has a book resting open on his chest. I remove the blanket from my bed and drape it over his shoulders, at least one of us should be comfortable. As I walk to the bathroom my legs give way, they can barely hold my weight, I'm weaker than yesterday. I feel the air begging to give me strength, but I refuse. I don't deserve to feel better, not yet, not ever.

I slip past Deklan into the second room. It's a cheap hotel, a cash only type of establishment that charges by the hour, but I'm told that the low profile makes it harder for our enemies to track us. Shay is sleeping next to Jason on a foldout sofa and Tripp is curled up on a single bed that looks too small for his long body. The last bed is neatly made, the polyester cover is still tucked firmly in place, and the pillows perfectly fluffed. I open the hotel door and step into the cool night air. It's gotten colder and the cement floor beneath my feet makes my toes shiver. I breathe the chilly air into my lungs until I feel snowflakes forming in my chest. I watch the exhale of my breath as it turns into a soft fog as it leaves my lips, the fog hovers in front of me for a moment before it floats away into the night.

"Cold isn't it," Aedan says from the shadows.

"Just a little," I reply.

I can feel his sadness lingering through the air between us. The earth aches for him, unlike myself, I feel Aedan welcome the strength of his element into his body. The energy enters through his feet, flows up through his legs until it makes its way to his core where it can ground him. It's probably the reason he's able to hold himself upright without the need of a wall for support. As I watch him I can see it's more than that, Aedan's stronger than I am and has less guilt to carry. It amazes me how he can find a reason to keep on going, it's a concept that keeps eluding me.

"Are you hungry?" He asks.

"No," I tell him.

"Are you sick of people asking you if you're hungry?" He asks with a small smile.

"I'm sick of everything," I reply.

"If you're okay with it I would like to take you to Ireland. Deklan has agreed. We will have enough men to protect you and after your birthday passes taking you to your father should be pretty straightforward," he says.

"I'm not going to the Vale and I want nothing to do with the Seelie, that world has taken everything from me," I say.

"But you owe..." he starts to say, but I cut him off.

"I owe them nothing," I cry.

"Of course not. I simply meant you owe it to yourself to find some happiness. You may be surprised to find that being among your own people can help," he offers.

"MY PEOPLE ARE DEAD!" I snap at him. He stands to comfort me, but I slam the door in his face as I storm inside.

Everyone springs to attention; the door has shaken the cheap hotel's foundations and the walls echo like in a nightmare. I walk past them, ignoring the concerned looks on their faces. Deklan has woken and his book is discarded to the floor. He starts to speak, but I ignore his words and climb back into bed. The dulled warmth of my body still lingers in the sheets and I pull the covers in tightly as I try to stop the chilly air from creeping in. Again, like every night since that night, I see their faces when I close my eyes. When sleep arrives I'm free of their haunting gaze and I'm blissfully numb.

-2-

Deklan

Adaline is still sleeping, and I need to stretch my legs before I tire and join her exhausted state. I close the door quietly and step into the other room. They have settled back to sleep after Adaline's outburst, but Aedan is nowhere to be seen. I step outside and find him sitting on an antique bench that smells strongly of damp wood and mildew. Aedan isn't a big man, but he's tall with broad shoulders and I'm surprised the decaying chair is able to hold his weight.

"She's falling apart," he says, sadly he's not referencing the chair.

"I'm aware, what do you suppose we do? You cannot compel her to function as you did her uncle. I'm out of my depth here Aedan, I admit I don't know how to help her," I say helplessly. "What about you? How are you holding up?" I ask him.

"I promised Seth I would keep Adaline safe, and I won't let him down just because he's no longer here," he says.

"That doesn't answer my question," I say, and he offers no more on the subject. "Are you confident about Ireland?" I ask.

"I am, she will be safer there," he replies.

"We leave for the stronghold in the morning then. Do try to get some rest, and as much as I hate to say it, you should really eat something," I tell him.

I wake Tripp, so he can keep watch while I get a few hours' sleep. I would go without sleep altogether if I could, but I'm afraid even I am not immune to that kind of deprivation. Tripp takes my place by Adaline's bedside and I try to make myself comfortable on his bed. Even now that he's a grown man I find comfort in his sweet grass like scent that lingers on the sheets. It's almost the same as when he was a child, except it's gotten more potent with age, almost like a fine wine. I think I knew all along my son wouldn't be like me. He is so much like his mother; how could I have ever thought he would become a wolf. I breathe his scent once more and relax into sleep.

There's little sign that the sun is going to make an appearance this morning, but I can feel it drawing near none the less. I wake the others, so we can get ready to make the journey to Aedan's stronghold. It's not my favourite idea, but I'm running low on options and trustworthy allies. Aedan has a loyal force back home and unfortunately, I don't think there's anyone in the King's service I can completely trust. Somehow Maura found us, and it wasn't from Aedan or Seth's actions. Wilber vanished during the attack on the estate, he is most likely dead, but if he's alive who knows what information he will tell his captives? Florence was badly wounded, so I sent her back to the Vale with Wren and Jackson where she can recover in peace. Right now, the only people I can trust can be counted on a single hand, and Aedan is one of them and he trusts his people inexplicably.

Getting Adaline moving is slow going at first, in her weakened state I'm surprised she still has the energy to fight us. I'm tempted to use some of the leftover sleeping potion to make her more docile, but I swore to myself I would never deceive her again. If we travel at the speed she's moving we might arrive only a few days before her birthday, and before then I need to find a way to heal her. I fear if we don't, she won't be strong enough to survive her transformation.

-3-
Tripp

After two questionable car services, one cheap commercial flight and a rickety car ride, that made the first two look like a luxury experience, we finally arrive in Ireland. The old man that's driving us to the stronghold speaks in drunken rambles that I can hardly understand, but Aedan does all the talking so the language barrier isn't an issue. After twenty minutes with the old man, I'm finding Aedan is equally as difficult to understand, which makes me wonder how much Aedan tones down his accent for our benefit.

I watch the textured hills that rise and fall in unique patterns across the countryside, it's like a patchwork quilt made of emerald greens and pale ferns has been thrown across the mountains. We pass through a small village that has been frozen in time, the beautiful structures would have been built in the eighteen hundreds and it reminds me of the simplicity back home.

The only sign of the modern world are the few scattered cars outside a well-lit pub. We cross a long wooden bridge and the car jerks each time its tyres get caught in an uneven plank, and there's quite a few. I pray silently that the bridge doesn't give way and drop us into the ocean. I don't think I'll ever be able to swim again, the very thought of it makes my veins shiver. I hold my breath as I try to forget the sensation of drowning and the scent of salt water that's filling my lungs doesn't make it easy.

The old man stops suddenly, he says something that sounds like a farewell and dumps us at an intricately woven gate that's guarded by high stone walls. So, this is Seth and Aedan's home, just Aedan's now, I remind myself.

As I set my sights on the estate I instantly wish I was here under better circumstances. The stronghold itself reminds me of a miniature version of the castle at court, I wonder if the house knows how lucky it is? It's free of the laws of our world, but it still has an otherworldly quality to it. My eyes follow the rich coloured moss that creeps up the stone walls, it's a beautiful mosaic of juniper and pea greens that encase the earth coloured stone. I smile as I feel the spirits of the trees brighten as a cool breeze travels down the hill. The trees that are scattered across the grounds are in an assortment of colours and sizes, which gives the estate the privacy people of our kind would want. Behind the castle, I can feel a powerful body of magic calling out to me through the earth. The intensity of it is overwhelming, it makes it hard for me to place the magic's origin.

"It's the yew tree in the grounds behind the castle," Aedan says. Like me, he has an affinity for the earth and can work magic close to my own but being a born fae my abilities are stronger and more pliable in this realm than Aedan's.

"I haven't felt anything like that since I left the Vale, is that why you chose to live here?" I ask him.

"In part, I grew up near here when I was young. The yew was small back then, only five hundred years old at the time of my birth," he comments.

Several vampires greet us as we approach the gate, all sharing the same paled complexion as Aedan, they fall from the trees like creatures of the night, silent and unseen until they want you to. A few women circle Adaline who's resting weakly against my father's side. Aedan whispers instructions to the Egyptian woman and the others link their arms tightly around Adaline as they whisk her into the castle. My father looks concerned, but Aedan nods his head to reassure him. Jason and Shay run ahead leaving Deklan, Aedan and I alone.

Aedan and my father continue knit-picking ways to help Adaline heal from this tragedy. I walk in an unsettling silence as they chatter. We step onto the cobblestone path when Aedan suggests a human therapist, he can fly someone in and erase their mind once Adaline's recovered.

I admit I have the same concerns that Adaline won't return to the girl she once was. Since Seth's death, she has been keeping her distance from me, and not just me, but everyone. I'm not sure if I'm grateful or unhappy with the distance after the way we left things on the beach. All I want to do is comfort her, but I don't want to overwhelm her, making her hate me in the process. Every time she looks at me my heart thumps excitedly, but then I look into her eyes and all I see is the void behind them. She's broken inside and it kills me. What she needs more than anything is someone else, someone she loves, someone that isn't gone.

"I think I know something that might help," I say aloud.

It's not going to be easy and there's a very good chance we may not be able to achieve it in time, but we don't have any other ideas. Judging from Aedan's expansive home and the wads of rolled hundreds I know my father has stashed in his side bag I doubt expense or space will be an issue.

-4-

SETH

The tips of my fingers feel numb, not so much numb, more frozen. I try to wriggle them, but the bones have stiffened under my icy skin. I try again, this time I feel a shiver move through me. The sensation closely resembles pins and needles but it's less intense, less tangible like it almost isn't real. The bones in my hands creak and crack as they start to move. One of my hands is higher than the rest of my body. My hand feels lighter, it's not weighed down in the hefty grain that's cradling me. A cold breeze swirls above the surface tickling my lone fingertip that's exposed, I feel the pull as the air brings the finger back to life. The breeze grows stronger, it finds spaces between the unknown grains and trickles into the cavity. My forearm starts to tingle, the pins and needles spread and intensify. I feel my elbow, it's a part of my body I have never given much attention to before, and I try bending it. It moves weakly underneath the fixed grain, I can hear the same cracking sound my fingers made when I forced them to respond. The prickly burning sensation keeps moving along my arm until it reaches my chest. My heart aches in response, feeling tight and fixed in place as it struggles to beat.

My lungs tremble as they inflate, the oxygen carried on the breeze forces its way in until my ribcage feels too small to contain the pressure. I open my mouth to release the air from my lungs, I breathe outwards and the grainy substance invades my parted lips. The organic bitter taste awakens my mind. Realisation dawns on me, I recognise the substance that's holding me, its soil. I'm buried in the earth, not just buried but sealed. My finger that's above the soil wriggles, spurring the others into action, I claw at the earth tilting my shoulders forward.

I feel the cool air brush against my forearm as it rises from the earth. My arm revels in the weightlessness of freedom, the eagerness to be uncaged sends adrenaline flooding through my body and I start making progress. I pull and push my body closer to the surface, but the pressure in my lungs is overpowering and my body begins to wean. Something blunt and moist encloses my exposed forearm. I tense as it tightens its hold on me. It tightens its hold and tugs at me, the force jerks my body forward pulling me from my grave.

I cough and choke on the soil that still clings to my mouth and throat. My body collapses onto something soft that's covering the ground. I expel the dirt from my airways, but my lungs still feel blocked and heavy. I lay immobile as my breathing evens out and my eyes begin to water. I rub the tears away with my hand, but it only helps the dirt find its way under my lids, making them water more. I rub and grind my fingertips against my eye sockets until they clear enough for me to see my own hand in front of my face. It's dark, I'm in a small clearing behind a lightless house, there's a shimmer of movement to my right. I look up to see a golden stallion staring down at me. The beast has traces of dirt around his mouth and nostrils, this creature pulled me from the earth and saved my life.

I try to stand, but I can't hold myself upright, my knees give way beneath me and I stumble. The horse lowers his impressive head until its chin is on the ground by my side. I reach out and grab hold of his mane. Once secure, he rises gracefully allowing me to stand against him for support. I look down at the place that was meant to be my grave. Pale blue flowers cover the patches of undisturbed dirt and the hole I was buried in feels shallow and cold. It shouldn't have been such a struggle to break free, but I know without the stallions help I wouldn't have made it out.

The horse keeps me straight as I walk towards the house. I enter through a kitchen door that's left swinging open. The horse is too large to enter so I steady myself on the first solid item I can find. I'm quick to notice that the floorboards have been shattered and broken.

23

Pieces of tables and chairs are scattered across this room and the next. I can see dark dried stains that resemble blood on the carpet and fragments of broken floorboards. What happened here? I ask myself. Perhaps this how I ended up buried in a shallow grave in the back garden.

I stumble through the rooms one by one, but most of the damage appears confined to the front end of the house. I enter the final room. It's barer than the rest. There is a mild sweet smell in the air, like flowers. The open closet appears to be filled with dresses and gowns, this room must have belonged to a woman. I close the door and make my way back to the kitchen. I open the fridge and the small light illuminates the room. I remove some juice and containers of cold meats placing them on the table. I don't suppose the owners will mind a few missing items of food given the state of the house. I turn back to the fridge and retrieve a bag of carrots. I tear open the bag, emptying the carrots onto the floor by the open back door. A carrot rolls over the lip of the door frame and onto the grass outside. The horse leans his head down and digs in, he enters the kitchen as much as his body will allow and has devoured all the carrots before I've sat back down. Poor guy seems hungrier than I am.

My throat still stings, I chew the food longer than necessary; the small pieces slide down my dry throat with ease and hopefully they can help clear the remaining dirt with it. The juice helps, it's cool and soothing on the abrasions in my throat, and I think the sugar does more than anything. I return to the fridge and find some celery sticks. I place them in my jacket pocket and make my way outside. The horse sniffs wildly at my pocket begging for his treats. I remove one and give it to him, in his excitement he almost swallows my hand in the process.

"I'm going to need your help horse. If you could tell me who I am and what I'm doing here that would be ideal, but I'll settle for you showing me the way to civilisation. If you can do that you can have the rest," I tell him patting the celery in my pocket.

The horse huffs, but he understands what I'm saying and starts leading me away from the house. I give him another stick of celery as a reward, which he gladly consumes in a loud elated breath. I lean into him as we walk. The steadiness of his breathing comforts me as we wander through the darkness. He leads me through a winding path of overgrown trees and rough undergrowth. The uneven ground makes the journey difficult, but the horse doesn't appear to be struggling. Once we are clear of the trees the moonlight reveals a sandy beach. The moon hangs high above us shining brightly as it guides our path towards the sand. The horse steps onto the shoreline, ignoring the fact that it tries to sink him and makes his way towards the water. He looks back as if asking me to hurry up and join him. I look out across the ocean and I can see the coastline of another island not too far away. There's no way I could swim it even if I wasn't in my weakened state. The horse grunts loudly, annoyed by my lingering. I step forward until the water washes against my shoes. The horse leans down so I can climb atop him. Once I'm secured on his back the horse starts forward, dragging us both into the ocean.

"Fuck, I hope you know what you're doing Horse," I tell him.

-5-
Deklan

I called the HBC cleaning crew a few days ago, and they should be arriving on the island today. House brownies have run our mortal realm cleanings for as long as I can remember, their main purpose is to ensure that the mortals don't find evidence of our kind in the form of bodies, but they also do the odd large-scale clean-up. A few years ago, they got organised and legitimised their services across all three realms. Brownies have always remained neutral and have worked diligently for both sides since the split. I'm confident they can repair the damages and remove any traces of our kind from the island before new tenants take it over in a months' time. Tripp had the brilliant idea of bringing the horse that Adaline was fond of to Ireland to help her heal. I emailed Milton, the head of HBC last evening, I asked him to procure the horse and ship it over, hopefully, the thing isn't dead already.

I dial Milton's number, he answers gruffly and informs me that his clean-up crew had arrived a few hours ago. When I hired him, I had informed him of the two bodies buried in the back garden that needed removal. I didn't say anything to Adaline, but in the event of a fae death the bodies are dissolved by magic fire and the ashes scattered back in the realm of their allegiance. It's a tradition we have practised since the great divide, that way the magic that flowed through the deceased's veins is returned to the boundaries that protect the fae realms. Despite the importance of the tradition, the last thing Adaline needed to know was that we would dig up her uncle and would-be boyfriend from their graves just to burn them.

Milton gives me a rundown of the invoice he's going to send and not surprisingly the damage was double what I had estimated. As he reads the list of services provided he says, 'disposal of one corpse'. I wait as he continues to complain about the difficult disposal the gargoyle blood caused, eventually he reaches the end of his extensive list, with no mention of a second body.

"What about the other body?" I ask him.

"My men only found one corpse under the blue flowers as instructed. There were some gargoyle corpses left behind, but stone removal is priced differently," Milton says.

"The corpse that your men removed, was it disfigured or intact?" I ask.

"They invoiced for a small removal bag along with a normal one. I would say the body was in pieces, that's usually the only time we use the small ones unless you had a child or small animal?" He says.

"No, we had no small animal or children pass. Did you recover the horse I emailed you about last evening?" I ask.

"No, the only horse we found was dark in colour with an injured leg. My men sent it to be healed on the farm before it's returned to the humans," Milton says.

Milton promises to send the invoice this evening and we end the call. The brownies don't make mistakes not when it comes to money or cleaning. What could have happened to Seth's body? I doubt Maura would have returned to claim a lifeless corpse, and what about the horse? Neither of them would have gotten up and flown away. What if Seth wasn't entirely dead? I discard the thought, the boy was gone when we put him into the earth, I listened to the stillness of his heartbeat. He was dead, of that I am certain. The last thing I want to do is get Adaline's hopes up, but Aedan is another story, he may be able to handle it better.

I make my way through the castles winding halls until I find Aedan sitting at a glistening oak table in a regal chair, his head hangs low and his elbows drill into the antique wood. I can hear the soft mournful sob escaping his lips. He hasn't cried since losing Seth if anything he's been impressively resilient. As I watch him drowning in his sorrows, I can feel how lost he is, he's as broken as Adaline is, the difference is he's better at hiding it. I step back before he notices my presence, I can't do it to him, I can't inflict false hope on a soul so clearly shattered.

I leave Aedan to his grief and decide to check on Adaline. The vampire women that collected her from the gate have settled her into a grand room that could rival the guestrooms at court. The bed has gold accents and the room is filled with an assortment of relics that Aedan and Seth must have collected over the centuries. I stare at the beautiful trinkets that lesser beings would have lost to time, Adaline looks at home here; her soft features blend seamlessly into the expensive surroundings. She is sleeping comfortably in the plush bedding and it almost looks like some of the colour has returned to her cheeks. A vampire woman who resembles Cleopatra sits by her bed watching something on a cell phone with her earbuds in. The woman didn't even glance up when I entered, but I could sense she was aware of my presence by the way she lifted her shoulders ever so slightly.

Knowing Adaline is safe, I walk down the old halls until I find my son's room. It's smaller than Adaline's with less extravagant furnishings, but it's still nicer than his bedroom at home. Tripp's sitting on the bed with a book in his hand, he hides the cover quickly, but I caught the word trauma on its spine. I can't deny the genuine feelings he has for Adaline or the anguish I feel on his behalf because his affections are not returned. The last thing I need is for Adaline and Tripp to be romantically involved, but I still don't want to see my son suffering such heartache.

"Do you need something?" He asks.

"Yes, I need your opinion on something," I reply. "I spoke to Milton, he informed me that there was only one body for removal. I believe the body was Adaline's uncle. Seth's body is nowhere to be found, and the horse you mentioned is missing. What do you think?" I ask him.

"I don't know. Could he be alive?" He asks.

"I was certain he was dead, we all saw it, but vampire hearts do beat slower than any other fae, maybe we were wrong?" I say, grasping at straws.

"He was definitely dead, I felt the earth when we placed him in his grave, trust me he was gone… What did Aedan say?" He asks.

"I haven't told him, I don't want to raise his spirits," I reply.

"I'll go, I can check for myself. Adaline would never forgive us if she found out that we didn't bother checking. One of Aedan's men is dating a porter of the leprechaun variety, I'll see if he can help," he offers.

I'm surprised by my son's willingness to try and locate the man who stands between him and Adaline, I don't know if I would be so gallant as to do the same. Tripp wanders off to find the vampire to ask for his lover's aid. Leprechauns are tricky bastards, but there is no faster way to travel than with a porter. I say a silent prayer into the night wishing for a miracle. As fond as I have become of Seth my prayer is more for Adaline's benefit. Wishing him back will mend the part of her that's broken, I just wish I could return her uncle too. I pull the book from under my son's pillow and flip through the pages, maybe the humans will offer something that could help because I'm willing to try anything at this point.

-6-
SETH

At one point I thought we weren't going to make it. Horse began to succumb to fatigue and faltered, but he pushed on despite the exhaustion. If the weather had been different and not in our favour we wouldn't have stood a chance at all. Horse is sleeping on the sand next to me, letting him catch his breath is the least I can do after all the effort he put into getting me here. The beach is empty at this early hour, the ocean is still, and the birds are beginning to wake. I can see the sun starting to rise on the edge of the ocean's horizon. The light turns the sky and ocean into a portrait of glistening golds and pale blues. As the sun moves higher in the sky the colours shift into pale pinks and robust oranges. It's incredibly beautiful.

I tap Horse on his side and tell him it's time to wake. He snorts loudly, disapproving of my nudges he snaps his enormous teeth in my direction making me jump. I can't exactly blame him for being irritable, it took a long time to get us here. I can see the island in the distance and the space between us doesn't look to be an impressive journey but looks can be deceiving. I decide to follow Horse's lead and have a rest for a little while. I lay my tired body against him, drinking in his warmth to find comfort.

"Wake up kid," a disgruntled voice says. "Wake up the tides changing," the voice repeats. The stranger kicks my leg forcing me to awaken.

"Where am I?" I ask the voice.

"Shit you must have tied one off. You're on Myrtle Beach boy. Why do you have a horse on the beach? You know they don't allow dogs, no way you'd be allowed a horse out here," he starts to prattle.

"We swam from the island," I say vaguely, still rattled with exhaustion.

"Jesus you did have a big night," he says.

I open my eyes to point towards the island right in front of us, but it's gone. Vanished as if it had never been there in the first place. I look at both sides scanning the ocean for signs of land but there's nothing, just an endless emerald sea. Could it have really been that far away? Maybe I've lost more than my memory. I lean against Horse using his mass to stabilise myself. Once I'm sure that my legs can hold my crushing weight I release my grip and take a tentative step. I notice I have lost one of my shoes along with the sock and my jeans are still heavy with water and traces of sand.

"You alright boy?" The man asks.

"I'm afraid not, I'm having trouble with my memory," I tell him.

"Gosh, come along then. My wife will have my head if I leave a loony stranded on the beach," he says.

"I'm not crazy," I reply.

"Do you know your name?" There's a long pause as I try to find the right title to describe me, but I can't place it. "See, you could very well be crazy," he says. "I'm John, I live not far up the beach, you and your pet can come to the house and we can find someone to help you."

By the time I rouse Horse, the old man is a long way ahead, and he looks back annoyed at our dilly-dallying. Horse and I hurry to catch up to him, but he's surprisingly spry. The walk is longer than I expected, and my body isn't responding well to this much exertion, Horse nudges me forward each time I misstep.

We approach a close grouping of trees with a small sandy path down the middle. As we walk up the crest I worry Horse won't fit, but he glides through the path with ease. At the top of the path, hidden amongst a thick cluster of trees and overgrown shrubs is a tiny green and white cottage. The paint on the house is in unexpectedly decent shape compared to the rusted pieces of cars and scrap metal that swamp's the front yard. The cottage has pots and urns in various shapes and sizes scattered across the porch, making it look like an obstacle course more than a place to relax. Every pot contains a different type of plant, each of them growing in abundance, the bright coloured flowers and creeping vines wrap around the fencing protectively like they are stopping the house from blowing away.

John walks up the front steps and removes his shoes at the door. He brushes off the sand from his feet and legs until he's satisfied he's clean. He holds out the brush he used on his trousers and waits for me to do the same. I remove my single shoe and sock then brush my pants vigorously. Once I pass his inspection he enters the cottage and allows me to follow. I hear a loud thump behind me and turn to see Horse attempting to climb the small staircase. I pat him on the head and tell him he can't come. He seems angry with me and turns away to sulk.

Inside the house, the layout is clean and simple, apart from the potted flowers and greenery that hang from one wall or another. I follow John silently until we reach a small kitchen, in the centre is a tiny round table just big enough for two and a woman is sitting at it sipping her tea. The woman is the same age as John, late seventies perhaps, both have greying hair and thick-rimmed glasses. John whispers something into his wife's ear and kisses her cheek lovingly. Suddenly my eyes see something else. No longer the small table occupied by an elderly couple. I see a grand glossed table in a great hall, surrounded by three beautiful figures, with faces I just can't place. I try to grasp the memory but as soon as I'm close the memory fades.
"My wife asked if you're hungry. I told you he's not right in the head?" John whispers to his wife.

"Sorry, I am hungry, and my horse is probably starving," I tell the sweet-faced woman.

"Well, you sit down, and I'll make you some lunch. John, you take some fruit and veg out of the crisper and give them to the boy's horse," she orders. "I do love horses, such sweet animals."

The woman begins fluttering about the kitchen, shifting back and forth moving one thing or another. In almost no time at all, she places an oversized pile of pancakes on the table before me. I forget all sense of formalities and scoff down the food in heaped mouthfuls, at one point I forget to breathe and begin choking. The lady sits patiently watching me until I become uncomfortable under her stare. I swallow another forkful and wipe my sticky lips on the sleeve of my jumper. I can still smell the salt and sand that lingers on it.

"Thank you," I tell her.

"You're welcome dear. You can call me Emilia," she says.

"Not that I'm not grateful, but why are you being so kind to me?" I ask. I don't know who I am, but I know there's something about my past that tells me that people didn't usually trust me. I can feel it, it's a sense of caution lying underneath the surface, like a silent annoying voice that becomes enraged as it tries to warn people away from me.

"Is there a reason I shouldn't be kind to you?" She asks. "The Lord wants us to be kind to our neighbours."

"No, you needn't fear me," I lie, but the voice in my head screams yes.

"Let's call the lawman and he can sort all this out for you," she says. Her offer stops my breath and I clench my fist around the fork in my hand. Alarm bells start pounding in my head, maybe I'm a criminal, why else would I shudder at the thought of the police? Am I on the run? I ask myself.

"No police," I tell her. She looks concerned, maybe she's thinking the same thing as I am. "Please, I don't want to be left waiting in a cold police station all day, I just need to rest and hopefully my memory will return, don't worry I'll sort it out," I say.

"Very well," she says. I can feel the intensity of her gaze as she considers what she's going to do. I figure she will call the police the second I leave. "We have a room out back if you want to stay for a while. If you haven't figured yourself out by the week's end we will have to call someone," she offers.

I accept her proposition and my mind relaxes some, but I can still feel the worries of my past teetering on the edge. I just need some time, time to remember myself and where I'm meant to be, by then someone will be looking for me, I just hope it's not the person who buried me in that grave.

-7-
Tripp

I'd be lying if I said Seth's miraculous return is number one on my wish list, he's probably the last person I would bring back from the dead if I had a choice, but Adaline's fading away and the truth is I care more about her wellbeing than hating a dead man, she needs him, and I need her to be okay. One of Aedan's men Roland is dating a Leprechaun named Leo, I met the pair last evening at dinner. Leo seems nice enough for a porter, but usually, their kind are charlatans. Leprechauns have a love of games and double-crossing, but if he's dating a vampire, clearly, he doesn't fit the standard mould. Leprechauns aren't tiny creatures in tall green hats as humans would have you believe, in fact, they are tall noble creatures. They are humanlike in appearance, but with far greater beauty. The only thing that gives away their true nature is their pointy ears and piercing spring green eyes.

Leo is willing to oblige my request if anything he seems overly excited at the prospect, but his partner Roland isn't impressed with our plans. Leo can only transport so many people at a time and that means leaving his partner behind, in case we have to bring back something as big as a horse.

I pack a small backpack and meet Leo in the courtyard by the impressive yew tree. As I step into the garden I feel the tree's energy. It's like nothing else I have ever seen. The trunk is a mess of woven roots twisting and turning to form a strong trunk. The branches start out high then swoop down towards the earth. The bowed branches look like hammocks, almost comfortable enough to sleep in.

"Amazing isn't shea," Leo says, his accent matching the one Aedan let slip in the car.

"Beautiful. We have trees similar to this in the Vale, but I don't recall any being this spectacular," I admit.

"The yew will give my magic a boost, if we end up having to bring a horse back we will bloody need it," he says.

Leo steps forward and places his hand on the yew. I can see the life force of the tree shimmering out of the bark and into Leo's hand. When he releases his grip, there's a glow about him. Nothing compared to the glow that encompasses Adaline when she's practising magic, heck even when she's not using it she has a radiance about her.

"Okay laddie, take my hand and hold on tight if you let go I'm likely to drop you into the Atlantic and I don't swim," he says.

I take his hand in mine, I make sure to heed his warning and hold on tightly. I close my eyes and ready myself to teleport. When Leo lets go of my hand I open my eyes and we are back on the island, I recognise the dark outline of the estate behind the trees. I don't have long to reminisce, because I lurch forward and vomit. It's the projectile kind of vomiting where my throat burns and the back of my nose has a vile acidic scent, that won't go away. I vomit a second time and my chest hurts from the heaving force.

"Shite sorry, that happens to non-porters. Clean yourself up laddie and let's get moving I have a party to plan you know," he says playfully.

"One of your folk finally found the pot of gold?" I joke.

"Don't we wish. Lady Adaline's party actually, Aedan hired me to plan the big event. Oh, it's going to be amazing. I had French truffles ported in especially and wait until you see the cake, sugar-coated violets," he swoons.

I don't have the heart to tell him that Adaline probably won't be in any mood for a party, but then again there's time until the big day, and things could change. He continues prattling on as we walk the length of the house. I'm amazed by the clean-up the brownies have done. The inside looks in better shape than before the battle took place. We make our way to the back garden where we buried Seth and Jerry. The ground has been filled in and I can feel the seedlings from the instant grass beginning to sprout. There are still remnants of the forget-me-nots growing in scattered patches. I place my hand on the earth and allow my magic to ripple through the rich soil. I can sense where Jerry's body has been recently removed, but the other grave is cold. The earth calls out leading me toward the stables. I follow its pull until I notice the tracks left in the solidified mud. Horseshoe prints and the faint line of sneakers have dried in the once damp earth. The son of a bitch is alive.

=8=
Adaline

The giant bed is comfortable, but my limbs can no longer stand being this still. I raise my head from beneath the covers and see one of the vampire women sitting by my bedside. When I first arrived at the stronghold she was the woman who tried to undress me and put me in a bath. Clearly, nudity isn't an issue with vampires because she seemed taken back when I refused her. Some of the women were dressed like they were from a different time, and I guess they probably are. I remember wondering if their outfits had been inspired by the time of their human birth, or perhaps a favourite era from their long lives. The woman next to me is wearing a gold gown with a gold-rimmed collar and an open v slit between her breasts. She has flowing loose sleeves that drape down to her knees. Her dark hair is sharply cut, and bold black make-up looks like something Cleopatra would have rocked back in the day. No matter what she is wearing the woman is naturally stunningly beautiful.

"Finally awake my lady. Shall I draw you a bath?" She asks, what is this ladies deal with baths I wonder. Do I smell that bad? I ask myself sniffing the air surrounding me.

"No thank you. What is your name?" I ask.

"Neema, my lady," she replies.

"You don't have to wait on me Neema. I'm sure you have better things to do," I tell her.

"Aedan has charged me to be your maid. I was in the service of many rulers in my life, do I not please you, my lady?" She asks.

"It would please me more if you were off doing your own thing," I reply.

She looks concerned and a little wounded. She absorbs my harshness with a courteous bow and leaves. I feel guilty. I don't want to be unkind to people, it's not in my nature, but I can't help it. I find myself only having three settings these days, exhausted, irritated or miserable. I start recalling the days after the plane crash. Granted I spent them locked up in a cold hospital ward and not in a lavish castle, but it all feels the same. In a few short weeks on New Year's Eve at exactly midnight, I will be eighteen and my power will be unleashed. Deklan keeps expressing his anxieties in no uncertain terms about my inability to handle my change. I don't want to think about anything further than my next breath, but my abilities let Deklan's fears sink into me. Some days I would happily accept my fate and meet my maker, I can even convince myself that giving up is the right decision. Then I think of Deklan and the agony he would feel if I was gone. I think of Aedan and Jason who lost their brother to save me. I couldn't hurt any of them like that, they would be as devastated as I feel, and I cannot be that selfish.

I can hear Neema lingering in the hallway outside, the scuff of her shoes makes it impossible to go back to sleep. I open the door and tell her she can draw the bath she desires so much. She looks elated to discover that her services are in need. After she finishes the bath she tries to help undress me just like before, I tighten my arms pinning the shirt at my side. She is reluctant to leave me alone to undress, which seems crazy, I'm a grown person who can undress easily enough. Her smile tightens, and she complies with my wishes. Once undressed I lower myself gently into the exquisite bath she has prepared. I can smell rose oil and feel the gentle fizz of salt crystals dissolving in the bottom of the tub as they tickle my skin. Neema sure can draw a bath.

I relax into the warmth and try to close off my mind. I hear the sway of the water as it swims around my exposed skin, it's more than the water. I can feel all of my elements moving around me in unison, like a single layer of energy hovering around me, it's tangible like a second skin.

I feel the life force of the air, the heat of the fire burning two rooms away and the balance of the earth surrounding the stronghold. I raise my hand from the water, my skin shines, coated with a thin layer of rose oil and water. With my magic, I lift the water from the bath creating a sphere of swirling liquid. It swishes and sways above me, I call more spheres into the air to join it. They float like weighted bubbles rising and falling with the wave of my hand. I feel the magic running through my veins and I allow a small amount of its healing energy into my broken heart. I don't take much, not enough to numb the pain, but enough to make it manageable.

I flick my hand back and forth swatting the water orbs into one another until I'm left with one large orb floating above me. I lean forward and let the water dribble out until it runs down my head and shoulders, like a scented shower. I think back to when I was a child and my mother would pour a jug of water over my head to rinse the shampoo from my hair. It's soothing and more pleasant than most memories I've been thinking about lately. I welcome the reminiscence and hide away in it. When the water cools I climb out of the tub and my stomach rumbles for the first time in a week. Neema has laid out a towel and a thick robe on the vanity, I dry myself and adorn the plush robe. I open the bathroom door to find Neema standing by my bed. I wonder if she has been standing there the whole time? She has laid out a gown that's a beautiful blushed pink. It has a shoulder to one side and a thin tulle belt under the bust. It has a scrunched flower on the side and a cascade of fallen petals that scatter down the front of the dress. She looks so pleased, I reach out with my mind and can feel the joy seeping out of her. She takes pride in this like it's a job and there's no way I can refuse something that's made her so happy.

"I hope you have undergarments for beneath that," I tell her.

She smiles broadly and retrieves a fancy corset kind of top and underwear the same colour as the gown. I slip on the underwear beneath my robe and look at the corset quizzically.

"Let me help my lady, I have done these countless times," she begs.

I allow her to assist me but keep a firm hand held against my breasts. Her vampire speed is an asset because she has the corset bound in seconds. Once the dress is secured to my body she collects a brush from the dresser and gestures for me to sit. She combs my hair expertly, weaving out the knots without causing me pain. In a flash, my hair is braided and twisted into an intricate fashion atop my head. Neema splashes some makeup on my ghostly pale complexion and some pinked gloss on my lips. When she's finished I look in the mirror and admire her work. She truly is gifted, and her satisfaction burns brighter when I award her a small smile.

"Are you pleased my lady?" She asks.

"I am, thank you," I tell her.

Neema excuses herself after my stomach rumbles a second time and I know with her abilities she must hear it too, hence why I'm not surprised when she returns with a plate of food. She places the mixed fruits and cheeses in front of me, she also has a plate of bread and paper-thin meats. She places a large glass of wine down in front of me which makes me widen my eyebrows. I sip the wine and discover it's not like I had imagined. It's sweet and has a little bubble in it, champagne? I wonder. Whatever it is I feel it rise straight to my head. Neema must see it too because she urges me to eat and for the first time in a long time I eat because I want to, not because I'm being forced.

-9-
Tripp

Leo and I ported to the nearest neighbouring islands and checked with local law enforcement but there has been no sign of Seth or any unidentified bodies that may have washed ashore. We reach our seventh station and there's still no news. Leo suggests that we keep looking and put up flyers or a notice in the newspaper, but how long should I spend on this person who I saw die before my very eyes. What if he is alive and decides to never come home, for Adaline that would surely be worse than him being dead. Should I put Aedan and Adaline through the torture of never knowing? If he really is out there he would have contacted someone by now, at the very least his brother. There's a voice in the back of my mind hinting at something I'm not proud of. I'm shameful to admit it even to myself, but there is an upside to Seth no longer being in the picture, Adaline's affections may be open to someone else.

Leo ports us back to the island where we started our search, one more walk around the beach and we are certain the island has no hidden inhabitants. I explain to Leo that there's no way Seth would have survived the journey to shore and that telling anyone else otherwise would only cause them harm. At first, he doesn't seem to approve but eventually, he understands my reasoning and agrees with my wishes. I take one last lingering look at the estate in all its glory. I grasp Leo's hand and ready myself to travel.

We arrive back in front of the mighty yew tree and it's as glorious as when we left a few days ago. I place my hand on its crisp abrasive bark. I like the roughness of it, it's a testament to its age and resilience. I draw strength from the tree, a power it shares willingly.

I feel a subtle warmth in my abdomen, the yews healing energy remedies the nausea that still claws at my stomach. Leo's magic makes him the quickest way to travel but I wonder if the pain is worth the reward.

Aedan's stronghold is different from when I left two days ago. Every inch of the walls has been draped in a steady wave of passion vines. The vines have more flowers in bloom than nature would permit. I place my hand on one of the flowers and I can feel the magic vibrating through them. The passion blossoms are the perfect medley of burgundy's and violets, in time passion fruits will start to grow in their stead, but for now, the magic keeps them frozen in a constant bloom. As I enter the ballroom I find Aedan weaving his hands back and forth like an orchestra conductor. Instead of directing music he choreographs the wonders of nature. I can see him starting to weave unopened moonflowers between his floral masterpieces.

"Where have you been?" Aedan asks.

"Checking on the clean-up," I lie.

"Adaline doesn't want to celebrate Christmas, so I've gotten an early start on her birthday party. I know she only agreed for my sake, but I'll take what I can get. I think this could be the first step in her moving forward," he says.

"What about you?" I ask.

"I need to focus on Adaline, no time for anything else," Aedan replies and turns his attention back to his flowers. "Your father put your attire in your room for you to try on, you should check the sizing. After Christmas, the tailor returns to Dublin." He adds.

I thank him and leave him to his work. Before I go rest I stop at Adaline's room. Her door is ajar and I can see her beds empty. I press my hand to the heavy door and push it open further. Adaline is sitting in a Victorian slipper chair that's a mix of greens and gold.

43

She looks thinner and the blush in her cheeks has faded since our time on the island. She's in a thick bathrobe and her hair is pulled into a messy knot on top of her head. I don't see how Aedan can think she's healing, to me she looks more wounded than ever. I step forward and the creak of floorboards gives me away. She turns to smile at me, her smiles kind, but it doesn't meet her eyes.

"I hear there's a big party in the works," I say.

"Yes, Aedan insisted. I refused but it seems so important to him and Deklan," she says.

"Is it important to you?" I ask.

"Not really, it feels wrong to celebrate anything." She says.

"Things will get better, it is possible to move past this," I tell her.

"I am trying," she promises.

"Save me a dance at your party?" I ask. She smiles and nods.

I arrive back at my room and my eyes are so tired I can hardly see straight. I have to take a second look when I see my father sitting on my bed. Next to him is a large garment bag and a box of new shoes. His eyes look bright and I see a flicker of hopefulness flash across his face, but it's a short-lived expression. I don't have to tell him there was no sign of Seth, which is good since my father could always tell when I was lying. Am I lying? I ask myself. Yes, there were tracks, but that was all, tracks mean nothing. He's dead I'm sure of it. My stomach twists echoing its doubt, I ignore the sensation and climb into bed.

-10-
Adaline

By Christmas Eve I have fallen into a rhythm. I keep to myself mostly, I bathe daily, I wear the dresses Neema sets out for me and I eat the food she delivers. Every second day or so I walk through the garden for fresh air with Shay and spend some time sitting under the yew tree. Aedan has been busy for the last fortnight decorating the stronghold, he hasn't used traditional Christmas finery, but stunning flowers and vines cover the outside of the castle walls as well as in. The smell perfumes the hallways and even the surrounding grounds have a sweetness to them. The lush greens are vibrant against the crisp whiteness of the snow that fell the last few nights.

Christmas morning arrives, I can hear the merriment from the vampires celebrating in the lower levels of the castle. They sing loudly and off-key to Christmas songs that are foreign to my ears. Neema and Shay stop by and ask me to join them, but I can't. I'm not ready to be happy yet, and I can't find anything to celebrate. They look disheartened when I turn them away, but I know they understand.

While the fun continues downstairs I start on my routine. I soak in a long bath until the steam turns to frost, distracted by the festivities Neema hasn't put out anything for me to wear, I seize the moment and slip into something comfortable. Dressed contentedly in my thick nightdress I run my fingers through my wet hair and curl up on the bed. I scan through the assortment of books Aedan has sent up, but none of them grabs my interest. I flick on the iPad Leo has given me as an early birthday present. I begin searching through the shows on Netflix and decide on a sappy Christmas love story, it will probably bring me to tears in seconds, but crying is proven to be cathartic hasn't it?

Fifteen minutes in, and the heroine's mother has died and she's lost her way in the world. The tears come heavily, I snort into a tissue and let them fall. A knock at the door startles me, I had hoped that everyone would just let me wallow the day away in peace. I wipe the tears from my face and open the bedroom door. Tripp is standing there with a large brown bag in one hand and a book in the other.

"Morning," he says. "It's getting pretty crazy downstairs; do you think I could hide out here? I feel like everyone's looking at me like I'm a piece of meat."

"I thought Aedan told you that you were going to be the main course tonight?" I tease and stand aside to let him in. "What's in the bag?" I ask.

"Essentials of course." He pours the contents of the bag on the bed. There's almost every type of chocolate I could think of and several bags of crisps and popcorn. "We don't have food like this back home, which is probably a good thing, or I would be the size of a house." He laughs.

Tripp and I make ourselves comfortable on the bed. We watch an Adam Sandler movie, and then another one. We eat more junk food than my stomach can handle, and I laugh, genuinely laugh. I thought the last thing I wanted was to be around another person today, but I was wrong. The book he had brought was actually a present for me, it's a lovely vintage style journal bound in leather. He hadn't wrapped it because he knew I wasn't in the holiday spirit, his thoughtfulness makes the gift all the more special. The music downstairs dies down, the laughter vanishes into bedrooms and eventually we stop paying attention to the movies, instead, we sit and talk. He tells me stories about his childhood and his time at the academy. I tell him about mum and the wild things she used to do. We talk until I can hardly keep my head off the pillow.

I must have fallen asleep, because when I wake its morning and I'm alone in my bed. The chocolate wrappers and crisp packets have been picked up and placed in the bin. There's a blanket tucked securely around me and the candle I had burning next to the bed has burnt itself out. I lay still for a moment assessing the usual unpleasantness that finds my body in the early hours. Today I feel different, generally, when I wake I have had to catch my breath, I've forced myself to keep the air flowing in and out of my lungs. This morning feels different, breathing comes naturally, and my shoulders feel less weighted. Despite the buoyancy I'm feeling, there's still something weighing me down, a sense of dread from my ever-coming birthday. Five days to be exact, one hundred and twenty hours until I become full fae or seventy-two hundred minutes until I die, depends on how you look at it but who's counting? I don't think this is what mum had in mind when she complained about the struggles of getting older. I need to focus on training again, the fact is I'm not ready to die just yet.

-11-
Adaline

Neema arrives with her arms filled with bottles of soaps and lotions. She begins drawing me a bath while I wait patiently sitting on the beautiful, but somewhat stiff couch. My skin begins to shiver, and I wonder if it's just nerves or is it something more. Today is the day after all. It's what everyone has been waiting for. Aedan seems untroubled by my upcoming change, but Deklan has been radiating a world of fear all morning and I had to ask him to leave my side because his distress was making me physically ill. He continued pressing the fact that I'm not healthy enough and I haven't had enough training, but there's little I can do about it in the next few hours. I was thankful when he stopped reliving his own change. It sounded so unnecessarily brutal. Why should someone need to suffer so much to inherit what's rightfully theirs? It just doesn't seem fair. Tonight, when the clock strikes twelve, at the moment between this year and the next I will have to fight for what's mine, whether I want it or not. If I triumph I will be made whole, if I fail it will kill me. No pressure, I tell myself.

Between Neema and Shay, no one has attempted to annoy me with party plans or their opinions on my circumstances. If anything, this is the most normal day I have had in a long time. Neema, Shay and I have lounged around on my enormous bed eating leftover junk food that Tripp and I had shared, and we even drank some sweet fancy wine from Aedan's cellar. Shay shares only a fraction of information about her extended life which seems short compared to Neema's. Neema worked for the Egyptian royal families until the fall of their rule, she even bore witness to the plagues of Egypt. Neema knows now that most of the plagues were caused by natural disasters, but when she relived the night the Pharaoh lost his firstborn child I could feel how real it must have been for them.

Both my friends have lived full lives and experienced so much. I'm envious of their shared experiences, both good and bad. I'm eighteen in a few hours and I feel like all I've experienced is misery. No passionate stolen nights or extreme moments of joy. I've never even had sex and, in a few hours, my life might be over. The fear of all the things I'm not going to do starts to overwhelm me. Maybe it's the wine talking or maybe I'm finally having an overdue breakdown, either way, I feel myself losing it. Neema and Shay start cleaning up the mess we have made and excuse themselves, so they can bathe and change for the celebration. Alone in my room with a slightly swimming head, I begin to panic.

A nervous wave washes over me, my stomach churns and my hands start to shake. What if Deklan's fears are right and this change is going to kill me. The air around me starts forcing itself in and out of me at an accelerated rate, it becomes too fast for me to count. My heart is beating wildly as it tries to keep up with my panicked breaths. The intense thumping hurts my chest like my heart is attempting to break free from its bony cage. I try to slow my breathing and calm myself, but it isn't working. Calm breaths, calm breaths, I tell myself. I can forget about the danger of the almighty change because this panic attack is going to kill me first. I try to get up from the bed, maybe the movement will help. It doesn't. I collapse weakly onto my knees and lower my forehead to the floor. The coolness of the floorboards soothes my pounding head, but my heart and lungs are still wildly out of my control.

"Adaline are you okay?" I hear Tripp's voice carry across the room. He walks around the bed to see me on the floor shaking in an upright foetal position, on the verge of inducing a heart attack. He places his strong hands on the small of my back and starts rubbing in a gentle circular motion. He whispers comforting sounds that are lost beneath my loud laboured breaths.

"I'm not going to survive it," I manage to say. "I'm not strong enough."

Tears start flowing freely and my nose begins to block as my insides expand and inflame. Breathing becomes more difficult. Tripp picks me up and carries me back to the bed. He brushes the damp strands of hair away from my face and tries to wipe aside my tears.

"What colour would you call my shoes?" He asks. I look at his shoes confused by the question. "I would call them charcoal; my father reckons they are navy." I look at his shoes and they are decidedly charcoal. While I ponder the colour of his shoes I notice my breathing has slowed.

"Charcoal," I reply.

"I knew it, no one wears navy... Do you feel better?" He asks. I nod as the air becomes less constrictive. "You are going to survive this Adaline. You are stronger than any person I have ever met. My father is an old fool who worries too much… He was wrong about my shoes, and he's wrong about this too. I promise you, you're going to beat this, I swear it," he says.

I look at him through my blurred vision. The gentle green of his eyes and soft lines of his face is comforting to look upon. My chest flutters, the sensation is nothing like the raging fires I felt for Seth, but maybe it's something. I remember the breathtaking flowers Tripp grew on Seth's grave. He did it for my benefit, he was able to look past the heartache I know he felt to do something kind for me. Tripp might be someone I can grow to love, someone who is kind and decent, maybe we can make each other happy. And most importantly, I trust him. I focus on the emotions rippling under his skin. His cravings and desire run deep, and his passion pours out of his body into mine. I can feel the affection he has for me, even after I almost caused his death. His feelings are compellingly strong. My breathing has evened out as I match his breaths. My heart is still beating wildly, but for a whole different reason. Lust. He wants me and as guilty as I feel about it I want him too. His emotions amplify my own and I lean forward to kiss him.

He's taken back by the assault of my lips, but he recovers quickly. He kisses me deeply until I feel the tingling reach my toes. My hands begin exploring his masculine body. The arch of his back, the rise and fall of his muscles. Before I even know what my hands are doing, I hear the rush of a zipper. I feel the cool metal between my fingertips and I realise where my body is leading me. Tripp freezes and pulls his lips away from mine. He looks at me intently.

"Are you sure about this?" He asks. The concern is clearly written on his face, but the want in his body is evident.

In a second everything flashes before my eyes. Moments of love and laughter, memories of sadness and heartache. I see images of the people I've loved and lost, pictures of faces that I'm never going to see again. Tonight could be my last night on this earth and I don't want to regret the things I haven't done. If I'm going to die I want to be able to cling to something positive.

"I'm sure." I pull his mouth back to mine and we fall into a linked embrace.

-12-
Tripp

Adaline is lying next to me with her eyes closed too tight for sleep. There is a blush in her cheeks that is brighter than her usual rose. I can hardly believe what just happened. It was a bliss like no other, she wanted me as much as I wanted her. I don't know if it was her loss or fear that allowed her to see me in a new light or if her feelings for me have shifted. No matter the reason it felt right for us to be joined together as one. If I can ignore the fact that I could be executed for my actions or the pit of guilt in my stomach that's growing larger by the day, then this moment would have been perfect. Adaline's lips quiver and a smile breaks across her face.

"Stop looking at me," she whispers.

"I like looking at you," I reply and kiss her cheek. "As much as I hate to say it I should probably go. It's almost time for your party, I'm surprised your lady maids haven't been in to dress you already."

"You make them sound like my slaves, they're my friends," she replies. "But you're probably right, you should go." I dress quickly and circle the enormous bed to crouch by Adaline's side. She shifts nervously as I stare deeply into her eyes. She breaks first and smiles with a small laugh.

"Don't forget you owe me a dance," I say and kiss her briskly.

As I open the thick wooden door I find Neema and Shay waiting on the other side. Both of them are dressed ready to attend the ball. Neema is in a long blue vintage gown while Shay wears a more modern styled grey. Before I have time to fabricate an excuse for my dishevelled appearance or why I'm sneaking out of Adaline's chambers, I'm assaulted by the judgmental expression on Shay's face. I close the door firmly behind me before Adaline notices their presence.

"Should I dig you a grave beside Seth's or are you happy to share his? It's still warm after all," Shay says coldly.

I don't offer a response, but her words gnaw at the already gaping wound in my stomach. As I walk back to my room the guilt expands like an overfilled balloon, the thought of Seth's grave and in fact, how empty it is, makes me feel sick. Nausea rises in my throat, I'm an awful person. I seduced Adaline by avoiding the truth. I kept Seth's unknown whereabouts to myself. I can lie to myself all I want. I can say I did it to spare Adaline or Aedan any more pain, but I did it for me. I took the chance that keeping this secret might make Adaline look at me the way she used to look at Seth. I'm disgusted with myself. I stand under scolding water, trying to scrub the filth and lies away, but I feel them embedded in my skin like a birthmark that's buried so deep that they can't be taken away with some soap and a loofa. I brush my teeth and spit out the poisonous deceit that clings to my tongue. I'm as clean as I can be, I'm still a horrible person but at least my sins can hide beneath my glowing complexion. I put on my suit and knot the silken tie around my neck. I tuck the tie underneath my buttoned jacket and look at myself in the mirror. I'm clean shaven and well dressed, the epitome of a gentleman, but it's a façade. A knock at the door startles me, but I welcome the distraction. Deklan opens my door wearing attire that matches my own. I don't recall ever seeing him in a suit before.

"That porter picked our suit sizes well didn't he? Still feels scratchy though," he says and smiles uncomfortably. "Don't think I've seen you in a suit since you were a little boy. Your mum always liked to dress you up in this fancy kind of getup," he says.

"I don't really remember," I admit sadly.

"She would be proud of you… I know I am," he says softly.

"Don't. We both know you don't mean it," I begin to say.

"Will you just shut up for one second? I admit I have made enough mistakes to last a lifetime. The biggest one was pushing you away, but you just reminded me so much of your mother and it hurt me to have you close. It was selfish, and I hate that about myself, but I cannot undo the past," he says.

"Maybe selfishness runs in the family," I admit. He looks confused by my reply. "There's something that I need to tell you."

I talk to my father like I never have before. I tell him everything. I tell him about Seth's missing body and the tracks Leo and I found. I tell him about the feelings I have for Adaline, I even tell him about our intimate time together. I hold back some of the details of course, but he gets the idea. When I come to the end of my sordid tale I can't stop myself from weeping. I brace myself for the disappointment and fury my father is about to unleash upon me, all of which I deserve. I'm taken back when his arms reach out to me and he pulls me into an embrace. I haven't hugged him since I was a child and I feel small in his arms.

"We can fix this, but not tonight. Adaline needs to focus on getting through her change and tomorrow we can right this situation. It's going to be okay, I promise," he says.

I never thought my father and I would be able to mend our fences, let alone be able to find the strength to have faith in one another again, but here we are. I trust him and what is outweighing the guilt that's eating away at my insides, is the love I have for my father. The same love I once had for him as a child. A feeling I had forgotten, a feeling I don't want to forget again.

-13-
Adaline

Neema and Shay announce their arrival outside my bedroom door. I'm surprised by their formality. The pair usually just enter my room of their own accord, which is no problem since I haven't done much lately, but sleep. Judging by the change in their behaviour I think it's safe to assume they witnessed Tripp's departure and have probably guessed what's transpired here. I have just enough time to cover myself with the robe that's on the chair next to my bed before they enter. I call out allowing them passage as I frantically try to smooth my mussed hair and calm the embarrassed flush in my cheeks. At least Neema pretends not to know about the transgression between Tripp and I. Shay, on the other hand, has dissatisfaction plastered all over her face.

"Please don't judge me," I say.

"I just want to know one thing," Shay says firmly, then a smile breaks her lips. "Whose better in the sack him or Seth? I don't like that boy one bit, but he sure is pretty to look at."

"I have no comparison, Seth and I never…" I blush. The shock on Shay's face and the instant look of sadness makes me feel worse than the thought that I have betrayed Seth in some way. Can you even betray someone who is dead? I ask myself.

"I guess, I just assumed," Shay replies with a gentle whisper.

"We didn't exactly have time, you know fighting for my life and all," I remind her.

"Enough sex talk, we have to get you ready. Adaline go clean yourself up while we get your dress sorted," Neema orders.

Glad to be removed from the vulnerable situation, I follow Neema's orders and draw myself my second steaming bath of the day. Since the awakening of my water element, I have found that no matter how hot the water is it never scolds my skin, but that might be more related to my fire element. I pour some of the oils into the bath, but the mix is nothing like the perfect balance of scents when Neema does it. I washed my hair this morning, so I tie it in a knot atop my head and lower myself into the tub. As my skin touches the water I smell Tripp's scent slowly leave my body. The aroma of fresh cut grass and raindrops fill the air for a few precious moments before it vanishes with the steam.

I replay the moment with him over and over in my head. The softness of his touch, the tender tingles that shivered up my spine as he kissed the nape of my neck. My toes tighten as the memory takes hold of my body. It was different than I had imagined. It was awkward, but not as much as I thought and at least he knew what he was doing, whereas I fumbled my way through relying solely on instinct. I expected it to hurt, given what my mother had told me, but the pain was short-lived and less intense than I had feared. It was wonderful, fumbles and all. It's an experience I don't regret, and I could definitely grow fond of it in the future. I hate myself for thinking it and it's not fair to Tripp, but a small part of me still wishes that my first time could have been with someone else, someone I loved more deeply.

Shay knocks on the bathroom door trying to hurry me up. I climb out of the tub and dry myself thoroughly. A small smear of blood on the pale coloured towel is a reminder that I'm no longer a child. I throw the towel into the hamper and wrap myself in a fresh one. As I open the bathroom door I find my bedroom has been transformed. Flowers and lit candles cover all the empty spaces and hanging from the canopy of the bed is the most exquisite gown I have ever seen, it even leaves my winter formal dress for dead.

Neema helps me into a corset and secures it tightly behind me. I have to convince her to loosen it a fraction, so I can breathe. Apparently, they didn't care if women could breathe or not in the old days. Once I'm satisfied that I can breathe without difficulty, the pair lowers the dress over my upraised arms and head. I slip my arms through the thin tulle draped sleeves until the scoop neckline sits in place. Its lower cut than anything else I have ever worn and the corset puts my breasts on display. I feel exposed. The torso of the dress is a tight fitted silken fabric with buttons all the way down the back. The soft tulle that's in the sleeves reappears at my waist and flows into a skirt of oceanic waves. The blue-green is stunning, and it makes my skin look flawless. There's a soft sparkle in the tulle skirt, it's subtle, just enough to make it special. I had worried the dress would be heavy when I first saw it, but its light and I feel light in it.

Once dressed Neema fixes my hair in loose supple waves pinning back a small section at the front. Neema starts to take my necklace off, but I stop her. I don't care if it doesn't suit the dress, I'm not giving it up. Shay shakes her head and Neema leaves the clasp alone without question. Shay does my make-up which she is surprisingly good at considering I never see her wearing any. My eye make-up is dark and shadowy with a whisper of green and my lips are a striking red. I'm glad to find I still look like myself, just on my best possible day. My face is still a little slender from the rapid weight loss brought on by grief, but my cheeks are slowly filling out. All my bruises and abrasions from the intensive training have healed thanks to a little magic and my skin is bright and clear.

"You look beautiful," Neema says. I blush adding some more colour to my cheeks.

"Are you ready for this?" Shay asks.

"Shit I hope so, it's definitely too late to back out," I reply. "Before we go down I just want to thank you both for everything. For helping me through all this. You are the best friends I've ever had and I'm grateful for you both," I say honestly. They both smile, Neema hugs me tightly and Shay offers a quick, but fond embrace. "Okay let's do this and I expect both of you to use your vampire speed to catch my clumsy ass if I fall," I tell them with a laugh.

"Promise," they both reply.

-14-
SETH

Emilia and John have welcomed me into their home, it was meant to be for a few days, but it's been almost a month. I have helped around the house and worked to clean up the yard in return for the shelter they have provided me. Emilia likes to cook. Each morning she makes an abundance of food and today is no different. I feel sick from overeating, and I'd bet I've put a few pounds on, but everything she makes is addictive and drenched in butter. She has even been making special platters of fruit and vegetables for Horse and had some hay delivered. Horse feels right at home in this small cottage hidden away from the beach, but as for myself, I still feel lost. Emilia has the radio playing and a music countdown has begun. Today is New Year's Eve, the date has been echoing an urgency in my mind. Since waking I have felt an overwhelming impulse that there's somewhere I need to be.

As I slept last night I had frightful dreams filled with grotesquely mangled faces, blood-soaked scenes and a blanket of death that touched everything. Now that I'm awake the dream still remains, and stronger than in my nightmares. As I turn a corner, a flash of horror appears before me, I reach out to touch the figures, but my fingers pass through the image like I'm trying to catch smoke. The faces I don't remember, but the feelings are too strong to overlook. Whatever my life had been before I awakened from the grave, it wasn't pleasant. It was a life filled with evil and violence. Why would I want to remember that? Perhaps my memory's gone by choice. A form of self-preservation, and trying to remember isn't in my best interests, but still, I can't shift this feeling of urgency.

I lay down on the tiny weak cot that has become my bed and close my eyes. A fragrance settles in around me. It's fresh and floral, like a scent that is trying to mimic the essence of life. I open my eyes and I'm still in the tiny spare room between bookshelves and storage boxes. The smell is gone. I close my eyes and it returns, it's a memory of a perfume and it's killing me that I cannot place it.

"Knock, knock. Do you want some lunch?" Emilia's kind voice asks from the doorway.

"I can hardly move from breakfast, but thank you for offering," I reply kindly.

"I don't know if it helps, but last night you were talking in your sleep. You kept saying a name, you got quite loud at one point. You sounded distressed," she says.

"What name did I say?" I ask her.

"Something like that singer woman. The famous one, oh you know she's curvy and has such a beautiful voice... Oh gosh, what is it? ADELE! That's her name, it was something like Adele," she says and wanders off towards the kitchen.

I roll the name around on my tongue until my head starts to ache, but it triggers nothing. I try saying it louder and still nothing. Adele, Adele, Adele. I say it like a mantra that's stuck on repeat. Why can't I remember? I try relaxing my breathing before I get frustrated and break another of Emilia's trinkets in defeat. I lay back down on the cot and pieces of a girl's face drift in and out of my mind.

At first, it's nothing notable like the curve of her chin or the way her hair fits behind her ears when she tucks it back. Then her lips fall into place, they are a gentle coloured rose and as I focus on those lips I can almost taste them pressed against mine.

The emotions linked to this memory is different than the rest. This girl makes my heart race in anticipation and I feel a sense of hope that's stronger than all the darkness of my past. I press a finger to my mouth, but all I feel is my own lips under the roughness of my fingertips. I remember kissing her supple lips. I remember the electric spark that ran through my body when her skin touched mine. In an instant, I remember everything.

"Adaline," I say to myself and bolt for the door.

I brush past a startled Emilia, and John only offers a glance as I sprint past him in his sitting chair. I step onto the front porch and that's when I notice something else. Something lacking, everything around me feels less and more at the same time. The sun doesn't shine as brightly and the only thing I can smell is the ocean drifting in on the breeze. There's something else missing, a hunger I could never forget. I turn on my heels and walk back into the kitchen. I look around the cluttered room until I find the sharpest knife. I pick up the blade pressing it against my skin. The blade slices through the palm of my hand cleanly. A steady stream of blood starts to flow, one thing is for certain, it really fucking hurts. I don't remember the last time I felt the rawness of real pain. The last time I can remember feeling anything close to this is before I was turned. The realisation dawns on me, I'm no longer fae, I'm human.

-15-
Adaline

Aedan greets me at the bottom of the staircase and I'm reminded of the last time I felt this uneasy exhilaration. I was happier then and Aedan had his brother standing by his side. I suppress the tears that are desperate to ruin my makeup and force a smile. When I reach the final step, he reaches out a hand to help steady me. I take his palm in mine and whisper my thanks.

"I know you agreed to this for me, but I do hope you will enjoy yourself tonight," Aedan says.

"I'm sure I will," I tell him.

Aedan escorts me down a long hall, Shay and Neema hurry ahead in a flash. I watch them vanish behind two large wooden doors with intricate carvings of knights with a strange crest in the centre. The door is closed and standing beside it is two men in formal suits. Aedan explains that in these kinds of proceedings someone inside will announce my entrance and then I am expected to walk in alone and perform a high bow to the guests. Practice for when I return to court he reminds me. He releases my hand and the doors open wide for him to be announced. When the doors close again I walk up to stand between them. I take a deep breath and my hands begin to shake. One of the attendants looks to me for the go-ahead but I'm frozen.

"Do you want an arm?" Tripp's kind voice asks from behind me.

"Dear god yes. I've never done anything like this before," I say.

I nod to the attendants and they open the solid doors. Tripp holds me steadily as we enter the grand hall. It's more like a ballroom than a hall really. There are beautiful tapestries of diverse colours and sizes covering the roof and walls. People must have spent forever creating the scene before me, but as I feel the magic lingering in the veins of the flowers and the sponginess of vitality in the leaves I realise it's all connected to Aedan's magic. Every inch of the room that's not covered in artwork has been filled with lush green vines. Small purple and white flowers bloom in a richness that balances me. As I look at the purple haze of the passion flowers I flash back to the balloons at my uncle's house and I struggle to breathe. Tripp squeezes his free hand against my forearm reassuringly, I bow to Aedan's clan as instructed, letting out a long breath as I do. When I rise they bow gracefully in return, most of them are unknown to me, but there are a few faces I recognise from when I have wandered through the stronghold. Tripp leads me over to Shay and Neema. He places a graceful kiss on my hand before he excuses himself to find Deklan. Left in the care of my friends I feel my unease lessen and the air returns to my tightened lungs.

I accept some of the champagne that's flowing freely and a few canapés that shuffle my direction. The soft music starts to pick up speed and people grab partners and dance merrily to the beat. They dance in styles I've never seen in person before. The type of old-fashioned dancing I remember from childish cartoons or classical dramas. I wish I could dance like that. Every move is deliberate and with purpose, the gentle touch of a partner's hands or the subtle stare of locked eyes as they spin round and round. It's beautiful, even the moment's where there is no touching to be seen.

Aedan introduces me around, not as a royal, but a guest of honour and the birthday girl none the less. People offer me well wishes and ask me questions about my time in Ireland. Unfortunately, I don't have much to offer in the way of small talk, but I smile politely and fawn on every word they say. After two hours, I'm exhausted, mentally and physically. I welcome the birthday cake and the uncomfortable singing because cakes usually symbolise the end of parties, which is a small blessing.

After I blow out the candles and the cake is served the band strikes up another slow song. Tripp claims my hand and pulls me onto the dance floor.

"I can't dance like them," I say gesturing to the glory before us.

"Don't worry it's your party we can dance however you want," he says and pulls me in close. "About what happened between us this afternoon, I just... I think I'm kind of in love with you. Which I know is crazy, we hardly know each other, and I know you have so much going on but, I just wanted you to know how I feel for you... You don't have to say anything, I just needed to say it," he prattles.

It's not like I didn't know he has strong feelings for me, but saying he loves me out in the open is different and it leaves me lost for words and I'm unsure how to respond. I decide to keep quiet and rest my head against his chest. He holds me tightly as we continue to sway. The room soon begins to spin and I'm not sure if it's due to the drink or the emotions rattling between us. I pull back and excuse myself from his embrace, so I can step outside to breathe in the cool night air. The stars gleam above me, and I steal myself a precious moment of solace before my battle for survival begins.

-16-
Deklan

I watch my son as he dances, Adaline is pressed firmly against him and the fondness he has for her is written all over his face. It's not an appropriate romance and I don't approve, but it's still nice to see my child happy. I reassure myself that I can allow him one more night of bliss, because if Adaline survives the night then everything will be different in the morning. Adaline will be eligible for the throne and any chance my son has with her will be no more.

Adaline goes outside while Aedan begins the farewells and starts sending his clan members to their rooms for the night. The great hall clears quickly under his expert management and in a few minutes the plates and glasses have been cleared, the band is packed and ready to go. I could easily see Aedan and Leo successfully running an expensive event management company together, exclusive to the rich and famous. Maybe they are missing their calling.

My son approaches my side and I'm happy to feel his closeness. The weight that usually hangs between us seems to have shifted and I feel more secure in our bond. I follow his gaze; his eyes are resting on Adaline standing out in the garden. I hear the increase in his heartbeat and I remember how his mother made me feel the same burst of excitement and fear. Young love, such a precious thing. I wish I could feel that way again, even if it's only one-sided like it is for my son.

The hectic ballroom is finally quiet, most of the candles have been blown out and the chairs are neatly stacked away. Aedan, Shay, Neema, Tripp and I wait in the empty room under dull lighting.

Each of us lost in our own thoughts, thoughts that are linked to a single focus. The five of us have done everything we could do, now it will all come down to her. It's becoming clear how easily Adaline connects to everyone and everything around her. She's the centre of our universe, it's no wonder she was gifted with the power of all the elements. How many other people could inspire the kind of devotion that Adaline can? It's not just her magic that does it either, the kindness of her heart allows her to bring monsters and men to their knees. Adaline's would be assassin is now her best friend, vampires and humans both gave their lives willingly to protect her, that kind of love is incredible really.

I watch as she shivers under the pale moonlight, I can see the goose pimples rising on her arms and shoulders, even at this distance. The light changes as a steady flux of shadows creep across the moon making her skin glow and radiate like a beacon pulsing in the night. I wish there was something I could offer to guarantee her safety, but it's not within my power.

"It's almost eleven. Shouldn't we be doing something?" Shay asks.

"Give her a few more minutes," Aedan replies.

I can tell she senses our presence closing in, her shoulders arch back and stiffen. I hear her breathe out a slow single breath that rises from deep within her lungs. Before we get too close she turns to face us all. She's our leader and we are her misfit monstrous entourage.

"Are you guys ready for this?" She asks, and I can't help but smile.

"It's best if you change into something more comfortable. If you're okay with it, all of us would like to be by your side this evening," Aedan asks.

"I can't believe any of you expected to be anywhere else, it's my big night after all," she jokes. In spite of her attempted bravado, I can hear the tremble in her voice. She's frightened, and she has every right to be.

While the womenfolk help Adaline out of her gown I wait outside her room with Aedan and my son. Aedan's handling the wait better than Tripp who is sanding the floor away with his feet. Tripp's anxious pacing is making my stomach solidify into a cement-like weight. I'm about to ask him to stop before I'm forced to make him stop, but Neema opens the bedroom door freezing us all in place. She nods her head inviting us in. The girls have moved the furniture, so the seats are focused around the bed where Adaline sits in a light velvety dress with long sleeves. She doesn't look as comfortable as when she was back home in Texas roaming around the house in faded sweatpants and t-shirts, but maybe I feel her discomfort more because I can tell her smile doesn't come as easily as it used to.

-17-
Adaline

I'm sitting on my bed with all the people I love standing around me. It feels like I'm in a hospital bed and my family has gathered to say their farewells to a person already deceased. It's like everyone has already prepared themselves for the worst without giving me a chance to prove their fears wrong.

"I feel like your all going to perform a séance or something. Maybe we can do something other than sitting in a creepy circle while you watch me without blinking." I suggest trying to change the depressed tone the night has taken.

"Wait one minute, I have the perfect idea," Shay says and vanishes from the room. She's back in seconds laying lazily next to me on the bed. I notice she has a bottle of alcohol in her hands and the cheeky grin on her face. "We can play a drinking game, like the ones in that stupid film you forced me to watch," she yells.

"The Breakfast Club kids smoked pot, they didn't drink… 'Never have I ever' is a drinking game." I offer.

"You call it what you want, I call it a reason to drink. Aedan hasn't been this loose with the booze in years," Shay laughs.

Shay starts the game by pouring shots into glasses I hadn't noticed she had brought with her. The questions start out silly and most of them have words and phrases I don't understand but I laugh none the less as they talk of relics from years before my time. I enjoy the sounds of their laughter more than the game itself, it's a nice distraction from the despair that's hanging above my head.

Everyone has had a turn and asked their question when the bottle is finally passed to me. It's my turn to say never have I ever followed by something I have never done, and I don't know what to say. There's a loud eruption outside my window disturbing the lull, I can see fireworks sparkling in the distance through the murky night sky. It's midnight. The bottle drops from my hand and I watch it fall in slow motion. I see Aedan reach out to catch it, but his movements are too slow, and his eyes are fixed on me. As I raise my head and look around, I notice everything has slowed to a crawl. Smiles fade to frowns and concern is plastered on the face of everyone in the room. I look down at the bed and see my hand is resting lifelessly floating inches above the rich coloured fabrics. As I step back off the bed, I can see my physical body floating stiffly above the sheets. Looking at myself I think of the game light as a feather stiff as a board, my eyes are closed but I can see the gentle rise and fall of my chest as my body continues breathing. It's still alive. I'm still alive I tell myself.

Bright golden lights flash in the corner of my vision. I look back at my friends and my body, and I know I need to follow it. As I pass my friends I realise they are blind to my current form. I look at my fingers and they seem solid, but if I move too quickly the colour of my skin fades until it's almost transparent. When I slow my steps, the colour returns. I follow the light through the castle, slipping past servants and vampires as ghostly as a shadow in the darkness. The light leads me to the back garden and a pale golden path stretches out toward the impressive tree in the centre of the grounds. I approach the ancient tree cautiously, what if this is a gateway to heaven and I haven't survived this? I reach out my hand to touch its bark, I half expect my hand to slip inside the tree like trying to touch air, but my hand rests firmly against it. I feel the roughness of its age and its power.

"Welcome home," a delicate voice says.

For a moment I think it's the tree talking. Until the most beautiful woman, I have ever seen pours out of the tree like steam escaping a kettle.

She's wrapped in an incandescent golden spark that flows behind her like a cloak. Her face is luminescent with light that escapes her skin as she moves. Her hair is an unending wave of flaxen feathers that flow down her back and disappear into the tree.

"Who are you?" I ask in a whisper, which still sounds too loud for her glory.

"I have had many names since the earth decided to speak. I suppose architect is the most accurate one, there was a time when you called me mother," she says.

"I have an abundance of mothers… Are you god?" I ask.

"No, I am not the god that humans pray to… I'm so glad to see you again, you had me worried for a while," she says fondly and clutches me close to her breast.

"I'm sorry I don't understand," I murmur into her feathery head of hair.

"Your frail little body needs time to grow first, don't fret… It will be confusing at first, but soon you will understand… We haven't much time are you ready?" She asks.

"Ready for what?" I reply.

"For your heritage my darling," she says.

Before I have a chance to answer she leans down and kisses my forehead in the centre between my temples. I feel a rush of warmth rip through my soul as it's forced back into my body. I open my eyes to see my loved ones hovering over me. Aedan and Deklan are each holding one of my hands tightly and I can see Tripp pacing in the corner of the room.

"She's awake, Adaline, are you okay?" Aedan asks. I take stock of my body as the air between the bed and my back becomes scarce. As the weight of my body lands back onto the lush bedding I notice that surprisingly I feel fine.

"I feel okay," I tell him.

"What happened?" Deklan asks.

"I'm not really sure, it's all muddled," I say. I know instantly that no one else would know about the woman I saw, I'm unlike other people and I know that, and she only appeared for me. I don't know how I know it, but I do. She spoke like she knew me and deep down a part of me recognised her too. She said I called her mother once, the word feels right, her presence felt maternal in nature.

"Is your transition complete?" Tripp asks.

"I think it's begun. I don't think it's going to be over in a night or hours like it was for all of you, I feel like it's a process. It will come with time. I'm sorry I can't be more specific, it's hard to explain but don't worry I'm not dying tonight," I reassure him. I feel their collectively held breaths leave the room all at once and their shoulders slump as they relax in unison. My body feels better than before, it feels stronger and more connected. I feel the tingle of cells duplicating as they repair the damage to my weakened muscles. Physically I feel better than I have in a long time, but on a level that I cannot describe, I feel like my soul still needs time to grow. No one moves at first. It takes them a while to adjust and I can sense they need time to grasp the fact that I'm not going to slip away into the death of night. Eventually, they seem confident that my current state isn't going to change, and they mosey off to bed. Tripp lingers in the doorway after the others leave, I can sense his worry. It's amplified more than the others. "I'll be here in the morning when you wake up, I promise," I tell him.

Begrudgingly he leaves, but I could tell he wasn't sure if he could trust my words and I can feel his presence lingering on the other side of the door. I lay down between the oversized pillows and allow myself to fall into a dreamless sleep.

-18-
SETH

Emilia bandages the cut on my hand after she's recovered from the shock of seeing all the blood. I tell her that it was an accident, but the furrow of her brow tells me she doesn't believe me. As soon as my wound is tended I try calling Adaline's phone and then my brothers, both go straight to voicemail. I imagine they disposed of them as soon as they left the island, I'd expect nothing less. I try calling Jason and any other number I have memorised, I'm greeted with only voice mails or disconnected recordings. I don't even know where they would have gone. Where would be safe for them to keep Adaline? It's late evening here but in Ireland its well after midnight. Maybe I could call the stronghold, perchance someone has heard from Aedan. What if I call and somehow tip off Adaline's existence and Aedan's involvement? I can't risk their lives like that.

I walk outside onto the front porch, Horse appears by the stairs, probably expecting another meal from Miss Emilia. I pat his head with my good hand while I look at the wounded one. This human form limits me, and I curse it, I already miss my ability to heal, although it's nice to be released from the addictiveness of bloodlust. How am I going to find Adaline? How am I going to get home? Without my vampire abilities, I'm useless. I have no money on me, no passport and absolutely no one who can help me get back to Ireland. Being human is also going to make it impossible for me to enter the Vale through any of the portals. I'm basically stuck. Maybe if I can make it back home I can wait for Aedan to contact the stronghold and I could find out where they are.

"Wife says your memories back," John says. I jump startled by his approach and wish I still had my superior hearing.

"I do. My name is Seth and I need to get back to Ireland," I tell him.

"You don't sound Irish," he remarks.

"I wasn't born there, but its home and someone's waiting for me," I reply.

"Well, I don't agree, but the misses has said we can lend you some money to get home. You can send it back once you get yourself sorted," he offers.

I turn to face him, and I can feel the shock that's settled on my face. I'm surprised by his generosity and not just for the money. I know I wouldn't have welcomed a confused stranger into my home and fed him and his horse for as long as they have. When did humans become this trusting? No matter the reason behind their generosity they have given me something greater than money and shelter, they've given me a sliver of hope in humanity, something I only started to believe possible when I met Adaline.

There's one number I know that never gets disconnected or changed. It flits and floats through the unsavoury side of our world and is only passed from one devious person to another. I received it when I had the charm made for Adaline. I will have to call Thomas, he's a shade that's allied with the Unseelie and his dark nature is the only reason I never called him in the first place. Unlike the Seelie, the Unseelie don't feel the need to hide from their true nature. King Addison is different than the Seelie King, he allows his people free reign of their dark desires. They can cause destruction and death until their black hearts are content, as long as they stick to one rule, no humans live to unearth our secrets.

As long as the secrecy of our kind is maintained King Addison doesn't need to step in. I admit I considered joining the Unseelie alongside Thomas when the vampire community was welcomed into the fold, but Aedan wasn't cut out for that kind of life and I couldn't leave him, not after everything we had been through. Thomas and I went our separate ways when I chose my brother over him. We parted on good terms though and as long as I don't cross him and have enough money for his services I'm confident in his willingness to help me. I just hope he hasn't changed his standards too much in the last few decades.

It's almost midnight which is peak business hours for Thomas. I thank Emilia and John for their help and I promise to return the money they have leant me. It's not much money by my standards and Thomas would die of laughter if I offered it to him, but I'm grateful all the same. I just hope Thomas will trust me to settle his payment when I arrive home. Horse follows behind me as we walk up the shoreline until we reach the small gasoline station that's long since closed. I find the phone booth like John had promised I would and at first, I worry it's no longer in working order judging by the amount of rust. I pick up the receiver and try regardless. I'm shocked and relieved when I hear a dial tone. I insert the change and start dialling his number. I can't remember if the last digit was a two or a seven. I try two. When an aggressive elderly sounding woman starts screaming on the other end I realise it must have been a seven. I dial again, this time changing the last digit.

"The base price is five thousand. Then I quote a service price depending on the type of service you require. If the price is too high then hang up now and don't waste my time," he answers.

"Hello to you too Thomas," I say and laugh, he hasn't changed a bit.

"Tell me that's not the son of a bitch that ran off to join the good witch?" He laughs.

"Guilty. How's the dark world treating you?" I ask.

"Can't complain. Nice penthouse, nice car and more women than I can handle. How's that goody two shoes brother of yours?" He asks.

"He's the same, making the rest of us look bad," I reply.

"That's enough small talk, why don't you tell me what you need. You wouldn't have called me for anything else," he says.

"I'm in a bind. I'm in a back-ass town in Louisiana and I need transport to the stronghold in Ireland and I have a horse that's coming with me," I tell him.

"Don't tell me you're eating fucking animal blood, how the mighty have fallen. Why can't you just compel some poor pilot to fly you back? It would be quicker," he says.

"There are complications and I need to go unnoticed," I lie, there's no way he would help me if he knew I'm now human.

"Okay, I get it. It will take time, fucking human terrorists have made large transports difficult lately and a few of my usual porters got themselves killed. It's been such an inconvenience for business, anyways it has forced me to return to old school smuggling, which takes longer. Deposit ten thousand now and ten thousand on delivery. Do you have the account numbers?" He asks.

"The thing is I can't access any funds until I get home. I'll give you thirty thousand when I arrive, you have my word," I offer.

"Fifty thousand on delivery and I'll agree to set up a safe house for you and your pet until you get picked up. Deal?" He replies.

"Deal," I agree

Thomas will have a man collect us within the hour to take us to a safe house until we start our journey. At least when using Thomas's services, I can be sure none of the fae in his employment will attempt to harm me. In my human state, there's little chance I would survive an encounter with one of my own and definitely not one of the Unseelie. The journey is going to be longer than I would like, but I don't have any other options and travelling with the horse won't make things easy. I have never been invested in the wellbeing of animals before, but Horse pulled me from my grave, literally, so I kind of owe it to him to make sure he is cared for. I can still feel the grit in my lungs and the weight of the soil pressing down on me when I think about my body being imprisoned in the earth. My breath catches in my throat and it's like I'm buried all over again. I try to think of other things but all I can think of is the broken look on Adaline's face before the world went dark. Her violet eyes were so red and swollen with grief, she looked destroyed. I just hope she hasn't given up on me.

-19-
Tripp

I didn't sleep at all last night. How could I? I recall the lifeless way Adaline's body floated above the bed and at one point I didn't think she would ever wake up. I felt my heart harden as it prepared itself for the worst. Then she woke, she opened her eyes looking more beautiful than ever and smiled as if nothing had happened. I'm struggling to make sense of it. My own change was as difficult as it is for other fae, it's supposed to be a test, after all, it's a chance to prove you are worthy of the magic being bestowed upon you. I think of the way the woods called to me before my birthday. I would sleepwalk into the densest parts of the woodlands, which was about twenty minutes away from our house on horseback. When I woke I was usually in the top of a tree, saying I was startled is an understatement. In my shock, I fell from the branches more than once. On one occasion on my way down I landed on a piece of rotting tree. I broke two ribs, my pinkie finger and had a hairline fracture in my femur. Not to mention the abrasions or pieces of broken sticks I had embedded in my bare feet from traipsing through the town. I'm just lucky I don't have the same affliction as my father. Month after month all his bones splintering and breaking as he shifted into his wolf form. Adaline's change is unheard of, then again Adaline is unheard of, she is like nothing our world has ever seen and that makes me worry. How can we protect her when we don't know what to expect?

I continue pacing outside her bedroom door, I feel my eyes trying to force sleep, so I pick up my pace. Between Neema and Shay they have checked in on her half a dozen times and she's still sleeping easily. I try distracting myself with thoughts of other things, but it's difficult.

Adaline's transition to Queen and what that will entail for the rest of us is a hard thought to ignore. No matter how hard I try I can't envision my life without her in it. I can see myself being her guard and friend if I'm lucky and anything more would be a blessing. I can see her father offering her hand to a son from one of the noble clans. A stranger will stand by her side and get to call her his own, the thought makes me sick, but I'm delusional to think her position would allow for a life with me by her side.

The only good thing about distracting myself with future fantasies and woes is that I don't have to face what my father's doing right now. He's upstairs talking to Aedan and not just about the weather. He's telling him that his brother might still be alive and that I covered it up. I told my father I would tell Adaline and I am going to, but I'm stalling. I need to work up the courage to tell her, which is the reason I'm on this side of her door right now.

"You shouldn't be on this property let alone outside her room," Aedan says from behind me.

"I didn't know what to think. I didn't want to give either of you false hope," I tell him.

"BULLSHIT! You wanted Adaline for yourself… YOU'RE A SELFISH SON OF A BITCH!" He screams.

Before I can react, he throws me against the wooden door. The cold metal handle is pressing sharply into my lower spine. He has his forearm weighted down against my throat crushing it with his force. His blue irises turn alarmingly dark. The walls of the stronghold begin to shake, his lips draw back exposing his fangs. I watch them extend as they reach out for my throat. Aedan lifts his arm from my neck just enough to let his fangs impale the rapid pulse beneath my skin.

As I feel the piercing puncture of his teeth sink into my flesh the door behind me opens inwards. Aedan and I fall onto the floor in a vicious snarl. Aedan punches me in the face and I feel blood escape the split above my eye. The blood spurs Aedan's rage, he lunges for me a second time, but he's blown backwards by a gale force wind. He crashes into a wall where he is pinned in place. One of my eyes is beginning to swell, but through my good eye, I see Adaline holding a gentle hand effortlessly controlling the air that's holding Aedan prisoner.

"What's going on?" She asks looking at me, but I can't answer her. I'm too ashamed.

"Tell her you fucking coward," Aedan says.

"Tell me what Tripp?" She asks lowing her hand releasing Aedan to the floor.

"I went back to the island…" I see concern flash across her face. Aedan is back on his feet and ready to attack, but he's waiting to gage Adaline's reaction. "Seth's body was gone. I found some tracks leading to the shoreline and I searched, I swear I did. Leo and I went to all the neighbouring islands and checked with the human police, but there was no sign of him. I don't know what happened, I can't explain it," I tell her.

"Are you telling me there's a chance he's alive?" She asks.

"I don't know. All I know is his body wasn't there and it looked like someone had walked away from the burial site. The prints looked old, they could have been from the cleaners," I say.
"Get out," she says softly.

"Adaline, please. I'm sorry…" I start to say.

"GET OUT!" She screams.

She hurdles another gust of wind that knocks the air out of my lungs and casts me outside like a piece of paper caught in a hurricane. Her bedroom door slams closed behind me and I hear her start to cry. I listen as Aedan speaks to her in hushed tones trying to soothe her. This is a mistake there's no coming back from, she is never going to forgive me.

-20-
Adaline

Once again Aedan is left consoling me while I cry like a defenceless child. I had opened myself up to Tripp in a way I haven't with anyone else. It was supposed to be a regret I wanted to tick off my bucket list in case I died. It wasn't meant to be something more than an experience, but it had ended up meaning more. The sadness I felt for Seth and my uncle's loss has been overwhelming and for a single second, I was able to envision a life beyond my heartache. I could see what loving Tripp could be like. I considered that one day my heart might mend itself and I could see a future. All that's gone now, Tripp's deceit has done that. Losing Seth and my uncle nearly killed me, and Tripp knew that better than anyone. If he really loved me he would have said something. He would have told me there was a chance that Seth was alive. There's no future for us, not ever.

My tears run dry, my nose is clogged and sodden. I feel wounded, but another emotion is rising within me. Fury. At first, the feeling seems justified, but I quickly realise the rage isn't my own, it's coming from Aedan. Calm and collected Aedan is consumed by anger. I squeeze the skin on his forearm to try and comfort him, but I'm bombarded with visions of death. One, in particular, Tripp's. Aedan envisions strapping him to a chair with rusted nail-studded belts. As the blood seeps from Tripp's wounds I see Aedan pick up a small rusted blade that still has enough sharpness to be damaging. He places the blade against Tripp's bruised and bloodied chest and slices into his flesh. He peels back a layer of skin like slicing the pith off an orange.

Tripp screams out against his restraints, but the sounds of the vision are muted. Like watching a horror film with the sound switched off. Somehow it makes the vision more terrifying. The screams I imagine in my head are distorted enough to make my chest ache in sympathy. I break free of the link between Aedan and me so I can rid myself of the horrors of his mind.

"Are you okay?" Aedan asks confused.

"How do you live with those kinds of images in your head? Every time you're hurt or angry is that what you see?" I ask him. I see realisation flicker across his face, he knows I saw what he was planning on doing to Tripp.

"More often than I wish," he says sadly.

"You can't kill him. I'm just as upset as you are, but we can't resort to that, it's not the kind of people we are," I tell him.

"Adaline, you have no idea about the things I have done. What you just saw was nothing. I'm sorry to burst your bubble, but I'm not as innocent as you seem to think," he says. His anger dulls, the only feelings escaping him now is his shame and guilt.

"I have no illusions about the things you and Seth have done in your lives, but people can change. Not always and it's not easy, but it's possible and you're not that person anymore," I tell him.

As I reach out to reassure him and see if his horrors have passed, my vision shifts and blurs as my hand touches his. I see an image of Aedan, but not the Aedan I know today. He's dirty and wearing rags. His hair is a long-matted mess, almost like dreadlocks. He's on the ground by a stream, its night time.

The grass and vegetation is vastly overgrown and, in the darkness, he's almost lost amongst it. As my eyes focus I see he has slashes in his skin, I can almost taste the fatty brine smell of his flesh as it still sizzles. He's been burned. I can see his exposed muscles protruding from the open wounds. He looks up at me, my position is substantially higher than him, I wonder if I am seeking refuge in a tree? It's too high for me to be standing. His eyes concentrate on me and he lets out a hissing cry. There's a feral-ness about him. Like a wild cat that's been wounded and cornered. My vision lowers until his face is close to mine. A gold droplet falls from my face and lands above his heart. He closes his eyes and his body relaxes. I raise my head and once again I'm high above him. I see that his wounds are beginning to mend, that's when I feel confident to leave him alone.

Just as quickly as my mind had left I'm pulled back to my bedroom floor sitting by Aedan's side. I let go of his hand and he watches me cautiously. I can see he's afraid of the harm his thoughts might inflict upon me. I ignore his concern and stand before him, reaching out my hand to help him up. He hesitates a moment but takes my hand in his and stands.

"What did you see?" He asks radiating shame and sadness, I feel bad for him, he shouldn't care what I think of his past.

"Nothing that changes anything. More importantly, how do we go about finding Seth?" I ask.

We scramble for an hour while we try to think of everything we can do to locate Seth. Aedan puts in calls to every Seelie connection he has but no one has any knowledge of his whereabouts. I wish I had kept my phone, but Deklan insisted on destroying everything when we left the island and at the time having no connection to my past felt like a blessing rather than a curse.

Aedan calls an old witch friend of his to do a locator spell, but she says its inconclusive, mixed results or some such nonsense. When Aedan disconnects another unhelpful call, a thought crosses my mind and I hate myself instantly for thinking it. It could be that Seth isn't alive, perchance someone did take his body and those were the tracks that Tripp had followed. Maybe Tripp had some merit in keeping this knowledge from me. Not knowing if Seth is alive or dead is worse than knowing his fate. It's the torture of the unknown that can gnaw at you.

"I think I should go and look for him. Maybe if I start back at the island I can pick up something that bastard missed," Aedan mutters to himself.

"Great I can be ready in five," I say jumping up to gather some clothes to travel in.

"You can't come," Aedan says.

"I buried him alive Aedan… I sat there while they scooped pile after pile of dirt on top of his broken body, don't you dare think for one second that I'm going to sit here twiddling my thumbs while he's out there alone," I say. I feel the fire starting to combust on my fingertips and the ends of my hair. The fires like a tether that's connected to my heart, it pulls at every fibre of my being.

"Neither of you is going anywhere," Deklan says abruptly as he enters the room.

-21-
Deklan

As expected Adaline is all too willing to rush into danger to save Seth and Aedan's no better. Theo and I have arranged for Adaline's safe passage to return home. I cannot let her put everything in jeopardy just to save a person who may or may not even be alive. Adaline doesn't want to hear anything I have to say on the matter. She excuses Aedan and me from her room, so she can change. As the door closes I can hear the shuffle of heavy fabric and the release of a zipper. She's beginning to pack a bag.

"Goddamit Aedan, you need to stop her. She is going to court in a fortnight. Until then we need to keep her safe and I need your help to do that. Seth wouldn't want you to do this, he would want you to make sure she's safe. If he is alive, he's a strong boy and he will find his way back to us I'm sure of it," I plead.

"He's my brother," Aedan says.

"I understand that, and I'm sorry but she is more important. He loved her enough to die for her, he understood that her life means more than his, or mine, or yours," I say.

I can see Aedan weighing his options. I hope as a leader he can see that doing right by his people is more important than his personal feelings.

It's true that Adaline has more power than all of us combined, but she's still too trusting of our world and incapable of protecting herself. Aedan finally takes a deep breath and steps back into Adaline's room.

He closes the door firmly behind him, I can hear the unhappy shouting as Adaline tries to convince Aedan to change his mind. I hear something made of glass smash against the floor, Aedan exits a second later.

"You made the right decision," I tell him.

"Your son needs to be out of my home within the hour and if something happens to my brother, I'll be taking your life and the life of your son, are we clear?" He asks.

I nod once, there is no point in pushing the uneasy peace, not now. I hear Adaline break another item against the bedroom door. I consider going in, but then I remember the flames I saw burning on her fingertips and think better of it. Aedan leaves one of his men outside of Adaline's chambers until he is certain she isn't going to run. I find my son waiting in my room when I return. He's cleaning up some scratch marks on his neck and eyebrow. I can see a dark bruise starting to colour on his cheek. He looks up at me and I can see the same look of dread on his face that he wore as a child, it's the way he looked when he realised his mother wouldn't be coming home.

When Adaline was born so much of my time was spent as her guard. The night of her near-fatal attack was no different. What I didn't know was that less than an hour before the attack my wife had been murdered. My sweet Chloe had come to court to find me, but she never made it inside the castle walls. The guards had found her body by a secret passage that leads into one of the towers.

Theo, his brother and I used to sneak through the passages as children. When Chloe and I were older we used its secrecy for our private affairs. It was simpler times back then, that was before the obligations of the world encroached on our lives.

The night I killed Adaline's attacker there was little time to act. We had to transport Adaline to the mortal realm quickly and I was unable to contact anyone in the Vale until things had settled down. A few days before I returned to court I was informed of my wife's death. My poor son had been unwell at the time of her passing and was in a nurse's care, I know now that's why she came looking for me. Our son was sick, she needed me, and I wasn't around for either of them. That's why keeping Adaline safe is so important to me. I can make sure I didn't lose the best thing in my life unnecessarily.

Between Adaline's anguish and Aedan's hostility towards my son, I know I need to keep him safe and that means him not being here. I can't have Tripp wandering around under Aedan's nose, tempting his vengeance. Tripp loves Adaline and I know he's not going to want to leave her side, but his presence will be a distraction to both her and Aedan.

"They were less than pleased," Tripp says, trying to downplay the situation.

"We expected them to react this way, I admit I was surprised by the intensity of Aedan's outburst... He wants you to leave and I think it's a good idea," I tell him.

"It figures but you know I can't leave, not now," he says.

"I need you to go for Adaline's sake. Theo has arranged for us to stay with Phedora at her temple. Theo has guaranteed that no one else would know of our arrival, but I need you to go ahead and check it's secure before we bring Adaline through," I plead.

"You're giving me a fake mission to keep me out of the way," he says sadly.
"Not at all. You're the only person I trust to do this and after some time has passed the others anger will have died down," I explain.

I'm surprised he agrees without much need for convincing. I don't know if it's because he fears Aedan's reprisals or Adaline's disappointment. I promised my son that I would help him right this mistake and I will. I just hope Seth comes home soon and his return can out shadow Tripp's mistake.

-22-
SETH

The safe house is in no way a palace, but it's warm and the fridge is stocked with food. Thomas had even gone to the trouble of stocking up on a supply of blood bags and specific requirements for Horse. None of the blood is of use to me, but I'm glad Thomas hasn't lost his touch and it's no wonder his business is still booming. It's been such a long time since I have had to worry about things like shelter and warmth. It makes me look at things differently, it's like learning to walk again and not knowing how to balance the distribution of my weight. I was a vampire longer than I was human, transitioning back proves more challenging than I would have thought. When I was a vampire all my senses were heightened, and I basically had anything I wanted at my fingertips. I could smell a drop of blood a mile away and now I can barely smell the food in front of me. I ate human food regularly as a vampire, but the taste was always dulled, it was nothing compared to the sweet allure of blood. Now the thought of drinking blood makes the contents of my stomach rise.

Horse, on the other hand, appears pleased with his accommodations and I can see he has no aversion to being waited on hand and hoof. Thomas's in-house employee has created a make-shift pen in the house's attached sunroom, complete with hay bed and horse friendly feeding trays. I just feel sorry for the poor guy who has to clean up after Horse when we leave. The giant beast isn't exactly house trained.

After taking Horse out for a quick walk around the block I settle myself into cooking a meal. I haven't done a great deal of cooking, but I can manage the basics.

It helps that the pasta and sauce jar have instructions clearly printed on the back. I test the pasta as instructed and know instantly that I've overcooked it. I grab the handles of the pot and thrust it into the strainer I have waiting in the sink. As I pour, the steam rises up and burns my fingers.

"FUCKING SHIT GODDAM SON OF A…" I scream aloud as I drop the pot into the sink. Horse pops his head over the split way door, he tilts his head to one side as he watches me intently as he tries to understand the cause of my commotion. "I'm fine Horse," I tell him.

If someone had told me a month ago that I would no longer be a vampire and that my best friend would be a horse that I named Horse I would have called them crazy. Yet here I am talking out loud to an animal that can't possibly understand or respond to me. If anyone is losing their mind here it's me.

I save what pasta I can from the dropped pot and sir in the sauce. I sit down at the table to eat and it's not a good meal by any standards, but the taste is pretty spectacular. With my memory back I can see what I missed as a vampire. As a human I can taste the richness that's been trapped in the tomatoes from their time spent on the vine and the sweetness of the garlic as its sweltered inside an oven. It's the best worst tasting food I have ever had, and I can't help but smile at myself for my accomplishment. I wish Adaline and Aedan were here, actually I just wish I had anyone here, even Deklan would suffice. Horse snorts in his room out back like he knows my secret wishes, sadly he cannot fill the void. I was never bothered spending time on my own before, often I preferred it. I liked the quietness that would settle in around me and alleviate the anger and violence burbling under my skin. Solitude gave my fire element less fuel to ignite itself, that's another thing I don't miss. The unending struggle I suffered with my element is definitely something I'm glad to be rid of but looking at the burn marks on my fingers and hand I wonder if it's worth it.

The bloodlust and constant inner struggle is something I had always wanted to trade away but being human is weak. I will eventually age and die, that's if something else doesn't get me first. How can I look after Adaline in this form? At least when I was a vampire if I wanted to live inside the Vale that was permittable. I could have stayed close to Adaline, even if we couldn't be together romantically. Now that I'm a human I wouldn't even be able to find the portal door, let alone be allowed to reside in the Vale. Adaline is worth any struggle and when I return home I'll have Aedan return me to my former glory. I don't know how I became mortal, but I know how to go back and it's the only future I can see for myself. My mind is set, and I'll welcome back the challenges of vampire life. As for now, I'm going to eat as much as I can and enjoy everything humanity has to offer because, in a short time, I will return to my dulled eternal existence.

-23-
Tripp

My father is able to arrange a horse to transport me to the portal, granted I think Aedan would have agreed to anything just to be rid of me. Unlike a car, horses can travel through the portal with ease. The Vale has no modern advancements like cell phones, cars or computers and any technology that enters the Vale is hit with an electric pulse that stops it in its tracks. As far as I'm aware, only King Theo has access to a cell phone that's spelled to travel through the boundary and getting your hands on one of those is impossible. The fates made sure of that when they put up the wall in the first place. I guess having a sister that can see into the future allows you to plan for things like social media obsessions and technological overhauls.

I saddle the stallion and latch a small saddlebag to a hook on the saddle. The bag is nothing fancy, but it contains the few precious items I was able to salvage from the island. A hand painted picture of my mother, a piece of bark from the tree that nearly killed me in my youth and a piece of cork from the night at Loora Lake when I was sixteen. Insignificant trinkets that mean the world to me. As I mount the impressive beast I remember the first time I took Adaline riding. I think I knew then how much I was going to love her. How her hair floated on the breeze, the way I felt the vibrations of her laughter in my heart. I wish I could go back and change things. I never should have lied to her, not about Seth. It was a selfish mistake that I'm going to have to live with, I just pray that one day she can forgive me. I look at the moss that is climbing up the side of the stronghold's walls towards Adaline's window and I wish she would appear. I'd be happy to have one more look upon her face, just a small sign to know there's hope, but she never appears. I feel my heart sink lower the further I get from the stronghold, by the time I gallop through the gates my heart is near impossible to find.

The journey isn't as long as I had thought but hours of silence is the last thing my mind needed. I follow the instructions on the map and each time I arrive at another landmark, the previous path vanishes, and the next segment of directions appears. As the sun begins to rise I pull up by a stream to feed and water the horse. The sound of lapping water is a nice distraction from the thoughts in my head. The weathers getting colder, I can see my breath escaping my lips only to transform into a thick veiled fog before my eyes. I pull out the map and find another path has appeared. Once the horse has had his fill of grass I take his bridle firmly in my hands and guide him through the thick brush alongside the stream. The path becomes more obscured the further I travel; the grass keeps rising higher and the surrounding trees block out the moonlight. Just when the growth is at its densest I feel the magic call to me. I don't need the map anymore. I follow the alluring scent of the portal's barrier, drinking in the energy that's seeping out of our world. At the end of the ravine a small ray of pale light returns, it's just enough to reveal a stone tunnelled bridge. All portal entrances are in a continuous state of flux. Manipulating themselves to become a part of the world around them. They become mirages, forgettable to the humans that pass by.

I remember when I left the Vale to train with the royal guard in the mortal realm. The portal I left through was in the form of a radiant tree that looked like someone had taken the time to cover it in gold leaf. It shimmered under the suns warmth forcing me to squint my eyes. Once I was on the other side I looked back for a final glance at the portals glory, but all I saw was a dying willow with faded leaves and rotting bark. Forgettable, just like this bridge. The tunnel is almost pitch black, but I can see the stream flowing freely from beneath. As I approach the entrance the horse increases his pace, he's urging me forward forcing me to move faster, and almost tramples me in the process. He settles down as we reach the opening of the tunnel, but I can hear a soft disgruntled huff under his breath. I step into the darkness allowing it to cloak me, for a moment I hold a panicked breath in my lungs, until the light changes.

A long stairway covered in overgrown roots and a thick layer of soil leads up toward a glowing alcove. I can see pale blue and white flickers of light floating above the ceiling. I recognise the lights immediately, sprites and will o' the wisps. In the dark times they were tasked with leading unwanted travellers away from our dwellings, now they protect the entrances to our world. As I climb the steps the wisps fall from the ceiling. They encircle the horse and me, so they can light our way. As we reach the opening I'm bathed in an otherworldly light. It's balmy and warms my skin as it hopes to find my bones. It heats my muscles and strengthens me. I feel my abilities grow more powerful with every ray of light they absorb. My heart skips a beat as I take it all in, it feels good to be home.

-24-
Adaline

"Do you want me to kill him?" Shay asks. Her offer though sweet is unnecessary. I hate that Tripp lied and tricked me, but I don't want him dead. I admit that for a second, I thought about it, the way everyone wishes someone gone in a moment of passion, but after seeing Aedan's thoughts I know I didn't really want that fate for Tripp.

"Normal friends joke about killing a boy whose broken your heart, but I worry your offer is serious," I say.

"Why wouldn't it be serious?" She asks confused.

"No more killing Shay, new leaf remember?" I reply.

"Your loss… Can we leave this room sometime this century? You have been sulking for days since Tripp left and we are still no closer to finding Seth. Maybe going outside would help," she pleads.

I sigh knowing there's no fighting her stubbornness. It didn't take me long to know that Shay won't stop until she gets what she wants and being cooped up makes her particularly defiant. She leads me through the castle until we are in the back courtyard standing in front of the tree from my dreams. The trees magic soothes me as it reminds me of the embrace from the golden-haired maiden. My skin warms at the memory and I feel a little dazed, Shay nudges my shoulder, shaking me free from my daydream. She sprints across the lengthy lawn like an animal that's been released into the wild.

"Bet you can't catch me," she mocks.

I reach out my senses, and I can feel the light in her soul that is ever growing. It's a glorious white light that touches my heart. I smile to myself as I remember the tiny flicker of a flame she once had when we first met. She's becoming whole again and the darkness that was cloaking her is almost a distant memory. She flits past me again nudging me a second time. She's back on the other side of the grounds before I have time to push her back. This time as she runs toward me I'm ready. I outstretch my hands and force the air toward her. I push hard forcing her into stasis. I feel her fight against it, but I raise her up until she's almost as high as the branches of the tree.

"That's not fair," she yells from above.

I laugh and send her flying across the grounds until she's resting atop the wall of the garden. I release her gently onto the stone, she shakes off the experience and leaps down landing in front of the hedge. She chargers again and I'm running toward her. I call the earth to rise up making Shay trip and roll to the ground like a fumbling child. I fall to my knees caught up in laughter, I giggle deeply until it hurts my chest to breathe. I worry I'm going to wet myself when I see Shay picking the clumps of snow out of her cropped hair.

"You're getting better," she says and reaches out a hand to help me up.

"I feel stronger, I don't have to force it as much anymore," I say taking her hand.

"Have you thought any more about going to court?" She asks.

"I've tried not to," I tell her.

"I would happily be Queen, imagine it, everyone waiting on me hand and foot. Giving out orders instead of following them," she says.

"You know you never have to do anything for me you don't want to right? I would never want you to be my subordinate," I say.

"I know, besides you're a pushover I would kick your ass in seconds," she laughs. "I know you're worried about this, and you and I are very different people... For what it's worth I think you would be a noble ruler and I would gladly follow you anywhere."

"So, does that mean you will stay with me at court?" I ask her.

"I swore you my loyalty... I'll be by your side for as long as you'll have me, besides we both know you're going to get yourself into trouble and need me to get you out of it," she says pushing me back to the ground with a laugh.

Shay and I run around the grounds attacking one another with our respective powers until the air becomes crisp and the light begins to fade. I'm confident that if we suffer another attack I will be more of an asset than a liability and Shay seems less concerned about my safety.

I wash up and change out of my sodden clothing before I head down to the dining hall. All of Aedan's kinsmen sit together at a long wooden table with various sumptuous foods scattered between them. I learned quickly that the tall silver jugs don't contain wine. I'm just grateful everyone has copper goblets instead of crystal glasses or I wouldn't be able to hold down my meal. I sit between Shay and Aedan, Deklan sits across from me and smiles as I begin piling the food high on my plate. It doesn't take a psychic to sense how happy Deklan is about my appetite returning to normal.

I eat quietly and listen to the roar of laughter and brotherly banter. Jason is sitting close to Shay and leans in to whisper something in her ear. I hadn't noticed how close they have become since Texas. I'm just glad to see them finding some happiness with one another, I know how badly Shay deserves it. I smile knowingly to Shay and she quickly averts her attention from Jason to refilling her glass. I stifle a giggle and Jason begins to blush, at least I think it's a blush, it's hard to tell with his pale skin. As I look around the table I notice an alarmingly male-focused presence that I hadn't paid much attention to before.

"Why aren't there many female vampires, are they with another clan?" I ask Aedan.

"Women have a lower survival rate. I think it's roughly one female to every twelve males that survive the change," he says casually.

"As if women didn't have it hard enough," I remark.

"I saw you training with Shay today. It looked like you had fun and it was nice to see you smile again," Deklan says.

"No thanks to your son," Aedan snaps.

"Aedan let it go," I tell him. The last thing I want is more hostility, especially with my abilities growing stronger each day. When everyone's tempers heighten it's almost impossible for me not to become swept up in it.

Deklan ignores Aedan's comment and continues to chatter about our journey to the Vale. I can still feel Aedan's anger quivering through the open space between us. I slide my hand under the table and take his hand in mine. I try channelling some of my own emotions into him like he's done for me many times. It's not something I have tried before, and it takes its time to work, but slowly I feel it. A peaceful calmness travels from me into Aedan. I feel him relax beside me and the air in the room feels lighter. He nods thanks to me before releasing my hand. I remember the vision of Aedan in the swamp, I knew the moment I experienced it that it wasn't a hallucination, but a memory. I'm just not sure if it was his memory or mine. I recall the torn clothing he adorned and the strange woven footwear he had strapped to his feet, his ensemble seemed medieval, almost like a peasant.

"Aedan, how old are you?" I ask.

"I was born in the late fourteen hundreds. I'm not exactly sure of the date, time was less important back then," he replies.

"So, you're roughly six hundred years old?" I reply.

"Give or take a few centuries," he replies.

"Time becomes irrelevant when you have an eternity," Neema adds. We shouldn't live forever I tell myself. "Don't look so sad Adaline it's not as awful as it may seem, everyone here has witnessed a great many things," Neema assures me.

"Immortality has its advantages," Aedan echoes with a sardonic smile pouring another unsavoury drink.

"Don't you find living for so long makes you numb to everything?" I ask.

Everyone looks at me like I've grown a second head. The room shifts from relaxed to uncomfortable. I'm ready to excuse myself before I insult them further, thankfully Shay jumps in with an anecdote and saves me from the intense stares. I should think more before I speak. Aside from Deklan who can age by choice, I basically just said everyone in the room is living meaningless lives. I'm really not Queen material, I've known it from the start and right now I think others are starting to see it too.

-25-
SETH

Horse and I have been at the safe house for few days and one of Thomas's footmen is due to arrive any minute to transport us back to Ireland. I'm out the front with Horse waiting patiently beside me. He keeps nudging at my pocket, he can smell the sugar cubes I have hidden there for his treat later. Thomas's man pulls up in a shady pick-up truck and a horse trailer that's more rust than metal. When he gets out I realise it isn't a man but a harpy. She is wearing a bulky hooded coat that attempts to hide her true form, but it doesn't quite do the job. If I was worried about the police pulling us over for the trailer's safety deficiencies, I needn't worry. If anything draws the human's attention it will be the bird-like woman driving the truck, maybe Thomas isn't as on point as I had thought.

"How do you expect to stay under the radar?" I ask the woman.

"Don't question my ability to do my job. Get in the truck or I'll terminate the contract," she says firmly. I follow her instructions and settle Horse into the back before I climb into the front passenger seat. "Thomas told me you were a vampire," she says.

"Yes," I reply.

"You're not a vampire, I can smell your frailty seeping through your pores," she says clearly repulsed.

"I've known Thomas a very long time and I recall he doesn't like being second-guessed. If you want to call and confirm what he told you, by all means, go ahead," I bluff.

"Point taken," she replies and starts the engine.

She doesn't play the radio or like small talk, which is fine by me. The silence gives me time to think. Unfortunately, all I think about is Adaline and what might be happening to her at this moment. Her birthday has already passed, and it kills me that I wasn't by her side. A horrific thought crosses my mind, what if she didn't survive her change? I discard the thought immediately before it has time to take root. If she was dead I would know, I'm certain. If she was gone I would feel her loss, and since I can still touch the invisible thread that binds me to her I know she's alive. Even without magic, the unexplainable connection between us is unwavering and it comforts me.

Before the attack, I had been so angry and hurt by Adaline. The way that guy had his hands all over her, the memory makes my stomach lurch and I feel my usual hostilities flooding back. I look down at my palms worried they will turn to flame, but the heat I've become accustomed to remains dormant. It appears the only fire I still have a connection too is the metaphorical kind that's in my heart.

"What's your problem?" The harpy asks, looking at me judgementally.

"You're not paid to ask questions," I snap.

She rolls her eyes and focuses on the road. I didn't notice the beautiful colourings of her feathers before. She has a thick black beanie on her head hiding her indigo feathered hair, but the light catches it every now and then, making it glisten like glass. I can see the start of her feathers sprouting from her wrist and up her forearm. If covered correctly she could pass through the mortal realm almost unnoticed, but I know what's underneath her thick layers. An expansive wingspan that travels from her wrists to her shoulder blades and razor-sharp talons that extend when provoked.

A few centuries ago I fought a harpy, she gave me an impressive slash across the back of my leg that charred with an acidic burn.

In return, I gave her an equally impressive laceration to her throat that ended her life. If I was to fight this harpy in my current state, even on her worst day she would destroy me in seconds. The weak don't survive in our world and Adaline needs me to be strong.

I continue to wrestle with the doubts and anxieties that are shadowing my sensible thoughts. Becoming a vampire for the second time in my life shouldn't worry me so much, but it does. I know if Aedan had the choice he would remain human without a second thought. There are things a human life can offer that our vampiric existence cannot. I feel guilty for wanting to throw this chance away and I wish it had been given to Aedan who's more deserving of the freedom. I twist my body again in the plastic covered seats as I try to seek physical comfort. The harpy turns on the radio trying to mask the irritating shuffles of my restlessness. I welcome the raspy sounding voice and allow it to drown out my thoughts.

-26-
Deklan

Our small troop is saddling up the horses and readying a carriage for Adaline, Shay and Neema to ride in. Adaline had insisted on the duo accompanying her to the Vale and I got the impression they plan on staying with Adaline indefinitely. I wonder how her father will feel about the kind of company she keeps. I was anxious about having them come along, vampires haven't exactly been welcomed as long-term guests at court, but I conceded to Adaline's request because it was the only way to make her come willingly.

Aedan and Jason direct our passage while Roland and I follow closely behind. Roland's boyfriend Leo had offered to accompany us, and I was grateful to have a porter on hand in case of an attack. Leo whistles happily as he drives the carriage, blissfully ignorant of the possible dangers that may lay ahead. The rest of us keep vigilant of our surroundings as we prepare ourselves for a possible assault. I can hear the girls gossiping and giggling like children from within the cart. One thing I have learned from watching these girls over the past few weeks is that no matter the age difference between them, or their race, women are women. They can go from fierce to fragile in zero point two seconds and no matter how much is going on they will continue to speak at great length like it's a challenge. As much as their chatter can irritate me I'm thankful Adaline is made happier by their presence.

The horse I'm riding begins to buck and snort. I hate horses and they have never been fond of me, given my animalistic nature. I tighten my grip on the reigns and try to straighten her stride, unfortunately, the beast is as stubborn as any other female.

After an hour we have to stop so I can switch places with Leo. He mounts the horse in one swift movement and gallops ahead with refinement. There's a slight flourish of eccentricity as he rides, which I can't help but roll my eyes at.

"Can I sit up front?" Adaline asks sticking her head between the thick curtains.

"No, it's safer if you remain out of sight," I remind her.

"Please, all the rocking is making me feel carriage sick... get it carriage sick," she laughs. I tell her no again, but she continues without any sign of ceasing. "Can I ride one of the horses instead?" She asks.

"Fine, you can sit up front, only for a little while though," I agree.

I begin to slow the carriages speed, but Adaline has already slipped through the opening behind me and is positioning herself by my side. She looks pale, then again Ireland isn't exactly the sunshine state in winter. Dark clouds begin rolling down the mountainside. I can smell the rain beginning to fall in the distance. It edges closer until it's almost upon us, I'm about to tell Adaline to go back inside, but then I notice something strange about the rain. Aedan and Jason turn back to look at us, equally as confused as I am.

"I can let it fall on us if you're worried about it drawing too much attention," Adaline says.

"I suppose its fine. Don't tire yourself out though," I tell her.

"It won't, I can hardly feel it," she says with a small smile. "Deklan, do you think my father will like me?" She asks. Like her? I can hear the fear trickling into her voice, it catches just in the back of her throat, but it's enough for me to notice. "It's bad enough that Leonora didn't care about me, but at least I had a mother who really loved me. What if the only father I will ever know doesn't like me?" She says.

"I promise he already loves you," I tell her.

"Love and like are different, you can love someone because your genetically predisposed, but you might not like them... I want him to like me, not because I'm his daughter, but because of who I am," she says. I had never thought of it like that. I think of my own father, I loved him, but I didn't like him.

"As far as I'm concerned if you were my daughter, I couldn't be prouder of the person you are," I tell her honestly.

I reach out my arm and hug her tightly. If Theo didn't like her he would have to be crazy. It's funny that someone so strong and confident still only needs one thing, unconditional love. Adaline relaxes against my shoulder as we head toward the mountain. The rain continues to beat down heavily, but we remain safe under the veil of Adaline's protection.

-27-
Tripp

When the fates constructed the boundaries between the three realms the sisters were forced to separate and lead individual lives. Phedora the fate of the past resides within the Vale. She lives amongst the Seelie and welcomes companions into her temple. Phedora is known for her wisdom, and she believes that all have the right to understand their past. Petra, the sister of the present lives in the mortal realm. I have never been to her temple, but from my understanding, her philosophy is to 'live in the now'. Rumour has it that she single handedly instigated Woodstock. The final sister Fallon is the embodiment of the future. She lives in Vargo with the Unseelie and is something of a bitch, at least that's what people say. She hasn't allowed anyone to enter her temple since its conception. Fallon foretold that if she and her sisters remained together the boundary would disintegrate. As it's their magic that holds the boundaries in place they were forced to separate. They sacrificed their family to ensure the fae would never be vulnerable.

I've been back in the Vale for almost a fortnight and after receiving a reply from my father I know Adaline will be arriving sometime tomorrow. My nerves have been on edge since I woke. I decide to take a walk through Phedora's garden to try and ease my troubled mind. Her temple is built of solid carnelian stone and when the light grazes its walls the temple glistens like fire. The temple is surrounded by fields of tall silphium flowers that sway gently against the breeze.

The beautiful medley of greens and golds is breathtaking and it's hard not to be caught up in it. I walk deeper into the flower maze until I'm lost beneath their remarkable stature.

I breathe in their sweet liquorish scent and allow the flowers headiness to overpower my worries. I'm glad I decided to walk barefoot, I dig my toes into the soil drinking in its richness. Unlike the mortal realm, the Vale hasn't been beaten and abused by its inhabitants. Fae understand the importance of being one with Mother Nature and not claiming dominion over her. Maybe if humans could understand this balance, they would stop assaulting the earth with chemicals and toxins that destroy her spirit. Mankind's stupidity astounds me, after all, the humans depend on the existence of the planet for their very survival, but they don't care enough about themselves or the planet to do anything about it.

A flash of colour that's out of place amongst the flowers catches my eyes, the pale crushed blue flashes a second time. I follow the mysterious colour as it moves through the flowers until I arrive at the heart of the maze. Standing in the centre is a young beautiful woman with pale blue hair that sways back and forth in the wind, her feet just barely missing the ground as she floats in an enchanted dance. Phedora. She turns to smile at me. She's more beautiful than I could have imagined. Piercing blue eyes with soft creamy skin. Her lightweight dress is a mosaic of crystals and gemstones that twinkle under the sunlight. Like myself, she is also barefoot, and her feet have splashes of dirt tracing up to her ankles.

"Nice to be home isn't it?" She asks.

"No better feeling," I reply.

"Forgive me for not being here to greet you. I was in the mortal realm visiting my sister. I told the King I wouldn't be back for another week, but my sweet sister is a bit much to handle when she's in one of her moods, so I came home early," she says and begins twirling around like a small girl chasing invisible butterflies.

"Your temple is beautiful I wish I had visited sooner," I tell her.
"You didn't need to be here any sooner, this is exactly the right moment," she says coyly.

"The others will be arriving tomorrow, I had better go back and have the attendants set up their rooms," I say and take a step towards the fiery temple.

"You know we all make mistakes, it's how we learn, and one needs to forgive themselves before they can be forgiven by others," she says.

I nod politely but don't respond. The last thing I want to hear right now is spiritual mumbo-jumbo or fortune cookie scripture. I forget her words and allow my connection to the earth to lead me back through the maze. As I walk up the slight curve of the hill I turn back to look at the buttery fields. Between the sea of green and bumblebee yellow flowers, I can see Phedora's blue head bobbing up and down as she dances. I step over the threshold of the temple and retreat to my room to hide until the others arrive.

-28-
Adaline

As we approach the valley between the two mountains the rain finally passes over us. I pull back my shield and the fresh scent of rain fills my nostrils. I breathe it deep into my lungs, rejoicing in the cleanliness of its fragrance. My eyes follow the line of the majestic shamrock coloured mountains as they stretch up into the heavens, disappearing behind the weighted clouds that linger at their peaks. I can't recall seeing anything so beautiful as the Irish countryside, I wish my mother could have seen this. I rub a finger along my healed tattoo, I love the delicate marking the more I look at it.

I feel a warmth in my chest that's aching to comfort me. At first, I think it's one of my elements trying to soothe my sorrow, or perhaps it's Deklan's emotions trickling into me, but it's neither. It's the piece of my mother that I always carry with me. It's the piece of her that's embedded in every breath of my lungs, it pulses in every beat of my heart, and it even lingers in the ink of my tattoo. I am comforted that a part of her will always remain, safely locked away in a place of love that she shares with my uncle. Before my change I had been finding it hard to locate the shattered pieces of my loved ones, honestly more times than not I struggled to find anything except for despair. Since my encounter with the golden woman, everything has altered. I feel different in myself and everything around me is so much more. More textured, more vibrant, and more fleeting. It's nothing I can place my finger on, it's just simply more.

Using the carriage has slowed our pace, I would have been happy to ride one of the horses alongside Aedan and the others, but Deklan had insisted on keeping me concealed.

I'm glad he let me ride up front with him for a while, but each time a traveller passed he would force me back inside with Neema and Shay. The last time an elderly man was on the road Deklan almost shoved me cleanly through the back window of the carriage. Neema's head is bobbing loosely with each shake of the carriage, while Shay is picking her nails down to the beds. I watch as her nails grow back a second after she had removed them. Her new nails show no signs of her nerves, they look healthy and strong. I look at my own nails that are chipped and weak, they still haven't grown back properly since I bit them off a week ago.

"If you had a choice this time around, would you become a vampire again?" I ask Shay.

"If it had been a choice the first time around perhaps things would have been different. Why, are you considering joining the dark side?" She asks with a cocked head.

"No, I just can't stop thinking about all the time you have. Never changing, never growing old, it's like your life is frozen," I reply. I couldn't imagine watching my loved ones grow old and die time and time again, while I lived a continued existence.

Shay opens her mouth to say something but holds back and gazes out the window thoughtfully. Neema sits upright, her eyes focusing intently on me. At first, I worry I have said something wrong, but she smiles and averts her gaze. Suddenly I sense it, a magical pull that's ten times stronger than all of my elements combined. I slide between Neema and Shay forcing myself amidst them like a piece of ham between two slices of bread. I slip my body through the window frame and climb into the empty seat next to Deklan. I smell the sweetness of grass growing across the hills and I can taste a hint of frost in the air.

"Can you feel the portal?" He asks.

"Yes, does it always feel like this?" I ask.

"Feels different to each of us. To me, it's hot, like when you approach a fire. I can almost smell the scent of cinders in the air," he says dreamily.

"It feels like coming home, like an inviting electrical current, and strangely it somehow reminds me of my mum. How far are we?" I ask.

"Just down that ravine, it's a bit of a trek on foot. We will set up camp here tonight and leave at first light," Deklan says pointing to an overgrown trench.

The sun is beginning to set, and the ravine already looks too dark to travel safely in the daylight. I can feel the magic influencing us to move forward, irritation bubbles under my skin. Aedan steps out of the tree's shade closely followed by Jason. I can vaguely make out the small nod of Aedan's head as he signals us to join him. Leo and Roland are charged with returning the carriage to the stronghold, so we say our farewells. Shay climbs on the back of Jason's horse and wraps an arm loosely around his waist. This time I'm positive I can see him blushing. Shay smacks him on the shoulder and the goofy smile on his face vanishes, but I can see a smirk form on Shay's lips. Neema rolls her eyes at them making me laugh. Deklan lets me have the final horse and walks alongside us. The beautiful mare snaps her teeth toward Deklan until he steps a few feet back giving us a wide berth. I stroke her neck whispering encouragement in her ears. Deklan scoffs at my words and before I have time to stick out my tongue at him the horse snaps once more in his direction.

"Good girl," I tell her.

"Stupid animals," Deklan mutters.

"Move your asses or we will never get set up in time," Shay hollers as she and Jason gallop toward the ravine.

I tap the mare's side and gallop after them leaving Deklan and Neema in my dust. I move with the horse's body. With each stride, I raise my thighs and hips the way Tripp taught me. I feel the beat of the horse's heart against my legs, a steady thump that drums in unison with my own. My vision shifts as the horse and I blend into a single being. I feel myself morph and shift until my human body no longer remains. My long legs make impressive strides across the countryside. My hooves feel so much stronger than my human feet. I'm enthralled by the clip-clop sound that my hooves make as they dig into the firm earth beneath them. I'm running alongside a herd of wild horses, each of them wears a suit of different colours with intricate markings. We slow as we approach the open stream, I lean down to take a sip of the ice-cold water and catch a glimpse of my reflection. Two bulging dark eyes, a long-drawn muzzle and a pitch-black coat. I have a flowing white mane that sways gently when the wind blows against it. I look around at the herd before me and quickly realise I'm different from the rest. I have a dazzling golden horn protruding from my forehead. The other horse's freeze, my ears perk up as I hear a foreign sound. The whistle of an arrow startles me as it grazes past my ear. The herd panics, but I know it's me the hunters are after. I gallop in the opposite direction heading deeper into the darkness of the ravine's overgrowth. I hear the shriek of more arrows being fired, one narrowly misses my flank. I take a sharp turn and vanish into the depths of the forestry.

I remain hidden amongst the trees and woven vines, the hunters continue searching, but my dark coat makes it impossible for them to find me through the darkness. A distant noise draws their attention away from me and once I'm certain they have moved on I creep out of my hiding spot. I lift my head, raising it out of the safety of the trees, I take a step forward and freeze. I hear another sound, its close, but it isn't hunters. I listen intently, it's a whimper, an injured cry.

I should ignore the sound, but I can't force myself to walk away. I tread carefully back into the vegetation and follow the sound. I expect to find an animal that has been caught in the crosshairs of one of the hunter's arrows, but it's a human man.

The wounded creature is dirty and reeks of burnt flesh, I've seen this scene before. My gaze intensifies, and I feel smaller as I'm drawn closer to the ground but as I look down I can see my human fingers clutching at the soil beneath me. My breathing is laboured, and my limbs feel weak.

"Adaline," Aedan says softly. I look up at him confused, how did I get here? "Are you alright?"

"What happened?" I ask him.

"When you got to the ravine you got off the horse and walked away. We tried to stop you, but you wouldn't let us. It's like you were in a trance," Aedan says.

It wasn't a trance, it was a memory and I was trapped within it. I could feel the crisp air that brushed against my mane. I could smell the dew that clung to the leaves as my coat brushed against them. I remember the fear I felt for the herd when the hunters came for me. I look past Aedan and I can see Deklan standing a few feet away, the others are even further back. Deklan is cradling his left arm to his chest, he's wounded.

"Did I do that?" I ask Deklan, the lowering of his head is all the confirmation I need.

"You didn't mean it," Aedan adds. "She's okay, go fetch the horses and set up camp, we just need a moment," Aedan yells to the others. Deklan hesitates a second but soon follows after them.

"I would never hurt him, not on purpose," I say as a sob sets in. "I just had to remember, it was beyond my control."

"Remember what?" Aedan asks.
"Who I was. I've been here before and so were you. You were different. You were human and badly injured, I almost didn't recognise you. It looked like someone had tortured you with fire," I tell him.

"It's impossible," he remarks.

"I think I healed you. I gave you something, a piece of me," I say dreamily as I remember the single teardrop I bestowed to Aedan. He lowers himself to the ground and sits beside me.

"I never told anyone about that night. You are right, I was still human then. The vampire who turned me was sadistically cruel. He used compulsion on me for years before he changed me. He forced me to harm myself for his pleasure. The night you speak of was by far one of the worst. I think because the pain was so intense I was able to break through the compulsion and I ran," he says with a sigh. "I was going to die that night. I found my way to the ravine in hopes that the water would help soothe the burns, and I could die with some semblance of peace, but it was too late. I felt myself on the brink of death, I'd lost so much blood and the pain was excruciating. I was just about to give up when I saw what couldn't have been possible," he says.

"I saw you," I say.

"And I saw the mother of horses. A beautiful mare that looked like she belonged in the heavens and not in the wickedness of that ravine. I thought she was a myth, there had been rumours across the land, but never for a second did I think she was real," he says.

"I remember your pain, your soul was shattered, and I couldn't bear to leave you, not like that," I tell him.

"How could it be possible?" He says.

"We live in a word filled with magic and you're almost as old as time itself, I think we can expect to discover a great deal of things we cannot explain," I say.
"We had better go," Aedan says offering me his hand.

"Aedan, when I left you that night you were still human, why did you return to your maker? Why didn't you leave?" I ask.

"I couldn't, my maker had acquired a new toy, a young man in fact and it wouldn't have been right to leave him to face that nightmare alone," he says.

I straddle Aedan's horse while he leads the animal on foot, tugging at its bridle every so often. I look mournfully at Deklan's wrapped arm as we approach and wish I could heal him like I had Aedan all those centuries ago. I still find it hard to believe I've walked this earth before, and in a different skin with four legs and a horn growing out of my forehead no less. It's crazy, perhaps crazy isn't the right word, maybe I should say peculiar instead and perhaps peculiar is something I should get used to because I can only imagine what fantastical beings reside within the Vale.

-29-
SETH

Our trip to Ireland has been unexciting and somehow very tiresome. Maybe tired is just my human body's usual state of being. I never felt this exhausted as a vampire and the harpy seems unaffected by the numerous hours of driving, the boat ride or the dodgy cargo plane that we spent way too long in. When we landed at Dublin airport I had never been so thankful to place my feet on solid ground. It was a fleeting moment of pleasure because soon we were stepping into another unsteady machine and Horse was being hitched to the back of it. The harpy has remained pleasantly silent for much of the trip, aside from the annoyed huffing sounds she made when my incessant movements on the plastic sheets would push her to breaking point.

Our vehicle rattles as we cross the bridge between the village and my home. It feels like a lifetime has passed since I stood atop the rafters of the bridge. I remember the ghost of a man that I had cast into the sea, I wonder if there has been any sign of his remains or if the ocean has washed my slate clean.

"It's pretty here," the harpy comments.

I look at the evergreen hills in front of us and the small stone homes disappearing in the review mirror. It is beautiful here, I had always known that, but there's a difference between knowing something and feeling something. For the first time, I can actually feel its beauty. I lower the window and breathe in the crisp ocean air. As I exhale my breath becomes visible in the chill.

When I was a vampire my core temperature never got warm enough to show my exhalation and watching it now is a lovely novelty. I breathe out once more, this time I wave the foggy breath thoughtfully with my hand.

"You're so weird. What the hell are you doing?" The harpy asks.

"Just drive," I tell her.

"Has anyone ever told you that you're not a pleasant person?" She says.

"Many times," I reply.

"And you have people who actually want you to come home? I mean, I'm being paid to spend time with you and trust me it almost isn't worth it," she snarks.

"I'm sure you're all peaches and cream," I comment.

"I am actually. I'm a people person, people love me," she says flashing her long talons and tapping them on the dashboard. I try not to laugh, but I can't help it and a small smirk escapes my lips. "Oh my god did you just smile. Holy shit I'm picking up a lottery ticket on my way home," she laughs.

I don't have time to respond because she slams her foot on the break forcing us to an abrupt halt. I begin cursing under my breath until I look up and realise where we are. The harpy has stopped outside the stronghold's gates, I'm home. I wait a moment before I open the door, there should be at least one guard at the gates, but no one greets us. I step out of the truck and approach the locked gate. Usually, I would just climb over the top, but my human body would surely fall to its death if I tried. I close my hand around the icy steal, I unlatch the hook on the inside and push the gate forward.

"Seth?" A voice yells from behind me.

My shoulders tighten as I turn to see Roland and his boyfriend approaching with one of the old carriages. Roland pulls up the carriage behind our truck, blocking the harpy in. His partner Leo has turned ghostly white as he spies her sitting in the front seat.

"It's okay, she's assisting me," I assure them.

"You son of a bitch," Roland says and welcomes me into a tight embrace, I flinch as his strength threatens to crush my brittle bones. He sniffs my neck, a sensation that's uncomfortable, to say the least. I wonder if this is what it feels like for a human before we sink our teeth into them. "Seth what happened to you, you're…"

"Human," I say finishing his sentence. "It's a long story. Have you heard from Aedan?" I ask.

"We delivered him and the others to the portal last evening," Roland says. "They should be heading through the boundary into the Vale in the next hour or so."

I've missed them, it's too late. She will be through the portal before I can reach her, I kick the dirt in frustration. Roland jumps back as the dirt cloud makes its way toward his pants. I let Horse out of his trailer and ready him to ride, Horse shakes and stretches like an oversized dog, he's glad to be free of the crate.

"You won't get there in time," Leo says. "If you give me a few minutes I can teleport you and this big fella," he says smacking Horse's flank affectionately.

The harpy is pleased to be rid of me and speeds off down the dirt path the second the carriage is out of her way. The truck moves much quicker without the weight of Horse and I holding it back.

Roland takes the carriage to the entrance of the stronghold where he is greeted by our men. Horse and I wait by the front gates, the fewer people that know I'm human the better.

I see Leo appear by Roland's side, he gives him a quick kiss and vanishes once more. Several minutes pass and I feel the anguish beginning to bubble under the surface.

"Ready?" Leo asks. I hadn't even heard him pop up behind me.

"Are you?" I ask.

"Nice to see you haven't lost your charm," he jokes. "Okay climb on, what's this boys name anyways?" He asks.

"Horse," I reply.

"Original. Okay climb on Horse and I'll jump on behind you," he says.

I raise my eyebrows at him. He laughs and smacks my shoulder playfully. I didn't care much for Leo's flamboyancy when I was a vampire and that hasn't changed just because I've lost the lust for blood. I climb atop Horse and take hold of his bridle. I'm aware that porter trips are by no means comfortable, so I brace myself. I feel Leo's elongated body appear behind me, he wraps an arm around my waist and squeezes more firmly than necessary. I feel the sinking sensation of nausea before we move. The sickness is worse than I remember. The swirling uncontrollable force makes it feel like my lungs are going to explode, while my stomach sinks to an all-time low. The three of us are standing beside a ravine I know too well. The portal itself changes but the ravine leading to it remains constant. I jump off Horse before I fall, and my feet hit the firm ground, my knees soon after. My stomach churns and I lean forward expelling all the greasy takeaway food I had eaten on the road. Just when I think I've brought up everything, an acidic bile creeps up my throat. I vomit the vile tasting acid onto the ground between disgusting coughs and gags.

"Porting isn't the most fashionable way to travel for non-porters, but I guess it's worse for humans," Leo says with a repulsed look on his face.

I spit a few inches in front of Leo's feet, trying to clear the burning acid from my mouth, but it's too late to help, the damage is done. I laugh when I see his face turn green. Leo hands me a flask he has hooked to his hip. I swish the whisky around cleaning my mouth with its delightful burn before discarding it to the earth. I look at Horse to see how he's travelling, and he doesn't seem affected in the slightest. If anything at all he appears bemused at my discomfort. I shoot him a glare, but it just makes him more pleased than fearful. I call Horse over and he leans down for me to straddle him. Once secure, Horse begins leading us down to the ravine. Leo ports ahead of us, probably trying to get away from the vomit smell that's decided its sole purpose in life is to cling to my clothing.

The ravine is as calm and beautiful as I remember, the rippling sound of the water makes my restless body feel at ease. In my darkest moments since returning from the dead, not seeing Adaline has been my biggest fear, I'll never forgive myself if I don't get to see her one more time. The fear of forgetting every inch of her face is becoming a constant worry. If I think about it too much more all of my fears will overwhelm me. I push the negative thoughts aside, so I can focus on the task at hand. I just hope I can reach her before she steps over the threshold.

-30-
Adaline

The electric thread I had felt yesterday is growing stronger by the hour, I felt it calling to me through the night, the connections so strong it makes my fingertips tingle with eagerness. Deklan, Jason and Shay left this morning when the sun climbed over the horizon, they are checking that there were no breaches at the entrance of the portal. I woke briefly as they left, without a second thought I snuggled back down into my sleeping bag and drifted off to sleep.

I hear people shuffling around outside my tent. I keep my eyes closed using the lull of the portals current to relax me as it pulses steadily through the earth like a heartbeat. The sounds outside become louder, I step out of the tent and I can see Neema has the horses downstream drinking from the river. Aedan is sitting next to my tent, his hair is messier than usual, I wonder if he slept at all last night? Things feel different between us since discovering our shared past. I have so many questions to ask him, but I know it's not the time. If someone had seen me as vulnerable as he was that night I wouldn't be able to look them in the eye either.

"I should have stayed human," Aedan says surprisingly. "You gave me a choice that night when you saved me, and I picked wrong," he says sadly.

"Do you regret the life you have?" I ask.

"Some of it. I don't regret going back for Seth. I just wish we could have both remained human... I shouldn't complain I have so much, but there are things I wanted that this life cannot offer," he says.

"I'm glad you're here, and you have your family," I tell him.

"I have soldiers, I have attendants…" he says.

"You have people that love you, blood doesn't determine your family Aedan. Trust me love and loyalty is more dependable than any bloodline could ever be," I assure him.

"You're always glass half full, aren't you?" He smirks.

"Maybe, but I know the reason I'm alive right now is not because of magic or immortality it's because of love. I'm standing here because people loved me enough to save my life and I think deep down you know it's the same for you," I tell him.

Aedan's eyes glaze over, and I worry I've brought him to tears until I realise his eyes aren't focused on me, but what's behind me. I turn to follow his gaze and I see Leo walking toward us. I'm confused, I can't see Roland anywhere. I look beyond Leo and see a horse heading toward us with a rider on its back. The horse has a familiar colouring, but all Aedan's horses are a standard deep brown, this horse is the colour of the sun. It takes me a moment for the connection to click. It's Apollo. Even at this distance, I recognise the beautiful beast. I can see the moment Apollo recognises me too because his front legs rise as he bucks the rider off his back. The rider falls to the ground while Apollo gallops forward in a blur, my heart rejoices as the earth vibrates with his excitement as he gallops towards us.

Aedan stands in front of me to shield me from the charging horse, I try to push him aside, Apollo won't hurt me he's just excited. It doesn't matter though, Apollo is too quick and is standing in front of us before I can force Aedan's body out of my way. I leap around Aedan and wrap my arms around Apollos neck. He huffs and snorts his excitement making me hug him tighter. I had been worried about what became of him after the attack, I had feared he was lost to the battle.

"You're a silly horse, you must have hurt poor Roland when you dropped him," I chaste and stroke his silky ears as he leans his heavy body into me.

"That's not Roland," Aedan says vanishing from my side.

I look to where the rider had been dropped, I can vaguely make out Aedan's figure tackling the rider. They rise from the ground in a haze and begin walking toward us. As my eyes focus I can see him, it's Seth. Aedan has his arm firmly wrapped around his shoulder as they walk. My heart stops beating, everything stands still and the only thing keeping me upright is Apollo's muscular body. Aedan and Seth are within range and I can see their faces more clearly. I watch as Aedan drops his arm from Seth's shoulder and a grim look falls on his face. They are speaking heatedly, but I can't make out their words. Aedan storms off in a huff. Seth shakes his head towards his brother and starts walking to me. I hold the air in my lungs for the longest time, this can't be real. If I let the air out of my lungs I'm worried he will vanish with my breath. I feel like I'm watching him walk in slow motion, each one of his steps makes another piece of the world fall away. Apollo nudges me unhappy that my attention has shifted from him. Seth's within arm's reach and I'm scared to make a move to touch him.

"Hey," he says.

"You come back from the dead and all you have to say to me is 'hey'?" I thrust myself into his embrace.

He wraps his arms tightly around my waist and I bury my head into his chest. I feel the cool breeze snapping at the tears running down my cheeks. I breathe him in deeply like it's the first time. I try to commit to memory the wholesomeness of his spiced scent, there's a hint of something sour beneath his usual aroma, but I don't care. I can't believe he's really here.

"I'll go away more often if you're going to act like this when I return," he laughs.

"Don't joke," I say and kiss him fiercely.

Our moment lasts longer than any kiss ever should, and Apollo makes sure we both know it. He pushes his head between us making me laugh. Seth pushes his head away making Apollo snap playfully toward him. I haven't felt this happy in a long time. I just wish my uncle and mother could have found their way home to me too. I pull back from Seth's embrace and look into his eyes. They seem brighter than I remember, his usual deep brown has more of a caramel glow. I notice something else, small patches of bruising and scars on his hands that should have healed, and a fresh bandage secured tightly around his palm. He has a light yellow and purple bruise that's fading under his left eyelid and there are fading claw marks along his neck. I reach out and touch the still healing wounds, but he catches my hand bringing the contact to a standstill.

"I'm mortal," he says and looks down at his feet like he's ashamed.

"I don't care, I'm just happy you're here," I tell him.

"I asked Aedan to change me back…" he begins.

"That's why he's so upset," I conclude.

"He will come around. I'm not good to anyone like this, I'm too weak to be of service to you," he mutters.

"Do you honestly think I want you because you're of use to me? If that's the case, we have bigger problems than you being mortal…" I say, but he doesn't answer. He's too busy looking at his shoes. I place a finger under his chin and bring his eyes to meet mine. "Are you still stubborn? Do you still know how to dance? Are you still going to look at me like I'm the only girl in the world?"

"For me, you are the only girl in the world,' he says.

"I want you because of who you are not what you are… do you understand me?" I tell him.

"I love you," he replies.

"I love you too, now stop being stupid and go talk to your brother. He might be right for not wanting to rush things," I say. He kisses me once more and I'm afraid to let him go. When I realise I can't hold him forever I soften my grasp, he takes his time pulling away, but he hears my words and wanders off to find his brother.

"Men, what are you going to do with them?" Leo says plonking his exhausted body into the grass beside me.

"Tell me about it," I laugh.

-31-
SETH

I knew Aedan wouldn't be happy with my choice, but I didn't expect him to be this opposed. Adaline didn't seem happy either, but I have to do what's best for her and for Aedan. Last time Maura attacked I died and they almost lost their lives. What hope would I have facing her as a mortal man? Aedan's angry now, but he will come around, he has too. Gosh, walking is tiring, maybe I shouldn't have indulged the way I have the last few weeks and eaten a salad or two. This body isn't conducive to a poor diet.

"I can hear you puffing a mile away," Aedan says appearing beside me.

"I did die you know, you could cut me some slack," I tell him. "Are you over your tantrum yet?"

"Have you changed your mind yet?" He asks me.

"No," I reply.

"Figured, that's why I have sent out an injunction to every member in the clan, Samuel is letting his clan know as well," he says.

"An injunction for what?" I ask confused.

"No vampire is permitted to change you. You need time to think about this decision and I won't let you make the wrong choice," he says.

"Aedan, I understand your reservations, but you don't have the power to make this decision for me," I say through a clenched jaw.

"You're no longer a vampire, therefore I control your seat. So, trust me I do have the power and the injunction will be enforced or the punishment is death," he says firmly.

Aedan's eyes turn cold and determined. I can feel my stern features morph into the face of a grief-stricken child. How could he do this to me? Aedan's gaze softens as he sees the hurt that his betrayal is inflicting on me. He places a kind hand on my shoulder attempting to soothe me, but it only makes me see red. I shove away his hand and punch my fist into his jaw. My fingers hurt instantly. Hitting him in my current state is ineffective and the only one who's injured is me. I may as well have blown him a kiss, it would have had the same effect on his unblemished jaw.

"How could you do this to me?" I ask.

"I'm doing this for you," he replies before returning to Adaline and Leo.

I sit on the velvety green hill and sulk to myself for a while. I think of every logical argument that might force Aedan to change his mind. The transition to becoming a vampire can be a long ordeal and that means Adaline's left unprotected for longer than necessary. I would tell him this very reason, but he would just wave it off and say he will protect her. Maybe I can play along, giving Aedan the time he thinks I need. After a few days of playing human, he will see what a struggle it is and he will lift the injunction.

I look up at Adaline, she's too far away for my ears to hear the sweet sound of her laughter, but I can feel its joy all the same. Horse is following her around like an oversized shadow, and he hasn't given me a second glance since he set eyes on her. Can I blame him though? Clearly, he has excellent taste. I had imagined every inch of Adaline's form the entire trip home and there were times I had wondered if she was as beautiful as I remembered, or had I simply built her up in my mind.

Looking at her now I know I haven't built up anything. Her hair is more vibrant than I remember, I can see splashes of coppery red that blend seamlessly into her auburn locks. Her cheeks are a blushing rose and her eyes appear more emerald than violet. My heart beats a solid thump, the force so powerful that it rattles my chest. I hear it beating louder until it's ringing in my ears, at one point the steady thumping feels so loud I think it's echoing across the mountainside.

"Never thought I'd see your sorry face again," A gruff voice says dimming the thunder in my chest.

"Deklan, I never thought I would be happy to see your ugly mug again either, but here we are." I stand and offer my hand to him, but he pulls me into a bear hug. "God I'm not that happy to see you," I joke as he squeezes me tighter. I can see Jason standing behind him. The joy on his face is clear, but it's obvious he remembers I'm not a hugger. "Screw it, he's not letting me go you might as well join us," I say to Jason. Deklan releases an arm and pulls Jason into our huddle. "This is not gay in the slightest, we should ease up before Leo feels left out," I say through a muffled laugh.

Deklan finally releases us from his iron grip so I can breathe again. Jason is quick to apologise for Aedan's injunction and for my death and everything else he can think of that he may have done wrong since the day he was born. I actually missed his incessant chatter. Shay and Neema offer polite welcomes as they come to greet us, but Shay keeps her distance. I still don't trust her completely, but she has helped keep Adaline safe and that's all that matters to me.

Adaline, my brother and Leo have convened at the bottom of the ravine as they pack up their tents. We walk over to join them, and I make a beeline for Adaline. She smiles warmly as I approach, I take her hand in mine and bathe in her warmth.

I bring the back of her hand to my lips and kiss it swiftly. After dying, ruffling a few feathers about a forbidden romance seems a senseless worry. I watch Deklan's eyebrows raise, but he doesn't comment and I'm thankful for the reprieve. I've been through hell and the only thing that makes any of it worthwhile is feeling Adaline's presence beside me.

-32-
Adaline

There's a shared sense of hope in the air, I can feel it in every beating heart in our circle. I also sense a lingering tension between Aedan and Seth, it has a bitterness to it that doesn't sit right in my chest. Aedan may have overstepped, but I'd be lying if I said I wouldn't have done the same thing if I was in his position. When Seth was a vampire there was always an expiration date looming over our relationship. We never spoke about it, but we both knew it was there. One day I would grow old and die and he would stay young forever. It's a selfish thought, but I'm happy he's human. His humanity was always challenged by his vampire urges. Every sentiment of rage and hostility was heightened, and he always seemed to be on edge, now that he's human I can feel the shift in him. The burden that weighed heavy on his spirit has lifted and his heart and mind have found balance. I wouldn't be able to forgive myself if he went back into the darkness just to protect me. Deep down another concern crosses my mind. What if this now fleeting existence isn't enough for him? What if I'm not enough? I ask myself.

"Are you okay?" Seth asks.

"Fine, still in shock I think," I reply, leaning against his broad shoulders as I try to hide my fears.

Deklan relays the movements he has planned and once we are through the portal it's a short ride to the temple. I'm excited to see what it's like inside the Vale, having heard so many stories about the mythical creatures that reside beyond the boundaries my mind is running wild with the possibilities.

Shay has told me about the fate Phedora whose temple will be hosting us on our journey. Unfortunately, she won't be at the temple when we arrive, which is a shame. I had hoped she might be able to help me understand the visions of my past, but I guess I'll just have to figure it out on my own.

The walk to the portal is long and haggard. We need to take our time with the horses since a single misstep could easily leave them lame or worse. Apollo walks behind Seth and me as we maneuver our way around the exposed rocks. Seth tells me about his journey back to us, but there's one thing he's failing to mention. He starts his tale with him and Apollo leaving the island, he never says how he made his way out of the grave we put him in. Honestly, I don't want the image of him suffocating under the earth in my head, there are some things you can't unsee, so I'm glad he refuses to share that detail. Apollo nudges Seth between his shoulder blades forcing him forward. Seth stumbles, catching himself on a rock before he lands in the moist mud beneath our feet. Seth begins muttering profanities under his breath as he shakes off the debris that has clung to him.

"That's not nice Apollo," I tell him through a suppressed laugh.

"Stupid horse, I should have left him behind," Seth says.

"I'm glad you didn't," I say.

Apollo snickers as I pat his head, Seth just rolls his eyes and I can almost forget that things have changed. A pit of nausea settles in my stomach, something else changed while Seth was gone, and I'm going to have to tell him. I know that he will find out about Tripp and me, it's inevitable, but I can't do it today. Things are tense enough amongst our group and I don't want to out shadow the only ray of hope we have found.

The trees grow thicker in this part of the ravine. I'm frightened Apollo might get hurt as he pushes through the foliage, but he doesn't seem fussed. The electric thread I felt earlier is no longer a thread, it's spread out and transformed into an oceanic wave. I feel it drift along the surface of the earth like the rhythm of a beating heart. My imagination starts running away with me as I try to envision the entrance of the portal. I picture a curtain of glowing wildflowers that move meticulously on the cool breeze, creating music while they dance. A medley of colours clouds my mind as they attempt to embody the euphoric pull of the portal.

"We're here," Deklan says gruffly.

I leave my imagination and allow my eyes to focus on the beauty of the portal, instead of my whimsical daydreams I see a rundown, overgrown bridge. There is nothing enchanting about the image before me. I can't help but sigh with disappointment.

"What did you expect?" Seth asks.

"Something otherworldly I suppose. It looks like the type of place you would dump a body if you never wanted anyone to find it," I reply.

"It's supposed to be hidden, we can't exactly roll out the red carpet," Seth reminds me.

Deklan and Jason step into the darkness of the tunnel first. After a few minutes, Shay and Neema follow. Aedan ushers me forward, pushing me into the darkness. I stop short, I'm terrified, and I know it's not the ominous tunnel I'm walking into that scares me. It's what lies on the other side.

"Seth, promise you won't let go," I whisper, taking his hand in mine.

"I can't come with you. Humans can't access the portal, but I can walk with you as far as it will let me," he says sadly.

"Why didn't you say anything?" I cry.

"Selfishness I suppose," he says placing a kiss on my forehead.
"Once you're through I can catch up with Leo and go home. I'll make some calls and find a way to get to you," he adds, and his eyes fall angrily toward Aedan. "You need to go to court. Once you're the Queen you will have the ultimate protection, hell you might even be able to change the rules and let me through the gates if I'm still like this," he says with a smirk. I squeeze his hand firmly wishing I didn't have to leave him a second time. I step under a hanging root and into the blackness. My feet are glued to the floor and the childish fear that monsters are lurking in the darkness returns. Seth presses a gentle hand on the small of my back to keep me moving forward. I step blindly maneuvering my foot from side to side before I take a step. My foot hits something solid, it's a wide staircase protruding from the solid clay wall. I place my foot on the first step and tiny lights above us flicker to life. At first, I think I have triggered a sensor, then the lights begin to move. A steady wave of gleaming whites and sapphire blues trickle down towards us. I lift my free hand and I reach out to cradle one of the lights. "Sprites are white, and the blue ones are wisps," Seth whispers behind me.

One of the sprites lands gently on my open palm. She's weightless like air, once my eyes adjust to her brightness I can see her tiny form. Her skin is formed from golden leaves layered over one another forming a thin human-shaped body. She has two very large oval eyes that glisten like polished onyx and a small black glassy dot between them. I lean closer and the black dot winks at me, it's a third eye. The sprite smiles and drifts back towards the others.

"Stunning," I say as I admire the tiny creatures.

I start walking up the stairs as the sprites and wisps light the path, I can hear Seth's breathing quicken behind me. I reach back, pulling him closer to me, I channel as much of my magic into him as I can, maybe I can wrap his body in a cloak of magic that will fool the portal.

The wisps begin tapering off and the sprites soon follow as they retreat into the darkness. The final wisp jumps out of our path revealing a sphere-shaped opening that's bathed in light. As the light falls on my face I'm comforted with a warmth that can only be described as love. It reminds me of when I was little, and my mother would hug me so tight it made my heart skip a beat. The path is decorated with rich coloured flowers in shades of reds, purples and glorious blues. Beautiful trees loom over us, woven together in twisted strands creating an arch. The heavenly rays seeping through the open spaces of the canopy creates a speckled path of light on top of the pea green blades of grass. I've never seen anything so exquisite in all my life.

"Shit I can't believe that worked," Seth shouts, shaking cobwebs off his coat like a dog. I roll my eyes at him. Only he could curse in a sanctuary as serene as this. "What?" He asks.

"Never mind," I tell him.

"I guess you don't have to hurry off and find someone to bite you after all," Aedan says smugly to Seth as he exits the portal with Apollo following close behind.

"Stop bickering. We need to get a move on it will be getting dark soon," Deklan orders.

I turn back looking down at the stairs to the darkness of the entrance of the portal, it's unassuming façade reveals nothing of the wonders that hide within, it's utterly perfect in all its unsuspecting glory.

-33-

Deklan

I can hear the tranquil sounds of the tree nymphs as they sing to the birds hiding in their branches. The calming tones soothe me, and my body tries to relax into the blissfulness of the sound. There are no signs of insidious enemy's hiding in the shadows and I'm tempted to release a sigh of relief, but I don't want to lure myself into a false sense of security. Theo has forbidden any hunters from using this portal entrance for the next few days which is allowing us the solitude we need to slip into the Vale undetected. I'm just glad to finally have something working in our favour.

Adaline has climbed off and on Apollo at least five times in the last thirty minutes. Just like with a child, something shiny catches her eye and she runs off to follow it. At one point I turned back to see she had slipped herself inside a fairy ring, luckily Seth pulled her back before the little bastards took her. I have to keep reminding myself that she isn't familiar with the dangers of our world and although we live in peace it only takes a single wrong move to find ourselves in trouble.
I notice movement in the trees above us, I lift my hand signalling our party to halt. The branches quake and shiver above us like something is gliding past, but it never settles its full weight on the branches. I pull out a sword from the saddlebag strapped to Neema's horse. The others move methodically forming a circle around Adaline, the rustling of leaves drowns out the heavy sounds of my heart beating in my ears.

"What's that?" Adaline asks in a whisper, pointing up at the canopy.

"I don't see anything?" Seth remarks.

I follow the direction of Adaline's outstretched hand, but I see nothing. The trees fall silent once more and the leaves turn still. Whatever was above us seems to have moved on.

"What did you see?" I ask Adaline.

"I'm not sure. It had fur that shimmered when the light touched it. It was hard to see through the trees," she says.

"Keep the weapons ready," I order.

We walk on eggshells until we reach the end of the forest's passageway. We lose the coverage of the forestry as we step onto a dusty road. The trees along the roadside begin to thin out as the hills lead down toward open fields. I order our group to withhold their weapons, out in the open like this the display of defence would draw too much attention. I'm glad to see the vampires are remaining vigilant, they are a weapon in themselves after all. Theo had offered a portion of the royal guard to accompany us back, but I'm afraid I can no longer vouch for their loyalty. I wish it wasn't true, but it only takes the right price or the right threat to persuade loyal men to commit unspeakable deeds.

The road to Phedora's temple is frequently travelled by merchants that move between the realms, but most merchants who use this entrance deal in forbidden services and restricted goods, so they tend to keep to themselves, which is exactly the kind of privacy we need. Not too far ahead I can see a stationary black carriage. I can make out three horses waiting patiently for their master to recommence their journey, but there's no driver in sight.

"Halt," I order.

"Can you smell that?" I ask Aedan.

"Yes, hobgoblins," he replies.

The acidic bicarb smell of a hob isn't something you forget easily. I remember the scent of the hobgoblin that made the attempt on Adaline's life when she was just a baby, the scent of the creature that killed my wife. Hobgoblins frequenting the Vale isn't unusual. In the uprising, they sided with the Unseelie and made their home in Vargo. It's possible that they are just passing through as they peddle their illegal goods, but what are the odds of us stumbling onto a party of the vile creatures with Adaline in our company. I don't believe in coincidences.

"Should we attack?" Shay asks, eager for a fight.

"Maybe they have trouble with a wheel or something," Aedan adds.

"Let's just kill them. We can't risk them seeing Adaline, they might be bounty hunters and what if they suspect something and make it back to Vargo. We will have more to worry about than the Queen," Seth says.

"How do you plan on killing a hob?" Shay says to Seth. He draws one of the swords from the saddle bag and holds the blade comfortably above his shoulder. "Here," Shay says throwing him a gun. "If you're close enough to use the sword they will be close enough to crush your skull," she adds.

"Adaline stay on Apollo, Aedan you join her. Everyone else keep your weapons ready but keep them concealed. If they make a wrong move we kill them all, no survivors," I order.

The horse's huff and snort as we make a slow approach to the motionless carriage. I can feel all our bodies synchronising into a single organism. The steady flow of adrenaline that filters into my bloodstream is urging the wolf in me to emerge. The beast is hungry for a fight but the man in me hopes it doesn't come to that.

The dark carriage has been pulled to the side of the road, heavy curtains are closed obstructing my view and the horse's reigns are tied tightly to the driver's seat.

This stop was deliberate. I sniff the air; the scent of the hobs is overpowering. My nose shifts through the other smells surrounding us. The musky scent of the horses, the fresh dew forming in the fields and beneath it all, there's something else, the scent of fresh blood.

I open my eyes as a hob leaps from the carriage. Six feet tall with pale lilac skin and a braided mohawk that rises as high as the creatures pointed ears. This creature could be the twin of the hob I killed eighteen years ago, I just hope he's ready to meet the same fate as his brother.

-34-
Adaline

The hob looks like something from a horror film. Fierce fangs are exposed as his lips pull back into a feral snarl. Deklan swings his blade toward the hob, but it leaps over him and his sword in one fell swoop. Shay and Jason lunge toward him as it tries to sink its claws into Deklan's shoulder. Neema's eyes glow red and her fangs extend as she leaves my side to join in the fight. As Neema approaches a second hob exposes itself from behind the carriage. Neema isn't quick enough and the violet coloured beast sinks its fangs into her arm. Neema rips her arm out of the hobs mouth leaving most of her flesh in its teeth. Seth starts charging towards Neema taking fire as he runs, the exploding sound of the gun is drowned out by a monstrous scream that escapes the carriage. There isn't time for me to focus on the source of the scream because Seth is hurtled across the road in a flurry of blood and dirt. Aedan leaps down from Apollo and runs to his brother's aid.

All the panic and anger burning inside me is making my skin start to sizzle, my arm stings and I feel a painful swelling pulsing in my cheek, as I look at my skin I realise the wounds I'm feeling don't belong to me. I'm absorbing the violence of the battle and it's too much to contain. My fingers begin to flame, I climb off Apollo before I cause him any harm. As my feet hit the ground an intense pain tightens in my abdomen. It squeezes my insides, contracting them until I'm brought to my knees. I look up to see where the pain is coming from. My friends are wounded in unspeakable ways, but each of them is on their feet still fighting. The contracting pain hits me again like a destructive wave, somethings wrong.

Fear and heartache out shadow all other emotions surrounding me. I try to stand, but it hurts, I reach down inside myself and release a scream that directs a powerful burst of wind outwards. The force sends my friends and the hobs flying in different directions. With the battle momentarily paused and the shock keeping everyone stationary I can focus on the suffering that's stronger than any battle. I run toward the carriage and pull back the curtains. Inside is a sweat covered female hob. Her belly is swollen, and her draped skirt is drenched in blood. She weakly holds up a small knife toward me, but she doesn't have the strength to use it. There's another contraction, the baby's dying I can feel it.

"Let me help you," I beg her. She lowers the knife dropping it on the carriage floor. I reach forward slowly and lift the damp skirt to her knees, I can see a small blood-covered head fighting to free itself. I can't explain how I know it, but the cords stuck around its neck. "You need to stop pushing," I tell her. She bites down on her lip so firmly I see blood starting to spill. I slip my fingers around the baby's head, but the cord is around its neck too tightly for me to loosen, I leave my finger between the cord and the baby's neck as I position myself. I'm going to have to remove it once the babies out. "Push now," I tell her. Her body contracts responding to the primal need to push, in seconds the babies out. I keep its head close to the woman's pubic region and flip the baby's legs over itself in a somersault fashion, I turn the baby to the side, rolling it around until the cord unwinds. On the second full turn, the baby is free. The baby isn't breathing, I scoop its mouth free of any fluid and lay it on its stomach over my lap. I thrust a firm pat on the babies back trying to clear any excess fluid. A single cry is expelled from the baby's chest. The hob woman cries out in relief, I place the baby on her chest. I back out of the carriage to give them both some space. I turn to see the stunned faces of my bloodied and bruised friends and two enormous hobs towering over me. The hob with the mohawk pushes me aside and climbs into the carriage.

"You helped her." The other hob says to me, the shock is written clearly on his face. "Why?" He asks.

"Because she needed it," I tell him. He still looks confused.

"Thank you. My name is Beetok and I owe you a life debt for saving my sister and her child," he says falling to his knees.

"Your welcome, but a life debt's not necessary, I'll settle for no more bloodshed," I reply. Beetok tilts his head in a formal bow and joins his family in the carriage.

"Adaline, it's forbidden for our kind to birth children outside of our realm. The child was born on Seelie grounds, it has to be put down," Deklan says tightening his grip on his blade.

"You will do no such thing, I don't give a shit about your rules. I forbid you from touching a single hair on that child's head, do I make myself clear?" I tell him.

"Adaline it's the law. Fae children absorb the essence of the realm they are born in. If a child is born outside of their allegiance the boundary can become unstable," Seth says.
"And I said I don't care… If any of you want to harm that baby you will have to go through me," I say firmly. I don't like throwing my power around, but the only way that baby is going to be harmed is over my dead body. The hob with the mohawk steps out of the carriage to face me, I square my shoulders bracing myself.

"Forgive our attack, we thought you were part of the guard," he says gesturing to Deklan and kneels to the ground before me. He withdraws a small blade and raises it high. Deklan's weight shifts to attack, but Aedan holds him in place. The hob slices the blade into his violet-coloured palm until blood begins to flow. He drops the knife and grips my hand with his bloodied one. "I Fealm, of the Unseelie, swear on my king and commander that I owe you a life debt, to be paid in full or I will offer my life to be taken in its place," he says to the heavens.

"Um… thanks," I reply. The warmed stickiness of his blood against my skin makes my teeth clench.

"What is your name, my lady?" Fealm asks.

"Adaline," I reply. He's still holding my hand as his blood drips between our palms and into the dirt. The moments becoming weird and I don't know if I should pull away or if that would offend him. God, I hope we didn't just get married, I don't think I would like to wake up to his protruding chin and nose every morning.

"How may I be of service my lady Adaline?" He asks. I feel everyone staring at me and it's making me uncomfortable, then I hear the baby cry in the carriage and my heart feels full. I lower myself to the ground and place a gentle hand on Fealm's shoulder.

"Our debt is settled if you promise to take that child home and raise it well. Raise him to be good and kind. Can you promise me that?" I ask.

"You have my word," he says with a fang-filled smile.

"You had better leave before someone else happens along your path," Deklan adds.

The trio is on their way as soon as the baby is swaddled and Neema has made sure the mother is safe to travel. The vampires and Deklan have all healed by the time we watch the carriage disappear over the hill. Unfortunately, Seth's human body has taken a rather bad beating. Seth shrugs it off clearly not wanting to appear weak, which isn't a word I would think of to describe him. Seth hobbles over to my side and wraps his arms around my waist. I'm afraid to hug him back in case I hurt his already wounded body. The back of his shirt is a damp mess of sweat and blood that's cool to the touch. A tear escapes my eyes as I remember his lifeless body having dirt shovelled on top of it, I can't lose him again.

"What you did was stupid," Seth whispers.

"We have that in common then... You're not indestructible anymore. You can't just run into battle like that," I tell him.

His shoulders tighten, and he releases me abruptly as if my words have offended him. He walks over to Jason with a small hitch in his step. He and Jason head down to the field to gather the frightened horses that have hidden themselves in the long grass. Apollo brushes against my side snickering in my ear, I run my hand back and forth over his gleaming coat and steep in his reassuring presence.

-35-
Tripp

I've walked around the temple grounds at least five times, Adaline was expected to arrive two hours ago and I'm beginning to panic, the sun has already set behind the rose coloured mountains and soon it will be dark. My bare feet feel the tremble of the horse's hooves before I see them approaching. As each of them passes through the temple gates it's hard to ignore the signs of battle. Most of them have ripped and tattered clothing, with remnants of dried blood. My eyes find Adaline and I examine her body looking for wounds, her hands are covered in dark dried blood, but it doesn't appear to be her own. As my panic subsides I recognise the horse she's riding and sure enough walking beside Adaline and Apollo is Seth. He looks worse than the others; he has grazes and cuts along his face and arms that haven't healed as they should.

"Hey son," Deklan says as he pulls me into a quick embrace.

"What happened?" I ask.

"Couple of hobs, but nothing we couldn't handle," he replies valiantly.

"Oh please," Adaline scoffs as she climbs down from Apollo. I don't need to see her face to know she's rolling her eyes. Now that she's closer to me I can see her clothes are as drenched in blood as her hands, but she doesn't move like she's injured. She wraps a tender arm around Seth's back and leads him into the temple. She doesn't even acknowledge my presence as she passes.

"She's still mad," I say to my father.

"She's not the only one," Aedan says, pushing past me.

"You're just lucky Seth doesn't know what happened, even in this state he would destroy you," Shay mocks raising an eyebrow.

I guess it was delusional to think all my sins could be forgiven after a short time apart. I help my father inside the temple, I can see burn marks on his arm that have almost healed and a few fresh cuts that are starting to close. His body heals quickly, and he looks younger than his years, but he's getting too old for this kind of life. I just hope he realises it before he gets himself killed.

Phedora's attendants flutter down the glassy staircase to greet us in a burst of excitement. They don't know Adaline's true identity, but they know we are under the protection of the King, so clearly we are getting the VIP treatment. Each of the attendants is assigned to two members of our party. Aedan and Jason follow their attendant down the hall on the first level, Shay and Neema follow another upstairs and Seth and Deklan are greeted by a third. Adaline looks around for her attendant but instead is greeted by Phedora herself. Phedora hugs her tightly before dropping to her knees and placing Adaline's blood covered palm on her forehead. I watch as Adaline stands over the blue-haired woman nervously. Silence seems too loud for this intimate exchange when I can't hold my breath any longer Phedora catapults herself off the ground and back into Adaline's arms.

"I knew it the second I saw you," Phedora squeals excitedly.

"Nice to meet you too... Do you think there is somewhere I can clean up, I'm covered in so many layers of disgusting I can't even tell you where it all came from," Adaline asks over Phedora's shoulder.

"Oh, of course, wasn't that baby hob just darling? I do love the way their little ears point out when they are so new..." Phedora prattles as she leads Adaline down the hall.

With everyone settled inside, I decide to wander back into the maze and enjoy the pull of nature. As I enter the maze I let go of my connection to the earth and allow myself to wander freely through the labyrinth. Every now and then I come to a dead end and have to turn myself around. Eventually, I make it back to the centre where I watched Phedora dance freely like a child. Part of me is envious of her childlike wonder, it's something I never really experienced. Between mum's murder and my father's detachment, I never really had the type of childhood where I could dance around like no one was watching. The earth tries tempting me to give in to my desires, I ignore its call and follow the path I had come. I arrive at the start of the maze, and I see Adaline standing just outside the entrance staring at the silphium flowers.

"I've never seen flowers like this before," she says.

"They are extinct in the mortal realm. The humans still have descendants of the plant, but the originals like this were killed off long ago," I reply.

"Everything's more vibrant here, the air's lighter and cleaner. I guess this is what life would have been like if people had taken better care of the planet," she says. I watch as she moves along the edge of the maze. The silphium flowers turn their heads and follow her path until she returns to stand beside me. "I don't want to be angry about what happened between us. I can't forget what you did, but I can forgive it," she says.

"I am sorry, I didn't mean for it to happen the way it did. I didn't intend to trick you into sleeping with me," I whisper.

"I know, it was my choice too," she says and reaches up to place a small kiss on my cheek.

"I won't say anything to him," I promise.

"I will, lies get us nowhere," she says.

She smiles weakly and walks back towards the temple. Deep down the crippling feeling that she would never forgive me was beginning to eat me alive, but it's not in her nature to be hateful. I could have understood if she did feel that way, but Adaline has more goodness in her than I have ever seen in anyone else. It's just one of the things I love about her.

-36-
Adaline

Anger is an emotion that comes so easily. It's fast and hot like the detonation of a bomb, after a while the debris settles and the fire burns itself out, leaving nothing but ruins in its wake. I could sense Tripp's remorse from the moment I laid eyes on him at the temple gates. I had tried to ignore him for Seth's benefit, but the culpability that weighed in my stomach wouldn't let me rest. I saw Tripp vanish into the beautiful labyrinth made of flowers and I waited for him to come out. I could have easily followed him inside, but I think I needed the time to build my courage. It's not easy forgiving someone who has hurt you, but living with the animosity is worse. I looked into his evergreen eyes and forgave him wholeheartedly, and on some level, I still have feelings for him. It's a tiny pang of affection that sneaks up on me just when I think it's vanished. Maybe that's something that will never go away, I just hope it's something that I can live with.

"What was that about?" Seth asks, standing by the temple door, nodding his head toward Tripp.

"Jesus Seth, I almost had a heart attack," I shriek. I release my startled breath and my heart finds its way out of my stomach and back into its rightful cavity.

"What was that?" Seth repeats.

"A goodbye…" I reply honestly. Seth raises his eyebrows but doesn't pry any further. "I'm exhausted, can we talk about it in the morning?"

"Go get some rest, there's nothing to talk about," He says and leans down to kiss me. The kiss is intense but not in the way I'm used to. I can feel his eyes looking over my shoulder. His body screams like a child that's pushed another off their bike and is riding away with it. I pull back from his embrace feeling more exhausted than I already did.

"Don't kiss me like that," I tell him.

"Like what?" He retorts.

"Like you did it only to spite Tripp, it was jealous and hostile. I don't want those feelings between us," I tell him.

"I didn't mean to," he says.

"We can talk tomorrow, I'm going to bed," I say and do just that.

-37-
SETH

Tripp vanished into the garden, moments after the exchange between Adaline and I. I was tempted to go after him, but still reeling from Adaline's disappointment in me I decided to sit on the porch and let my emotions cool down. The fire element that used to swell within me was a pain in the ass and trying to control it was a constant struggle, nonetheless, at least it gave me something to focus on. Now all I have are the emotions themselves and the jealousy I felt as I watched Adaline with Tripp overwhelmed me. She only kissed him on the cheek and the moment seemed innocent enough, but I can't deny the insecurities that arose within me. It's obvious that Adaline is too good for me, and I've never tried to tell myself anything different. When I was a vampire at least I had something more to offer her, even if it was only protection, and now all I have to offer is me.

When I saw them together my greatest fear was realised, she's going to see that I'm not worthy and someone else is better suited. Deklan's son, as much as I hate to admit it, is a threat. He can offer her things I can't, a family, security within the Seelie and the fact he doesn't need to drink blood to sustain himself doesn't hurt either.

My human eyes catch sight of a dark figure approaching the temple. Had I still been a vampire I would have spotted him a mile away. As he gets close I feel my jealousy building itself back up like Jenga blocks on the verge of collapse. Adaline had said it was a goodbye between them, but I'm scared about what she was saying goodbye to.

"Hey," he says through the darkness.

151

"Patrick is it? We haven't been formally introduced," I reply.

"Who needs formalities when you set my neck on fire and tried to kill me," he says slowing his walk. He is only a few feet away and I can properly see the lines of his face, he looks wounded. I disregard his evident pain because flashes of him and Adaline on the beach return to the forefront of my mind.

"Patrick, I think its best that you and I keep our distance, and since I won't be leaving Adaline's side I guess that means you will be keeping your distance from her as well," I say firmly. He regards me for a moment and his expression changes.

"Human right?" he comments with a sly smirk plastered on his face.

"It's temporary I assure you," I remind him.

"Either way, we both know neither of us will be worthy of her. Don't worry though, I'll keep my distance," he says as he brushes past me.

The sky is dark and dim, but hundreds of fireflies have emerged from their hiding places to dance along the mazes flower tops. The moon sits high tonight behind the rose-coloured mountains, its pale light has a blushed colour to it that trickles down the mountainside. The light stretches across the fields until it casts a misty fog against the temple and its surrounding walls. Phedora's temple is supposed to be the embodiment of clarity and wisdom, but tonight it feels shrouded in shadows.

-38-
Adaline

I must have been more exhausted than I thought because I slept through the night without burdened thoughts troubling my unconscious mind. No longer having the guilt of Seth's death on my conscience and being able to forgive Tripp seems to have gone a long way to easing the pit of anguish in my stomach. There's still one thing I need to do and that's tell Seth about what transpired between Tripp and I. Technically, I know I shouldn't feel guilty for my actions, since the death of your boyfriend gives you the freedom to date whoever you want, but it doesn't excuse how quickly I negated the affections I have for Seth just to offer myself to someone else.

I place my feet on the cold mosaic floor as I climb out of bed, and an icy shiver climbs up my legs. The shiver stretches up my thighs, through the arch of my back, and across my shoulder blades until it's released at my fingertips. I collect some fresh clothes from my travel pack and tiptoe across the floor until my feet sink into the thick rug. I lift off my nightgown and feel a cool gust of air as it caresses my body. I turn to see my bedroom door is wide open and Phedora is standing in its frame. I clutch my gown to my naked chest, but it's too late she's already seen everything.

"DO YOU MIND?" I yell.

"Oh," She says playfully and closes the door, unfortunately, she stays on the wrong side. "Forgive my forwardness, I just can't believe the form you have chosen," she says.

"Turn around," I tell her as I hastily slip my clothes over my head. "I can't help the body I was born with," I comment as I turn to face her.

153

"You don't remember do you?" She asks with a slight tilt of her head. "Here," she says as she removes a necklace from under her dress. As I look closer at the trinket I realise it's a small vial containing a gold liquid. "Do you remember giving me this?" She asks.

"No, I hadn't met you before yesterday," I reply, looking closer at the vial. "But it reminds me of something…"

"Your last life. When you were the mother of horses," she adds.

"How do you know about that?" I ask.

"I know everything that has ever happened. Sometimes certain things are harder to see, but still, I've seen it all. Before you left us, you gifted each of my sisters and me with a vial of your tears. Strongest magic in the world are the tears of the mother horse, it's partly how my sisters and I keep the barriers up," she says staring at the dreamy golden liquid.

"Do you know how I came to be here now?" I ask her.

"You promised you would return, I just didn't think it would be so long. Then again, your life is longer than ours," she says.

"Are you saying I'm immortal?" I ask.

"You were never immortal, but you also never died. This body you have chosen is different though," she says as she examines my form. "It's frail."

"Have you seen the architect? A woman with feathered golden hair, she appeared to me during my transition," I ask.

"Can't say I have, but you have been around a lot longer than me, perhaps she's from before my time," she says sweetly and begins bouncing back towards the door.

"How old are you?" I call after her.

"Ladies never reveal their age…" she hollas.

I run after her, but by the time I reach the door she has vanished, and the corridor feels cold without her childlike laughter. The first thing I'm going to do when we reach the castle is ask for a history book on the fae world, because I feel like my mind is going to explode trying to make sense of everything.

-39-

Deklan

We are taking the day to rest before leaving for court, the events of the last few months have really taken a toll on all of us. My son made himself scarce this morning, and I wish we could have spent more time together. It's now early afternoon and everyone else is huddled in Phedora's sitting room. It resembles something close to a hippy commune more than the formal lounge it's supposed to be. It's draped in an array of silken fabrics and plush cushions that cover every surface of the floor. Attendants continue handing out goblets filled with copious volumes of lavender wine. Despite the laughter in the room it's hard to ignore the ever-present tension between Seth and Aedan, they aren't even making eye contact, and won't directly address one another. The uncomfortableness of the situation is making my shoulders rigid with anxiety. Adaline makes her best efforts to try and mend the fences between the two brothers, however, I think even this is beyond her power.

An attendant arrives with empty hands, I know at once he has come for me. He informs me that the Tarrax has arrived to deliver my message. I pull the scroll from my pocket and make my way to the garden. As I open the gate a floral scent catches on the breeze and I find Adaline trapesing after me.

"Do you mind?" She asks. "I just need some fresh air,"

"Not at all, I'm sending a message to your father," I say raising my forearm and let out a high-pitched whistle.

The Tarrax takes its time to land, but eventually, it perches itself on my arm and stretches out its impressive wingspan, the bird is almost too heavy for me to hold. I watch Adaline's eyes open wide in astonishment. The birds really are beautiful creatures, long elegant necks with small white beaks. Their pure white feathers don't look thick enough to keep its massive body warm and the tips of its long wispy tail look like dandelion seeds drifting in the wind. I attach the scroll to its ankle and stroke its long neck. I gesture for Adaline to approach. She walks toward us slowly, I can see she's worried she might frighten it away, but the Tarrax don't scare easily. If they do feel under threat their white feathers turn to a blackened ash and a toxic poison dispenses from their talons, it's one of the reasons that makes them ideal messenger birds for the royal family.

"Is it a boy or girl?" Adaline asks as she ruffles its feathers.

"Tarrax are gender fluid, they change as needed to reproduce. When they are white they are in male form, black they are female," I tell her.

"Does it have a name?" she asks.

"Cinder. Cinder's one of your father's favourites," I tell her. "Cinder will tell him we are leaving at first light tomorrow," I say. I lift my arm and Cinder takes to the sky disappearing amongst the clouds.

"Can I ask you something?" She says looking at the sky.

"Of course," I respond.

"Do you think Seth will forgive me? I know you're aware of what happened… between Tripp and I. I can sense your discomfort whenever we are in the same room," she says uncomfortably.

"I never have been good at hiding my emotions. My wife always said my face said more than my word, my sons the same in that respect. I know he loves you, but I also know where your heart belongs… Now, I'm not saying I approve, but I understand," I tell her.

"I never meant to hurt Tripp or Seth. I have never wanted to hurt anyone in my entire life," she says sadly.

"Truer words were never spoken," I say and hug her tightly. "I believe it would be impossible for someone to stay mad at you."

I look up and meet Seth's gaze looking down at us. "Speak of the devil. I'll be inside if you need anything," I say.

-40-
Adaline

Deklan walks back to the temple at an impressive speed, he smacks Seth on the shoulder in a friendly gesture as he passes him which makes me smile. Seth lingers for a moment, maybe he can sense that somethings been eating away at me since his return or maybe he can feel the shift between us.

"Are you okay?" Seth asks.

"I'm fine, I just saw my first Tarrax," I say.

"Silly birds, they can turn at the drop of a hat," he remarks looking up at the sky.

"Seth, about Tripp and me," I begin to say.

"Don't, I don't want to think about it," he says coldly.

"Seth, I need to tell you..." I begin to say, but he cuts me off.

"Do you love him?" He asks barely looking at me.

"I care for him, but I love you," I say honestly.

"I hate that you feel anything for him... I HATED WATCHING YOU KISS HIM ON THAT BEACH!" He screams. I reach out to touch him, but he steps out of my grasp. "Please don't... I woke up in the coldest darkest place imaginable, I couldn't breathe without being consumed by darkness.

The only thing that kept me going was you, even when I didn't know who I was, deep down I knew I had someone to live for… at least I thought I did."

As he storms off his pain explodes with a physical force that crushes my chest. He might as well have stuck a blade in my heart. I collapse to the ground and try to find my breath beneath my sorrows. The rain comes heavily, dark clouds close the sky in our shared heartache. When Seth was gone I had wished and prayed to every God to bring him back to me and now I'm responsible for pushing him away. The smell of rain usually comforts me, but as the drops fall on my skin I feel no relief. My skin starts to shiver, and my clothes are made heavy as they absorb the water. I feel like I should just lay here in the dirt and give up.

"Poetic isn't it, dying from pneumonia after everything we have gone through to keep you alive," Shay says from behind me. "Can you do your umbrella thing? I'm not a fan of the rain." I raise my hand and cast a small shield that follows Shay as she walks towards me. "I take it you told him," she says and sits down beside me.

"Didn't get a chance he was so angry about the kiss on the island I never got to tell him the rest. I can't blame him for hating me, when he finds out how far it really went it will kill him," I reply.

"He's just pissed off, we both know that boy is hella high strung, he will cool down eventually," she says nudging my shoulder with hers. "Trust me, he just doesn't know how to handle his emotions, he's like a child. He can hardly judge you, he's no saint."

"I understand though, I'd be just as upset if he had kissed someone else," I admit. I feel Shay's emotions tighten, she's putting up a shield between her emotions and me. "Don't worry Shay, I know about your past with him. You don't have to hide yourself from me, besides it was long before Seth and I ever met." Her breath catches in the back of her throat and I feel a wave of guilt drift out of her that sinks into the earth. "It was before we met right?" I ask.

"It was one time, the day you met him. It didn't mean anything though, not to him… It was before he knew you," she adds.

"I don't have the right to be mad at either of you," I say to her.

It's true, I don't have the right to be angry, the day I met Seth feels like a hundred years ago, but I still feel hurt. I feel my heart shatter into pieces so small it resembles a fine powder that threatens to drift away on the breeze. I stand up dropping the shield between Shay and the rain and walk back into the temple. I lay down on my bed and watch the bold flashes of lightning that illuminate the sky through the window. A lightning bolt strikes a tree somewhere behind the mountains and the sky turns amber.

-41-
SETH

I have never cared enough about anything to feel this kind of grotesque betrayal that's rolling around inside of me. First my brother with the injunction and then reliving the moment Tripp had Adaline pressed against him. The sudden downpour only heightens my increasing rage, a nearby tree is the target of my fury. I punch my fists into its bark until I can no longer feel the sting of the cuts and my hands become a mangled bloodied mess. I can feel a warmth in my hands and it reminds me of my fire element. I think of the way it used to burn and explode inside of me as it enticed my emotions and desires. The power begins to build, I wait for flames to emerge from my skin, but the fire remains dormant. The heat I'm feeling isn't otherworldly, it's just the warmth of my human blood pumping out of open wounds.

"Are you finished breaking your hands?" Aedan asks. I swing around and punch him in the jaw. My blood is streaked across his face and his eyes grow red and his fangs expose. "Here," he says biting his wrist and offering me a sip. I smack it away, his blood will only heal me, but I need his venom to change me.

"Turn me and I won't need healing," I spit.

"Are you coming back to the temple or are we going to court without you?" Aedan asks.

"There's no reason to go back," I say.

"You mean besides going back to the girl that clearly loves you. Sometimes I could snap your neck for being so insipid. You were dead Seth, it broke her, it broke me. She was destroyed, I thought we were going to lose her too, have you even noticed how thin she has gotten? She wouldn't eat, wouldn't drink and when she did it was because Deklan forced her to. I did everything I could think of to keep her going after losing you. You're a selfish smug asshole... Who cares if she did something stupid, it doesn't matter. She loves you and you still don't deserve her," he rants.

"I didn't realise…" I start.

"No, you didn't. I know you went through hell and I'm sorry for that, but we all went through hell, Adaline more than the rest of us. Try and remember you weren't the only person we buried that day," he snaps.

"I'm sorry," I say. I hadn't considered how hard it had been for them, not really. The only person whose emotions I have been thinking about are my own.

"I don't need your apologies, but Adaline needs your forgiveness and you need her, so stop being a dick and be grateful," he says.

I hug my brother tightly and for the first time since his refusal to change me, I don't have any animosity toward him. Aedan and I walk back to the temple under the cloak of darkness. A shadow passes over us and I hear the change in the air as the steady beat of wings overpowers the sky. We pause looking up at the heavens searching for the figure casting such an impressive shadow. The wingspans too large for it to be a Tarrax.

"Gargoyles," Aedan says sniffing the sky.

I stare frozen at the blank space beside me, Aedan is already back at the temple before I can force my feet to move. I run after him as close as I can, but my body won't work as quickly as I need it to.

By the time I reach the temple doors there is no door to be seen. Only chunks of broken red stone resting in pieces at my feet. I step over the disturbed threshold, the only sounds escaping the temple is silence. I open the chest by the entrance and grab one of the swords. Mechanically I start checking the passages of the temple. The lower levels are clear aside from the antiques that have been tossed to the ground, I discover two attendants on the floor in one of the halls, both of whom are dead. I hear glass breaking upstairs and a woman's painful cry. I hurry towards the chaos, climbing the stairs two at a time. On the second level, I see Adaline on the ground holding Phedora in her arms as she lays bleeding.

There are remnants of a dead gargoyle or two by pools of thick black blood that's burning into the floor and beside them is Jason's body. I can see his neck has been broken which thankfully is a wound he can heal from. Deklan's tying a tourniquet to stop the blood flowing from the gaping chunk of flesh that has been bitten out of his leg. He fumbles with a torn piece of shirt. I run over and help him tie off the blood flow at his thigh. Stopping the blood is enough to allow his natural healing to kick in and rebuild the severed artery. Aedan's standing over Adaline and Phedora looking more frantic than I have ever seen him.

"How do we save her?" Adaline asks.

"I don't know, I, I..." Aedan rambles, running his blackened hand through his hair.

The fates do not age, they do not get sick and as the oldest creatures in our world they don't die, but I guess no one has ever tried before. Not with their lives being linked to the boundaries. If she dies the barriers will crumble down around us, leaving nothing except destruction in their wake.

Phedora's blue hair is mattered and stained with streaks of dark blood that's starting to turn stiff. Her face is whiter than the snow coloured dress she's wearing. She's clutching at her chest as Adaline begins to cry. Phedora wipes a tear weakly away from Adaline's face and I see her shoulders stiffen. Adaline's expression hardens, and she begins ripping at Phedora's dress, tearing at the fabric ravenously.

"What are you doing?" I ask her.

"I can save her..." she says absently.

She removes a small vial that was hidden beneath the layers of Phedora's dress. I step closer to get a better look. The vial contains a gilded substance that swishes back and forth as Adaline rolls it between her fingers. She unscrews the metal cap and spills a single golden drop on Phedora's tongue. The colour comes back to her cheeks instantly and her blue eyes open wide. I watch in astonishment as the torn slivers of skin across her abdomen begin closing, knitting themselves together like a piece of fabric being joined by a seam.

"What was that?" I ask.

"Just a little of her magic," Phedora replies sweetly.

"You pushed me out of the way and saved my life, I owe you so much more," she replies.

"Where are the others?" I ask Aedan.

"They took them, Neema, Shay and Tripp. One of the monsters had a message for us," Aedan's says.

"What was it?" I ask.

"Maura sends her bests," Adaline says.

-42-
Adaline

She's taunting me now. Taking my friends is her sick way of getting back at me for having the upper hand during our last encounter. This has become more than an assassination for Maura, it's a game. Unfortunately for her, I'm no longer a tiny mouse caught in her trap and I'm going to make sure she knows it.

Aedan and Seth are downstairs helping Deklan with his wounds and realigning Jason's neck and spine, so he can heal in the correct position. Phedora's stomach has almost completely healed, there are faint red marks on her ivory skin that show how badly she had been injured, but for the most part, you wouldn't know her stomach had been ripped open. I help her into a fresh set of clothing and position her comfortably into her bed.

"You shouldn't go after her," Phedora says.

"I'm not letting her hurt any more of the people I care about," I tell her.

"In your first life you were the symbol of purity and nourishment, mankind looked to you for guidance. You watched as humanity found its place in the world and the destruction that followed. When your current form was no longer able to help people the way they needed you changed. For eons you shifted forms, becoming what was needed to save us, but no matter what form you took the one constant was the hope you brought to us. "This isn't like your previous lives if you die here you're not coming back," she says. "How do you expect to continue your work if you die?" She asks.

"It could be why I chose this body to be my final vessel," I tell her.

"Because you want to die?" She says.

"I don't want to die, but maybe it's time I stop coming back," I tell her.

"Promise you won't go after her," she pleads.

"Please don't make me lie to you," I tell her. "Rest."

I close the door behind me and whisper a silent apology into the empty hall. The temple is hollow with all the attendant's dead. I can feel the others downstairs, I don't bother going to see them, instead, I go to my room to pack. I change into some warmer clothes and borrow some of Shay's heavy-duty boots. I sneak into the kitchen and steal a few pieces of dried fruit and some bread and cheese. I grab a leather pouch and fill it with the water I had collected from the well this morning. In Tripp's room, I find a leather belt with a sword attached and a small blade that I slip inside my right boot. I'm ready. I slip outside through the back gate and cut through the maze, I had sensed the hob Beetok watching the temple not long after we arrived yesterday. I didn't alert anyone to his presence, his intentions were noble. Once I'm on the other side of the maze I make my way through the thick brush for about forty yards until I reach Beetok's camp. He's sitting beside a small fire that's shaded with propped branches and he has an animal that's turning on a spike above the flames.

"If you want to repay your debt now is the time," I tell him.

"How long did you know I was here?" He asks.

"You followed us once your sister was through the portal, you're a good tracker and I need your help," I tell him.

He doesn't question my offer, he takes hold of the stick that's sitting above the fire and sinks his fangs into the cremated creature still sizzling on it.

He chews loudly, and the sound makes me cringe. I guess this is the Vales version of take away food. He stands and smothers the fire with his boot. He scoops his small collection of belongings and shoves them into the animal skin that was his shelter and throws it over his shoulder.

"Where are we going?" He says through a full mouthful of meat.

"Bristeal Mountain, do you know it?" I ask. One of the injured gargoyles had whispered the name in his mind and I was able to catch a glimpse of Maura and her men setting up camp at the bottom of the mountain. I just hope the element of surprise is enough to help me defeat her. Beetok nods and begins parting the foliage with his gargantuan body, I look back towards the temple. I'm doing the right thing I tell myself.

-43-
Tripp

I passed out at some point from blood loss, luckily Shay gave me some of her blood, so the gash in my side has closed over and I've healed enough to be able to stand. The three of us are locked in a small iron cage made of thick chain linked metal. Shay tries breaking our confinements, but the skin on her hand begins to blister and liquefy. The smell of cooking flesh makes the contents of my stomach begin to rise.

"Fucking bristeal thorn, it must have been added to the metal. I can't break it," Shay spits.

"Who else did they take?" I ask, gripping the bars to pull myself upright.

"Just us," Neema replies.

"Why bother taking the three of us, there's no way my father will leave Adaline unprotected for a recovery mission?" I say.

"This isn't about killing Adaline anymore. Maura wants to torment Adaline. She will probably put our bodies on display for her to find, then when she is distracted with grief Maura will kill her," Shay says coldly.

One of the gargoyles approaches the front of our cage, he removes a padlock the size of my head and discards it to the ground. He opens the cage door wide enough to fit his arm inside and wraps his enormous hand around Neema's leg.

As he begins to yank, Shay feebly attempts to fend him off. Neema bites down on his dense forearm and even draws a little blood, but both the vampires are too weak to fight. Once Neema is out of the cage he snaps her neck in one swift movement and drops her to the ground. He returns the lock to its rightful place and slings Neema over his shoulder like a trophy.

"I'm going to rip your fucking head off," Shay spits at him.

"Don't worry my men are lovers, not fighters, they will take very good care of her." The beast taunts.

Gargoyles are infamous among our kind for their less than reputable nature, it's one of the main reasons they weren't invited to join the Seelie. In the beginning, gargoyles were guardians. They only tortured and dismembered the wicked. They made their homes on the rooftops of human dwellings, as mankind grew the gargoyles numbers decreased they limited themselves to churches and places of worship. Gargoyles were once the epitome of purity and goodness, that was when they still protected the innocent. Just like with all things, the world transitioned, humans changed and so did their fae counterparts. The gargoyles became just as malicious as humanity did. Mortal's buildings of worship morphed into temples of sleaze, sin and lies. What people forget is that our homes are more than just stone and dirt, they are a reflection of ourselves. Homes are places of love and warmth, they are supposed to be a sanctuary. Sadly, the gargoyles took on the corrupted desires of their masters and lost all sense of morality. They became as dark and menacing as the places they protected and the stone in their hearts mirrored the stone walls of their homes. Poor Neema is going to experience their depravity first hand.

As the monster drags Neema away all I can hear is the deafening sound of my pulse drumming in my ears. For a time, I hold my breath so tightly, I feel myself on the edge of collapse. I fear that I will hear Neema's cries, but there's nothing. Just the steady roar of drunken laughter in the distance and the flickers of light as their shadows pass by the shelters they have tied to the trees.

I can see Shay's attention shift; her ears perk up towards our captors. She closes her hands around the poisoned cage, allowing her fingers to burn. I reach out to pull back her hands, then I hear what's making her intentionally harm herself, Neema is awake. Her choked scream comes in waves. Scream, after scream, after scream. Each time she suffers one of the monsters laughs louder. I can feel their sick pleasure rippling through the earth. What's more disturbing than their enjoyment is feeling Neema's pain. The earth is drinking up the spills of her blood, every rip and tear sinking into the soil. The earth shouldn't know this kind of suffering, no one should. I tighten my hands around my ears trying to block out the horrific sounds, but her distress keeps finding a way in. Shay screams profanities and unrecognisable abuses, I'm not sure if it's because she's trying to shift the monster's attention or drown out the sounds of Neema's torment. Another scream pierces my ears, and all the while Shay's fingers sizzle against the metal, cutting deeper and deeper into her disintegrating flesh. The horrific sounds and smells become embedded in my skin. Consumed with disgust, I lurch forward expelling everything inside me, gagging and choking until the screams in the distance seem to dwindle.

Neema's cries finally fade to whimpers as the sun begins to rise. They tortured her all night without disruption. I can't speak for Shay, but for me having to stand by powerless while Neema suffered was how they tortured me. Each time I thought the nightmare had ended I would close my eyes and then the screaming would start again, even now that the torture has stopped I can still hear her pain ringing in the back of my mind.

The monster that took Neema away is carrying her lifeless body back towards us. Her clothes are gone, her olive skin is pale and coated in blood and dirt. Her skin is bruised and broken, she looks like she has clawed her way out of a grave made of cement. The cage door opens, and he tosses Neema's body inside. Shay looks over her friend's laboured body, but most of her physical wounds are superficial and in various stages of healing. I slip off my shirt and gently place it on Neema. She whispers something that sounds like a thank you before her eyes roll back and she passes out.

"I'm going to kill every single one of those bastards," Shay says and rubs a soft hand over Neema's forehead. The gesture is extremely maternal, a quality I didn't know Shay had, maybe I have misjudged her. As the sadness pours out of her it makes my heart ache in sympathy.

"I'm going to help you," I say and offer her my exposed wrist.

-44-
SETH

Deklan has been slipping in and out of consciousness infrequently over the last few hours. Aedan has offered him blood, but the stubborn prick wouldn't take it, luckily when he was down for the count I placed a few drops of Aedan's blood directly into his wound. It's not as effective as if he had ingested it, but it's going to speed up the healing process. I can see blood starting to seep through his bandages again. I stand and begin unwrapping them. When I did this two hours ago his calf muscle was still missing, and I could see a mess of blue and red coloured veins wriggling like worms trying to fuse themselves together, this time he's made more progress. His calf is a tapestry of meaty muscles and flexing veins. The first layer of skin has begun to spread across the open spaces as it tries to restrain Deklan's insides. The flimsy skins translucent, like plastic wrap with less sheen. I'm careful not to disturb his improvement and wrap the leg once more. As I seal the dressing I hear him curse in a whisper and I finally let go of the breath I've been scared to release, he's going to be okay.

I leave Aedan to watch over him and go looking for Adaline. We had left her upstairs watching over Phedora while she recovered. I open the bedroom door quietly, expecting to find them both asleep, but the chair by the bed is empty. Phedora is sleeping soundlessly in a cocoon of blankets and Adaline is nowhere to be seen. I find my way back to her room, it's also empty. I already know she's gone, but I search every room in the temple in the hope that I'm wrong. I smash my fist through a reflective glass sculpture that's outside Phedora's greenhouse.

Like so many times before the glass pierces my skin and blood flows without restriction, unlike the other times when my anger has gotten the best of me the blood continues to flow instead of clotting. I kick the remaining framework of the artwork and stomp on it until it's no longer a thing of beauty.

"You're bleeding again," Aedan says from behind me.

"SHE'S GONE!" I yell, shaking my bloodied fist at him. Aedan bites down on his wrist offering me his blood. "After all this, you still won't do it? You know what we have to face, and you still don't care enough about me or Adaline to change me back."

"Drink or bleed out…" he says. I bring his wrist to my lips and drink in the vile tasting blood, it's coppery and overpowering with warmth. The mild thickness of it makes me gag, but I continue to force it down. Once I feel the cut on my wrist heal, I release his hand and wipe the spilt blood from my face. "Now that you're settled, do you have any idea where she would have gone?"

"Obviously she's gone after Maura," I say with a roll of my eyes.

"Obviously," Deklan says stumbling out into the hall. "And you two are the idiots that left her alone. Did you honestly think she wouldn't try to save her friends? Morons the pair of you," he snaps and makes his way to the chest by the door.

"We have no way to find them," Aedan says.

"The bastards reeked of bristeal trees and sulphur, my bet is they have made camp by Bristeal Mountain," Deklan says.

"Makes sense, the volcanos current blocks tracking spells. I'll get the horses, it will be quicker than on foot," Aedan says.

"There are guns in my room and a bag of bristeal bullets in the brown bag, fetch them," Deklan tells me.

174

I find his guns easily enough, but the bag takes longer. It's small and only has six bullets inside and a bottle of clear liquid. I open the lid and sniff the substance; hypnoval. I remember the sweet smell from my early years before I was a vampire. I had just made my way to London after spending years living in absolute poverty. I worked on a ship to gain passage to Ireland with other riff-raff hopefuls. We had plans to build a better life for ourselves, maybe even stake a claim in one of the Anglo-Irish colonies. I was also no longer welcome in London due to a string of thefts and petty crime, so Ireland looked like an adventure. Aedan approached me on the street a few weeks after I arrived, little did I know when I stepped onto the Irish shores I had walked into plague and famine. Any offer that came my way was like a dream. Aedan wasn't the well-dressed man he is now, he was cleaner than I was, but dirt still coated his fingernails and his beard was roughly shaven. He wore his hair long back then, I now know it was to cover the bruises. Aedan offered work on behalf of his master, I remember how refined his master looked sitting across the street in his carriage, I began walking to the cart before I verbally accepted Aedan's offer.

The first night in my new home I was given more food and wine than I had ever eaten in a month. The wine had a sweetness to it, the same sweetness as the hypnoval I'm holding right now. My master would hide it in my food, so I remained in a docile state, he preferred his slaves pliable. Not long after, I discovered the hell I had stepped into. Aedan bore the brunt of our master's torture, one night he was so badly wounded I didn't think he would come back, but he did. Our master turned him that night. Aedan became one of them, as a new vampire he would take off for fortnights at a time, always returning covered in blood, with a thick coating of shame painted on his face. Every time he stepped out the door I wasn't sure he would return, I could see how difficult his new life was for him to navigate.

Every time he came back his maker would hand him a glass of wine laced with the same sedative he gave me. I always thought Aedan took it willingly to numb the pain of his life until the night he killed our maker.

In truth, Aedan had been taking the drug in a higher dose for years so he could build up a tolerance. His nights away were spent trying to control his urges so he would be strong enough to kill the creature who made him. On the last night of my humanity, Aedan had been gone for a month, my maker had given up hope of his return, so he gave me the bite. Aedan returned hours later while I was still paralysed in a state of torment, he slipped a dose of the sedative into our maker's wine, he was already high on the night's torture so he didn't notice the unusual sweetness of the wine. As he dozed by the fireplace dreaming of the next child he would steal, Aedan sunk his fingers into his chest and pulled out his heart. I remember watching the organ burn among the sizzling coals, my maker's body shrivelled up and died in front of me. That night I finally saw Aedan smile and he hasn't stopped since. I guess freedom can do that to a person.

I place the sleeping potion in my pocket, unsure why the compulsion to take it with me is so overwhelming. I zip up the bullet bag and slide a gun under each arm. Adaline's coming home, and Maura is finally getting put into her casket, permanently.

-45-
Adaline

For a large creature, Beetok is lighter on his feet than I would have imagined, and his tracking skills are impressive. After a few hours, we are far enough from the temple to set up camp and get a couple of hours sleep before starting again at first light. I didn't think ahead enough to pack something in the form of shelter, but Beetok's covering is big enough for us both, even with his large body. He offers me a fur-lined blanket while he collects some firewood. When he returns with his bundle he digs a small ditch and places the branches down. I wave my hand and bring them to flame.

"There's a lot a talent in those tiny hands," he says eyeing the fire.

"I sure hope so," I tell him. Maura has a great deal of help on her side and I only have myself, but she ran from me once, I can do it again.

"Are you going to tell me what's at Bristeal Mountain?" Beetok asks.

"Don't worry you don't have to fight. I just need you to point me in the right direction," I tell him. He frowns at me and I don't need to be able to sense his feelings to know he expects more. "A vampire took three of my friends and almost killed the others. I'm going to get them back," I offer.

"One vampire did all that?" He asks unconvincingly.

"She has minions in the form of gargoyles," I say.

"Hmm gargoyles, never liked them, no morals that lot," he scoffs.

"Forgive me, but aren't you allied with the bad fae?" I ask.

"The Unseelie aren't bad, we just aren't all good. Gargoyles are like the distant cousin you wish you weren't related to. Honestly, the sides don't matter it's more about what rules you want to live by. For example, your King wants the Seelie divided from humanity, he wants you isolated from the world. King Addison on the other hand, allows the Unseelie to mingle with the humans as we please," Beetok says fondly.

"By mingle do you mean murder?" I ask.

"Everyone's different. My clan lives in a small village in Vargo, we are a family and we frequent the human world for goods and services, but we never go out intentionally to kill people," he says.

"Why doesn't the Seelie King want to associate with humans?" I ask.

"Not sure really, happened back when the last treaty was renewed. You see, King Theodore and King Addison are brothers, both rulers by birthright, but King Theodore is older. When they disagreed on the terms of the treaty Addison left the Seelie. When he surfaced amongst the Unseelie it was a huge blow to Theodore's ego, but it didn't matter, eventually, Addison became King on his own. You should have learnt all of this during your studies, couldn't your family afford schooling?" He asks.

"I grew up in the mortal realm," I reply.

"You're lucky, I don't exactly blend into the mortal realm and witches veil is too costly to use all the time. Last year my brother in law got us both a dose and we watched the phantom of the opera in New York," he smiles.

"You like opera?" I ask in disbelief.

"Didn't your mother tell you not to judge a book by its cover?" He snaps.

"She did. I'm sorry, I was just surprised. Does the witches stuff make you invisible?" I ask.

"No, it makes us appear human to mortals, our own kind can still see us though, but the veil only lasts a few hours," he says and settles down by the fire. "You ask a lot of questions, I'll put it down to your upbringing," he adds.

"I like to understand things, Goodnight," I say and relax into sleep.

-46-
Tripp

Neema has been sleeping for a few hours, her face flinches every so often and she scrunches the corners of her eyes. When her body is still she looks peaceful, almost childlike. Then a wave of anguish washes over her dreams and she cringes again. I clench my fists until they are white-knuckled and taught. I've been letting Shay drink a small amount of blood from me every hour since they returned Neema back to us. I hope she will be strong enough to tear the heads off those godforsaken beasts the second they open the cage door. The only downside to our plan is I'll be completely defenceless, but after the torture, they put Neema through I'd happily die if it meant she got her justice. Justice doesn't seem like the right word. I let the word sit on my tongue and it feels wrong. For what they did to her, they deserve so much more. More anguish, more brutality, anything that makes them suffer greater than she did, and there's only one word that feels right, revenge.

Neema's eyes open in a small slit, and for a second, she looks like she had before, delicate, respectful and graceful, then her body changes. Her eyes darken, and her lips turn into a fine grim line. She tries to raise herself into a sitting position, but she's too weak and falls back. I place a gentle hand on her shoulder to help support her weight. She flinches, I've never had a woman be afraid of my touch before, I don't like it. I know I shouldn't take it personally, but revulsion still hurts.

"I'm sorry," Neema says relaxing against my hand.

"Don't you dare apologise, we should have stopped them. I should have helped you," Shay tells her, and I can see her stone features break if only for a second.

"We won't let them get away with it," I tell Neema, she smiles weakly.

"Please don't... Don't tell anyone about this," Neema says holding back the tears.

Shay and I nod in agreeance. What could be worse than suffering through hours of torture and rape? Looking at the panic on Neema's face I know exactly what could be worse, reliving the horror and having others know the horrific intimate details of your story.

The sun's rising higher, it must be nearing midday. I offer my bleeding wrist to Neema once Shay has finished with it. Neema looks at it not wanting to take a sip, but I can see how dry her lips have become and her colouring has lightened more if that's even possible. I push my wrist closer giving her a reassuring nod. She closes her cracked lips gently around my wrist and I can feel my blood spilling into her mouth. Her bite is gentler than Shays, perhaps it's because she's still weak, or it could be because her natural instincts are more tender.

Shay coughs loud enough for it to be a signal, one of the monsters is approaching us. His skin is more pastel lime than the finger paint green of his kinsmen and his hair is cropped short against his scalp. He's carrying three large carved bowls, liquid splashes loosely as his colossal feet step over the rocky patches of earth. Shay arches her back into a half standing crouch like a mountain lion ready to pounce on her prey.

"I brought water," The gargoyle says. Shay spits at his feet, but the dryness in my throat aches for anything that will moisten it. "It's not poisoned," he adds and takes a sip from each bowl.

"You tried to stop them," Neema says to him. "Why?" She asks.

Uncomfortably he looks down at the ground, his bulky fingers fumble with the padlock. I make eye contact with Shay and shake my head, this guy isn't like the others, but attacking him will cause him to react just like the rest of them and Neema and I are too weak to help fight.

"Let us go," I ask. "We never did anything to you or your friends."

"They're not my friends," he snaps. "They're family."

"Please," Neema asks. I can see a tear glisten down her cheek and it's not just for show.

"I can't, I'm sorry," he replies.

"What's your name?" Neema asks him.

"Mikael," he replies.

"Thank you for trying Mikael," she says genuinely. As he looks up to meet her gaze I notice the abrasions and scattered bruising across his face. I wonder how hard he fought his brothers for her?

Mikael opens the cage and places the water bowls inside. I see Neema's hand close around Shays' wrist keeping her in place. Mikael wraps the chain around the cage and replaces the lock. I notice the absence of the clicking sound the lock makes when it's closed correctly. Mikael takes a long breath as he looks at Neema.

"Wait until dark," Mikael whispers and heads back to camp.

-47-
Adaline

The Vale has so much of the mortal realm in it. Trees look like trees, the sky is an oceanic blue and the grass is thick with life, but it's the subtle differences I notice that set it apart. The way the leaves have an irresistible fragrance that filters the air as I inhale it or the richness of the pigments in the flowers. Everything in the Vale is pure and unblemished. The fae doesn't have cars or aeroplanes encroaching their environment, so there's no layer of smog obstructing the rays of glorious light that peak through the clouds. This is how the world should be, this is the beauty and wonder that should still exist outside of the Vale and it breaks my heart that it doesn't.

"What the hell are you looking at?" Beetok grunts.

"Sorry, I was catching my breath," I tell him and push my aching legs forward. "It's so beautiful here, what's Vargo like?"

"The Vale has normal seasons like the rest of the world, Vargo lives in a persistent winter. Everything is coated in a blanket of white, it makes growing food difficult and we eat a lot of fish. That's why we travel between the worlds so often, but everything needs balance," he says. "There she is," He adds. I look above the canopy and see the sharp incline of the mountain before us. "That's bristeal trees growing along the mountain, its thorns are toxic to vampires and a number of other fae. Unlikely that woman of yours would choose here to set up camp," he says.

"I think she chose it specifically for that reason. Where do you think they would be?" I ask.

"The other side, there's a small area that was cleared for farming before the last eruption. We can be there just before the sun goes down, but from here out we need to be silent…That means no more questions." He says pointedly.

Eruption? The word gets stuck in my mind. I release my abilities, the mountain muddles my potency, but I can feel something. It's the steady rumbling of lava flowing through the mountain like veins, the volcanos flow is calm, it won't erupt today. I pucker my lips and follow Beetok's path. I carefully place my steps inside his footprints as they are cast into the soil. My legs quiver, weak with exertion. Beetok doesn't look dazed in the slightest, I imagine he could walk for weeks without fatigue setting in.

Beetok was right about the sun, it's setting by the time we reach the encampment. I can hear the roaring of laughter and a large fire in the centre of the camp beckons for me. It wants to draw me in, but it's not passion or warmth the fire is craving, its vengeance. The fire can feel the rage that's trickling through my veins, I suppress the urge to walk in with my anger burning on my skin, and instead, I focus on my other elements. I breathe in the air as it counts the bodies that are drawing its life force into their lungs, I can feel ten hearts beating in rhythm with the vibrations of the earth and further down the encampment I feel another three lives. These hearts beat weaker than the rest and there's something else. It's more than frailty, it's a brokenness cloaking them. Dear God what has Maura done to them?

"You can leave now, I'll be fine from here," I tell Beetok.

"I can't leave you, I can hear how many of them there are. You won't be able to defeat them alone," he says.

"This isn't your fight," I tell him.

He answers by withdrawing a long-angled blade from his side and marches towards the camp. I guess we are doing this together after all, I drop my pack to the ground and stretch out my fingers pulling the energy from the earth. Air is quick to join the party and strengthens my lungs. The fire burns brighter in the distance eager for battle. One of the gargoyles has stepped away from the safety of his pack to take a leak. Beetok removes his head in a single movement. I gasp in shock as the severed head rolls towards my feet, black blood pools at the tips of my boots seconds before the head shrivels into dust.

"If you plan on getting out of here alive you're going to have to toughen up," Beetok whispers.

I swallow the lump that's formed in my throat and bring flames to my fingers. I step soundlessly on the grass as we absence ourselves from the coverage of the trees. I see the other gargoyles lingering by the fire. Nine, I tell myself. There are only nine things standing between me and my friends. A pit of guilt settles in my stomach. Killing is never something I have wanted, my heart aches at the thought of it. I was foolish to think I could do this, I'm not a killer. It doesn't matter because Beetok's volcanic battle cry shatters any second thoughts I'm having.

His fighting is like nothing I have ever seen. He stabs his sword into the back of a monster severing his spine, as he falls Beetok recovers his weapon and swings it toward another. In seconds he is flooded by attacking gargoyles while I stand frozen. Beetok becomes buried beneath the hoard, he screams. The flames in my hands grow until they consume every inch of my skin. I run towards the onslaught throwing fire toward them. The monsters shriek as their tough hides begin to sizzle. They forget Beetok and turn their attention towards the real threat, me.

-48-
Tripp

I drank the three bowls of water that Mikael offered. The water was enough to renew my physical strength and any other healing I needed, I syphoned from the earth. The three of us are the strongest that we are going to be while held captive and the time is now. The sun has gone down and the darkness is setting in. In another half an hour it will be dark enough to aid our escape. It took all day to convince Shay that running was a better option, she was resolute in seeking immediate revenge, but it's a fight we won't win, not tonight.

"She's here," Shay whispers, the tone of her voice enthralled.

"Maura?" I ask.

"Adaline," Neema replies.

Before I can respond a shrill scream drowns out all other sounds. The single cry is followed by several vicious snarls and a faint gurgling sound I can only compare to the time I had drowned. I can almost feel the liquid seeping into my lungs, I cough expelling the phantom water from my throat. Shay unlatches the padlock from the cage, her hand burning as it slips back through the chain link.

Shay and Neema are running towards the action while I stumble behind. I break through the edge of the camp and enter a war zone. Shay is piercing the shoulder of a gargoyle with her fangs while Neema is beaten down by another. I send my magic into the bristeal trees urging the thorn-covered branches to aid Neema's defence.

The plants extend and swirl around the beast, encasing him enough to give Neema the upper hand, but she doesn't need it. Mikael comes to her defence by removing the heart of his brother with his bare hands. He drops the still beating heart to the floor as the monster turns to dust. Neema's frozen, Mikael touches her shoulders gently trying to wake her, by the time I reach them she's woken from her daze. I can feel the earth gnawing at her fear, the trauma from last night is flooding back.

"Get her out of here," I tell Mikael. He doesn't second-guess my instructions, he simply scoops Neema into his arms and runs.

I pick up the dead gargoyles axe and begin swinging it at Shay's attacker. The axe pierces the beasts love handle, and he arches his back trying to remove the blade. Shay takes her opportunity and sinks her teeth into his throat ripping it out. She spits the mouthful of flesh to the ground as it turns to dust. Shay smiles savagely while black blood drips from her parted lips. She launches forward tackling me to the ground. Limp bodies fly overhead nearly missing us as they are propelled into a pile of bristeal thorn branches, I can hear the painful cries as the thorns dig into their bodies. I tilt my head back looking for the source, I see a female form encased in fire.

-49-
SETH

We were hours behind Adaline when we left the temple and between my mortality and Deklan's still healing leg, Aedan's plan to take the horses was the right decision. We arrive at the base of the mountain in the early evening. Despite travelling at full speed and pushing the horses to run further than they could handle we are still too late. When we climb down from the exhausted horses the smells of battle and smoke filters through the air.

Aedan runs ahead, to my surprise the gargoyles lay in dusty piles of cement and the few that haven't been killed lay unconscious. The hob we had met on the road is standing beside Aedan, both are wearing a stunned expression on their faces. I step forward fearing the worst. Adaline stands in the centre of the chaos. Her hair has turned scarlet, her skin has an electrical fiery current flowing around her naked body. Every inch of her is covered in layers of ash or the remnants of scorched fabrics that was once her clothes. She's staring down at a wounded gargoyle.

"WHERE IS SHE?" She yells.

"She didn't say. She left not long after we returned with your friends, she just told us to hold them," he spits through the curdling blood on his lips. Adaline leans down until she is inches from his face.

"You are on the wrong side of this. Unless you want me to destroy every single one of your kind I suggest you take the men you have left and run. Don't assist Maura, don't step foot back in the Vale and if for one second I think you're coming after me or the people I care about, you're dead," she says.

Her hand turns blue as the flames burn brighter. She presses it to the gargoyle's face. His scream echoes through the trees, and I actually grimace. She pulls back her hand when the mark is deep enough to leave a horrific reminder of her power. It's impossible to deny how commanding her presence is. At this moment I can finally see her for everything she is, a powerful force of nature. Adaline is the kind of person whose devotion for her people is placed above all else. At times I have worried she was too soft to make the decisions that rulers need to make, but looking at her now I'm fearful of her, I'm anxious about her power and the path it's going to lead her down. The wounded gargoyle knows he's met his match and scrambles to his feet. Adaline stands steadfast while he collects his wounded and retreats on foot. When the remaining gargoyles vanish into the forest Adaline collapses to the ground defeated. I can see goose pimples rise on her exposed flesh, she shivers as a cry escapes her lips. Aedan approaches and drapes his jumper over her bare shoulders.

"They're on the run we have to go after them," Shay demands.

"They aren't coming back, not after what Adaline did to them," Deklan says.

"We can't let them get away with what they've done," Shay screams.

Tripp pulls Shay aside and whispers something to her. I can't hear what he says, but whatever it is, it makes her stand down.

"Where's Neema?" Adaline asks. "Is she okay?"

"She's okay, one of the gargoyles helped us, he got her out of here," Tripp says.
"I need to leave, I can't be amongst all this death any longer," Adaline says, still huddled on the ground.

Aedan scoops her into his arms and carries her through the bushes while the rest of us follow in silence. Even though she won the battle after the long trek back to the temple it somehow feels like she lost a war with herself.

-50-
Adaline

"Wake up," A voice says gently. I try to ignore it; my eyes are too taken with sleep to open willingly. "Adaline, we're back at the temple." This time I recognise Aedan's voice.

I force my eyes open and the torch lights that line the temple walls makes them sting. I close them tightly, but instead of blissful darkness, I see flashes of blackened blood and the slow rolling of dead eyes as they fall back into their sockets. When I attacked the creatures, my objective was to injure not kill. I knew my limits the second Beetok removed the first one's head. On our way back to the temple Beetok said three of them had gotten away, excluding the one that's by Neema's side. He said the few that escaped were a little worse for wear, and none of the deceased had been killed by my hand. I felt relieved when he told me that, I still feel guilty about the pain I inflicted on them, but at least I'm not a murderer.

"Do you want me to take you to your room? I can run you a bath," Seth offers. I look at the dark circles under his eyes and the frustration hiding in the corners. Seth looks smaller, that's when I realise Aedan is still holding me high in his arms.

"No, I think I need to be alone," I reply. Seth reaches out a hand to help me down as Aedan lowers me. He releases me from his embrace only when he's certain my legs will hold me. Aedan's jumper hangs on my body like an oversized sweater dress. I feel my nakedness beneath the fabric and hug myself tightly, suddenly feeling vulnerable.

When the bedroom door closes behind me and I hear the footsteps travel down the hall, I sink down onto the cold floor and cry. I don't bother trying to stifle the sounds of my sobbing or cull the fierceness of my tears. Those creatures died tonight, not creatures, people. Sure, they looked different and they had a different set of ethics, but they were still living beings. I felt their deaths, and I became their pain. The earth cried out in agony as it experienced the indescribable suffering of battle. I know the gargoyles were not by any means noble and the harm they inflicted is unforgivable, but I can't just brush aside their deaths.

My tears run their course and my muscles have stiffened against the tiles. I force myself to stand and take off the jumper. I position myself before the crisp white empty tub, I reach my dirt covered hand forward and unlatch the window. I use my abilities to pull water from the well outside until the bath is full. I lower my hand into the icy water until my fire element warms it. The hot water stings at first, even though there's not a single cut on my body. I wriggle my toes relaxing until the stinging feels pleasant. When the water turns cold I climb out and dress mechanically. I slip on woollen socks and comb my hair. I look in the mirror at the stranger before me. My face has gotten thin, my cheeks still have colour, but it's more red than pink and my hair is no longer a plain auburn, but more of a fiery scarlet. I'm changing, and I wonder if it's for the better.

"It's too late to come home my darling." The golden woman says appearing in the mirror.

"Are you real?" I ask.

"Define real… This was your decision and I'm sorry that I can't help you," she says with a sad smile. Her golden feathered hair sways back and forth hypnotically. The gentle movements distract my train of thought and put me into a lulled trance.

"What decision?" I ask dreamily.

192

"To become a part of this my dear," she says stroking my cheek in the mirror. I close my eyes and I can feel the warmth of her hand on my cheek. I reach up to touch it, but it's not there. I open my eyes and see her loving face still trapped inside the mirror.

"Can you tell me anything useful?" I plead.

"Mortal lives don't come with cheat sheets, besides you made me promise not to intervene, and I've already done too much," she replies.

"I have been known to make mistakes," I retort.

"I miss your humour," she says with a lyrical laugh. "I'm sorry, but I have to go." She strokes my cheek once more and vanishes just as mysteriously as she came.

The sun is creeping through the windows, but the temple remains still. I walk down the halls until I find the kitchen since my stomach won't let me sleep any longer until it's had its fill. Tripp is sitting alone at the table and I'm reminded of the night we first met. I consider turning back before he notices me, but my stomach grumbles its annoyance.

"Can't sleep?" I ask.

"No," he replies, but he doesn't turn to face me. I can feel his discomfort, I'm just thankful that it's not my presence that's causing it.

"Are you okay?" I ask placing a kind hand on his shoulder.

A scream penetrates my ears and it's far worse than the sound of any battle. The anguish of the cry rattles me to my core. An image of Neema flashes between the connection Tripp and I have formed. I feel everything Tripp felt during her torture. The things that they did to her and the pleasure they took inflicting it, it all floods into me. I want to vomit, Tripp pushes my hand away severing the link between us.

"You can't say anything, she doesn't want anyone to know," he says.

"I just… I keep hearing it every time I close my eyes. I swear there was nothing I could do to help her…" he trails off into tears.

I pull Tripp close to me and try to soothe his guilt. All the pain I had felt during the battle didn't belong solely to the gargoyles after all. Everything I felt through the earth had stemmed from Neema's suffering. It had been trapped in the soil and at the time I couldn't decipher her pain from what was happening in front of me. Nausea rises higher in my stomach, I feel sick with guilt for feeling remorse for those creatures. Letting them go was a mistake, I should have killed them.

-51-

Deklan

Adaline's holding my son tightly while he sobs. Her features as tormented as the mournful sounds that are escaping him. Adaline senses me lurking, she offers me an encouraging smile and nods her head. She releases her hold on Tripp and for a moment I fear he will drift away without her grounding presence. Adaline passes me saying nothing, but a gentle squeeze of her hand on my shoulder encourages me to go to my son.

Watching my grown son weep is a hard pill to swallow. My own father would have smacked me alongside the head for behaving as such. I always wanted to be different than my father, it was a promise I made myself a long time ago. I broke that promise when my wife died and now finally I have a chance to change it. Tripp tries to pull himself together as I approach, although he isn't doing a very good job of it.

"I'm fine," he says through a blocked nose and hoarse throat.

"Do you want to tell me what happened?" I ask.

"I can't. It's not my story to tell," he says, which seems to hurt him worse than if the pain was his own.

Taking Adaline's lead, I bridge the space between us and wrap my arms around him. He's tense at first, but he soon softens into the embrace. He lets out a loud breath and drains his remaining tears into my plaid shirt. When his tears have run dry and his eyes are swollen with sadness I loosen my hold, so I can really look at him.

195

"Whatever happened, it's not your fault and I'm proud of you," I tell him.

"I've done nothing to be proud of, I couldn't help either of them," he mutters under his weakened breath.

"I'm proud that you care enough about someone else to feel this way. I don't know what happened, but I've found myself in powerless situations before and it's an almost unbearable kind of suffering," I say. "You need to get some rest, I'll mix you something to help you sleep."

"Thanks, dad," he says.

My heart swells at the word, I squint my eyes before they have a chance to spring a leak. I pour some water into a pot and place it over the wood fire stove that's still burning brightly. I collect some herbs from Phedora's garden and stew them in the water. I want to give him a drop of the sleeping potion I used on Adaline, but as I retrieve the brown leather bag I realise the potion is nowhere to be seen. I shuffle the contents of the bag back and forth hoping to loosen the vial from its hidden place, but it doesn't come free. I must have lost it in our travels. I still have some jasmine and lavender extract in my satchel which helps aid sleep. I add a few drops to Tripp's pillow on my way back to the kitchen, hopefully between the drink and the extracts my son should have a peaceful night.

The water has come to a roaring boil, its high-pitched whistle hurts my ears as I remove it from the stove. The mixture I have made should help suppress any nightmares and make sure he sleeps through the night. When the liquid cools enough to drink I pour it into a cup and hand it to my son.

"It will help you sleep," I say.

"Thanks," he replies. He blows on the hot liquid and the steam rises around him making him look more like a ghost than a man. He scrunches his nose at the smell but drinks it down anyway. "You never told me what happened to mum. Was that when you felt powerless?" He asks.

"It was," I say and pull out a chair to sit next to him. "Your mother had come to court to see me that night. The creature that tried to kill Adaline killed your mother. I'm told it was quick and she didn't suffer."

"You never saw her?" He asks.

"No. I had left with Adaline and was in the mortal realm by the time they discovered your mother's body. It's the main reason Theo came to the mortal realm so soon after the attack. He had wanted to tell me about your mother in person." I feel tears begin to well in my eyes as I remember the night Theo told me about my sweet Chloe. "Funny enough Adaline reminds me so much of your mother, headstrong, unwaveringly kind, determined…"

"I guess mum wouldn't want us to be at each other's throats all the time," he says.

"I don't suppose she would," I reply.

Like a puff of smoke that vanishes in the darkness of night, I feel all the hostility and anger that had been simmering between us for years dissipate. I hug my son once more and send him to bed to rest. I take a small sip of the broth I have made, it wouldn't be a bad thing for me to get some sleep either. I walk down the silent halls of the temple in a haze. As I reach my door and my fingers grasp the handle a shiver runs up my spine. The hairs on the back of my neck rise and the wolf inside of me readies itself to attack.

"It's only me," says Phedora. Her blue hair hangs limply over one of her shoulders, it seems to have lost is typical buoyancy. As she approaches I notice the absence of the dance she usually has in her step.

"You startled me. Are you feeling better?" I ask.

"Much, the magic heals quickly," she says with a soft smile.

"That's good. I'm going to bed if you don't need anything," I tell her.

"No, I'm fine... I'm sorry about your wife," she says hesitantly.

"What about my wife?" I ask brashly.

"It was a shame, her death. It was unnecessary, betrayals of the heart are always the worst," she says sadly.

"My wife never betrayed me," I snap.

"Oh," she says surprised. "I didn't mean it like that, forgive me, my word choice was poor. I'll let you rest," she whispers as she tiptoes back down the hall.

I feel like the tiny thing slapped me with a sledgehammer. Infidelity was never a problem that entered our marriage, but between Phedora and the broth, my mind is beginning to wonder. I climb into bed and begin reliving every day I spent with my wife. She was tentative and loving. She always called me out on my bullshit and sometimes we fought, more often than not it was about how often I was away from home. My wife was my childhood sweetheart, she's the only woman I have ever been with and I know in my gut that she was never unfaithful. Phedora has had one too many drinks tonight I'm sure. Thankfully the darkness of sleep finds me before my doubts can take root.

-52-
SETH

When I wake the sun has already begun filling the sky with warmth and I can hear birds singing in the distance. Their cheerful song fools me for a moment, but only just. I can't deny the way Adaline looked at me last night, when Aedan put her down I reached for her, but she couldn't look me in the eyes. I spent most of the night tossing and turning until my mortal brain admitted defeat and thrust sleep upon me. I know the only way I will understand this emotional pit that's in my stomach is by talking to Adaline, but I'm worried she will tell me what I fear the most. I reacted like a child when she tried to talk to me about her and Tripp. I hadn't considered her feelings or what she had been going through and deep down I know she isn't the disloyal type.

Aedan is already gone when I arrive at his room. I should have known he would be up early. Deklan, Tripp, Aedan and Jason are standing by the garden gate at the front of the temple as I descend the stairs. Jason's colour has returned as much as it can for someone who suffers a vampire affliction. He smiles at me as I approach, I return his warmth and pat his shoulder firmly.

"I was just saying we should travel in two parties. The smaller group will have Adaline, smaller groups draw less attention," Aedan says.

"And I keep telling him he's wrong. Adaline should have all of us by her side," Deklan replies.

"I think we can all agree Adaline is capable of defending herself. She has proved it time and time again. Just yesterday she single-handedly turned a hoard of gargoyles into lapdogs that went running for the hills," Aedan snaps.

"Just because she has power doesn't mean she's capable of using it when needed. Let's not forget she let those monsters live," Deklan retorts.

"Why are you always talking about me instead of to me?" Adaline pipes in appearing behind us.

"I'm sorry," Deklan says bashfully.

"You're right that it was a mistake to let them live," she says looking at Tripp. Something unspoken passes between them that makes my jealousy blaze. The only person I want her sharing secrets with is me. "I won't make that mistake again, I know better now."

"So, when will we leave," I ask Aedan.

"Dusk. Adaline, myself and Deklan. The rest of you will leave in the morning," he replies.

I tried to dissuade Aedan's decision, but he won't budge, and Adaline is supporting the decision. This human form keeps me at a disadvantage. I can think of a million reasons why I want to go with Adaline, but it all comes down to her safety and what's best for her. The truth is that I'm a liability. Travelling with me by her side would place a bigger target on her back than she already has. While my brother and Deklan continue to disagree with one another I keep a steady gaze on Adaline, she still can't bring herself to look at me. Jason and Tripp start shuffling their feet and focusing intently on the thick blades of grass surrounding their shoes. Deklan finally concedes, mostly I think it was because he could feel the tension building between Adaline and I. Everyone is quick to wander off and busy themselves with preparations for our journey. Adaline and I are left alone. I watch the rise and fall of her shoulders as she brushes the dirt back and forth with her foot and traces circles in the soil with her eyes. The silence between us is unnatural and I miss the hum of her constant chatter.

"If you want me to return to Ireland I can," I finally say. "I know that I'm no good to you like this, but I can't handle waiting around for you to end it."

"I don't want to end it. I love you, I told you before I don't care if you're human," she says, but tears are forming in her eyes.

"Then what is it? I'm sorry for how I handled things the other day. I hadn't really had time to process what happened on the Island, but I'm fine with it. Could you please just look at me," I say.

"Something else happened when I thought you were gone," she replies. The tears that had been brewing have finally spilt over her lids and are running down her rosy cheeks. I suppress the urge to wipe the tears from her face.

"What happened?" I ask.

"It was the night of my change. I thought I was going to die and you were gone, and mum and Jerry were gone... I was looking for something to cling to," she rambles.

"You had sex with him didn't you?" I say. I had known from the moment I came back there was something between them, but I never thought it had gone any further than the kiss they shared on the island.

"I'm so sorry, I wanted to tell you, but you were already so hurt, and I was scared of losing you all over again." she begins crying heavily. "I'm sorry."

I'm too shocked to respond. I feel sick in my stomach, I imagine the two of them together and all I can think of is crushing Tripp's face between my fingers. I conjure up the sounds of his wailing cries, I imagine the thrill I would feel as I flick white-hot flames against his exposed skin. I hadn't noticed my attention had fallen to the floor until Adaline raises my face to meet hers. The pleading and regret on her face wounds me, but I can't shake the feelings of disgust and betrayal.

"Have a safe trip," I tell her.

I step onto the stone path that leads towards the road and I keep walking. I see flashes of my past, images of my mother, the pain I endured at the hands of my father. The brutality of my life with my maker. It all still stings like salt in an open wound. All the heartache and misery I have suffered in my long life is hitting me in violent waves. Still, all of it feels like nothing compared to the pain that just stabbed me in my chest.

-53-
Adaline

I waited for Seth all day, but he didn't return. It was foolish of me to think he would be able to move past this, I just thought our love was bigger than our mistakes. I wish things could be different for us, I wish I had made better choices for myself, but I must deal with the consequences of my actions. A dark shadow looms over me, blocking the last of the sunlights fading rays.

"He'll come home," Shay says, following my gaze toward the road.

"I don't think he will, but thanks for trying. How's Neema?" I ask.

"She's okay, her and the gargoyle are with Phedora. I think Neema's going to stay at the temple until she feels well enough to travel to court," she replies.

"Is there anything I can do for her?" I ask.

"Just make sure you get there in one piece or all of this has been for nothing," she snaps.

"I never wanted anyone to suffer for me," I reply, sinking deeper into guilt and sadness.

"I didn't mean that," she adds. "I'm just angry at the situation."

There's so much guilt radiating from Shay it's hard to focus on myself or the pain I'm feeling.

Neema had suffered unspeakable assaults when she was held prisoner, but Tripp and Shay didn't escape unshaved either. Listening to another person be brutalised and tortured for hours on end with no way to help it, it would drive anyone over the edge.

"Aedan and Deklan are almost ready to leave, they asked me to collect you," Jason says appearing as silently as ever.

"I had better go. If Seth comes back," I begin to tell him.

"Don't worry he will be back when it's time for us to leave. I know him, he just needs some space. The second he realises how good he has it he will come running back," Jason says kindly.

"Thank you, Jason," I reply.

I'm grateful for his optimism and his unwavering belief that Seth will come home is a sentiment I try to cling to. I give both him and Shay an extra firm hug and make them promise to be careful on their journey. After I collect my bag of mostly borrowed possessions I find my way to Neema's rooms. She hasn't been outside since we returned from the mountain which is understandable. There's silence outside her bedroom door, but I can feel the slow unsteady beat of her heart hiding behind the door. I lift my shaking hand to knock, the door swings open before I have a chance.

"You breathe loudly when you're nervous," Neema says. Her usual serene expression and modest smile are absent.

"I wanted to check on you before I left, Shay said you wanted to stay here for a while," I say.

"If you want me to join you at court I will my lady," she whispers.

"No, I want you to look after yourself. If you want to come to court when you're feeling better I would love that, but only if you wanted to of course. I would never want you to do anything you're not comfortable with," I say trying to reassure her doubts. "I brought you something," I add. I unclasp the necklace from around my neck. "This pendant is charmed to warn you when there's danger, it will burn hot if it senses trouble. Phedora helped me store some healing magic in it as well, she said it will help restore you."

"I can't, it's yours," she says waving her hand.

"Please, I want you to have it, besides I won't take no for an answer," I say. She lowers her head and I latch it around her neck. It hangs lower on her delicate frame than mine. "It becomes you," I smile.

"Thank you," she says with a tear forming in her eyes.

I hug Neema close to me, I feel the deep ache within her. There's no scarring, but my arms can feel the cuts and tears the gargoyles had sliced into her flesh. They bled her until she was too weak to fight. I feel the way they forced themselves upon her. I fight the bile rising in my throat, I draw all the energy my body can contain from each of the elements and propel it into Neema. I wrap her in a cocoon of glowing warmth and strength, as I release my hold I feel her mood brighten. It's just a fraction, but it's enough to keep her fighting.

Aedan and Deklan are already saddled and waiting for me as I walk through the arch of the temple doors. Tripp is standing nervously beside Apollo. Apollo makes snickering sounds as I approach, his excitement radiates through his hooves and tickles the earth beneath him. I run my hand along his smooth flank and despite my sadness, I smile. Tripp hands me the reins and smiles, but his smile doesn't come as easily to his lips as it once did.

"Be careful," he says.

"You too," I reply, giving him a quick hug.

I straddle Apollo easily and settle into his movements. Aedan gestures for me to pull up my hood on the long cloak I borrowed from Phedora, it makes it hard to see, but never the less I comply with his instructions and conceal myself under the heavy fabric. We begin fading into the darkness, I look back once more hoping that a pair of warm brown eyes will meet my gaze. My heart sinks when I have to pry my eyes away from the road behind me and face the solitary road ahead.

-54-

SETH

I try to stop myself from going back to the temple. I've made up my mind. Determined to go back to the mortal realm I begin walking, but no matter what path I choose it always leads me back to Adaline. I can see glistening red flickers of light shining over the treetops. The sun is setting and the last few rays of sunlight catch in the temples crystal walls. I've already started walking back to the temple when I realise my heart has beaten the battle with my mind.

I can see Jason and Shay convened in the front garden, with the loner gargoyle and Beetok beside them. All their heads are facing the same direction and their backs are to me, I follow their gaze and see Adaline riding away. I place my foot on the edge of the tree line ready to run after her, but something stops me in my tracks. Adaline is looking over her shoulder, there's a mournful expression on her face. Her stare stretches past our friends and lingers on my hiding spot. I know she can't see me, but my heart stops all the same.

I stare at the empty road long after Adaline has ridden off. The others remain outside for a while until one by one they trickle back inside the temple, except for Tripp. He sits down on the stairs and buries his head in his hands. He looks different than when I met him on the Island, younger in a sense. Despite his youth and damaged appearance, it doesn't dissuade the rage that's growing inside me.

My body moves before my mind has time to catch up, and in a few quick strides, I am standing at his feet. He doesn't raise his head to look at me which makes me furious.

If you're going to sleep with someone else's girl, the least you can do is face them like a man. I'm livid, my hands feel hot to the touch. I can almost feel the pleasurable tingle that the fire used to bring to my palms, but my hands remain as unextraordinary as the rest of me. I shake off the absurd notion that the fire will return and clench my fists at my side.

"If you're going to hit me can you just get it over with already?" He mumbles between his cupped hands.

"You couldn't wait, could you? You must have been so overjoyed when they buried me. Pretending to be her friend, taking advantage of her when she was grieving. You're pathetic," I say. I can taste the vileness that stings him with each of my words.

"You're right," he says standing upright. He's taller than me and the stairs give him an advantage, but he looks too wounded to be much of a threat. "Go on," he says squaring his chin.

I wish I was a better man who wouldn't hit a wounded dog when he was already down, but I'm not. I tighten my fist until I can feel the blood drain out of my knuckles as it flows into my palms. I pause, only for a fraction of a second, then my fist connects with his jaw. I can't stop myself from grimacing. It's a sick type of pleasure you feel when inflicting pain on someone else, it's a pleasure I used to revel in, now it feels almost wrong. He turns back to face me expecting more, but I can't do it. His eyes are hollow with dark circles underneath, his lip has started bleeding. He doesn't even flinch as the blood drips down his chin and onto his cream coloured shirt.

"Touch her again and I'll kill you," I tell him, but my words have lost their venom. I push past him as I climb the stairs.

"You can confront me for the second time in twenty-four hours, but you couldn't man up and go after her? I don't think I'm the only pathetic one here," he calls behind me. "She loves you and for the life of me, I can't understand why," he adds.

That makes two of us. I tell myself.

He doesn't have the right to comment on the way Adaline feels for me, it's none of his business, but a small part of me is glad that he knows she didn't choose him.

-55-
Adaline

The road is quiet for most of the journey. We take small tracks that lead through heavily wooded areas with almost no wildlife to speak of. The lack of animals probably has something to do with the awful smelling moss that Deklan insisted we wipe all over ourselves not long after we left. It smells like cat pee with a hint of molasses, he swore it will confuse and deter anyone following our trail. I don't doubt its repellent powers; the way I smell right now even I don't want to be around me.

Apollo is enjoying the journey and stops to smell every interesting plant we come across, it makes me wonder if he knows this world is different from the one he was born into. Deklan groans every time he lowers his head, but I'm just as eager for the distraction. Aedan hurries us along with a gentle hand until we arrive at a lake. The lake looks black under the darkness of night, at least until the wind casts a breeze across it. The movement transforms the lake into a glorious masterpiece. A luminous blue light traipses along the edges of the water, moving back and forth with the steady flow of its ripples.

"It's so beautiful," I say.

"You can touch it, it's safe," Aedan says.

"We don't have time for this," Deklan snaps.

Aedan ignores him and climbs down from his horse. I hurry down and follow after him. I secure myself on one of the large rocks and lean down to run my fingers through the water.

It's warm and the incandescent lights follow the path my fingers trace as they move through the water. Aedan picks up a rock and rolls it around in his fingers smoothing its rough edges before tossing it across the lake.

"Can you please just get back on your horses? We are almost at the walls," Deklan scolds.

Aedan and I both laugh at his fatherly tone and we climb back on our horses. We follow a small stream that stems from the lake as it bends and weaves through a forest that's blooming with life. The creatures here don't seem as bothered by our foul scent, secretly I hope it's wearing off, so I can meet my father not smelling like I've bathed with a skunk. Snake-like creatures as big as my arms scamper up trees while impossibly small birds dart back and forth teasing them. As the bird's glide on the breeze their silver wings glisten in the moonlight and cast a mirrored light across the undergrowth. Deklan stops abruptly causing Apollo to snort in a most unsatisfied manner. We have arrived at a high stone wall that sprouts up into the canopy. I peer through the open spaces in the trees and I can see that the wall is actually the base of a tower. Deklan starts scratching a section of moss away from one of the stones until it's clearly exposed. He pushes his hand firmly on the stone until it sinks inside the wall. I hear a faint clicking sound and a weight drops revealing a darkened doorway before us.

"Leave the horses. I'll have someone collect them once we are inside," Deklan orders.

I tie Apollo's reins to a tree and promise him I'll return. He doesn't seem pleased to be left behind but looking at the constricted passageway it's clear that I can't bring him along. The three of us step through the doorway and Deklan closes the entrance sealing us in complete darkness.

Deklan reaches out a rough hand and takes mine to guide me and I try my best not to stumble. Aedan stays close at my heels and clearly needs little guidance to find his way through the blackness. The tower smells musty, traces of dust tickle my nose and threaten to force a sneeze. We climb an endless staircase in complete darkness, I misstep often, but thanks to my guardians I never fall.

"This is it," Deklan whispers.

I hear the crank of a handle and the rushing sound of air as its sucked out of the forgotten chamber. My breath tightens in my chest. I can't believe it, after all the lies and losses, after everything we have endured, I'm finally home.

-56-
Tripp

The cut on my lip is beginning to scab, it would heal quicker if I could stop myself from brushing it with my tongue. Seth had every right to come at me the way he did, in truth I think he went easy on me which makes me feel more pitiful. He hasn't said a word to me since we left the temple which is fine by me. Our party attracts a few odd glances as we pass through villages on our way to court. I'm glad Mikael stayed behind with Neema, because Beetok sticks out like a pig in a toddler's beauty pageant, despite being wrapped in layers of colourful shawls that Phedora was so kind to provide. Beetok sneezes noisily making the horses jump.

"Could you possibly be any louder?" Shay says like it's an accusation, not a question.

"These rugs are bothering my allergies," Beetok replies.

"We should have left him behind," Shay says to Seth.

"Adaline was happy for him to come, let's make the best of it," he says calmly. "But if he puts us at risk when it comes to a fight, leave him behind and protect yourself," he says to Shay and Jason who attempt to stifle their laughter.

It's mid-evening by the time we reach the village nearest the castle walls. Adaline should be entering the castle through a secret passage with my father and Aedan. My party will be going directly through the front gates.

Spending two days away from Adaline has felt like a century and my heart jumps excitedly at the thought of her being so near. The Talbot castle was built into the edge of a robust mountainside. Lush green foliage wraps lovingly around its walls camouflaging its sandstone bricks. We follow the dirt road beside Lunar Lake, the stream's current is slow today. The glowing water cascades from the peak of the mountain that the castle is built into. The water escapes between the spaces in the rocky terrain and creates dozens of tiny waterfalls that encase the castle in a steady stream of mystical light.

As we cross the bridge into the grounds of the castle I peer over the edge at the blackened water below, a silver sparrow swoops down to steal a drink from the cool water only to be pulled under by one of the maidens of the lake. Mermaids have always made me uncomfortable, beautiful to look upon, but deadly to any creature small enough to become their dinner. The five of us approach the drawn gate, it takes me a moment to realise the others have cleared a path and are waiting for someone to step forward and take the lead. Quickly it becomes apparent that they are waiting for me.

"I'm Patrick, son of King Theodore's right hand. We are here under the order of the King," I shout to the hooded guard that stands atop the tower.

"Here goes nothing," Seth mutters under his breath as the drawbridge begins to lower.

-57-
Adaline

My eyes take their time to adjust to the sudden change in lighting. I still have hold of Deklan's hand as we emerge from behind a woven tapestry that's secured to the top of the wall. I duck my head past Deklan's broad shoulders so that I can peer down the length of the long hall. Large arched windows filter a ghostly white moonlight that illuminates the coloured stones in the floor. I look up expecting to see lit torches lighting the rest of the hall, but instead, I see evenly spaced floating orbs of fire. They are the same kind as the ones I've created in the past, only more red than blue. I wonder what fae could manage to keep these alight all evening. Deklan makes his way through the maze of halls without difficulty until we come to a passageway with a single guard posted outside of an ornate bejewelled doorway.

"Wait here," Deklan orders. He rounds the corner, marching forward with purpose. The guard's body language changes. His shoulders arch and his knees bend just a fraction as he closes his fingers around the small dagger that's strapped to his side. I step forward to warn Deklan, but Aedan holds me back. "I would have killed you twice by now. Go find Wren and tell him I've returned," Deklan orders. The poor guard doesn't look much older than a boy, the young man swallows his fear and scampers off.

Deklan waves a hand beckoning us toward him. It's only when I begin to walk that I notice I have forgotten how to breathe. My racing heart is fighting for the oxygen in my blood, its angry with me for depriving it of its needs and beats wildly in revolt.

Aedan places a soft hand on my shoulder to reassure me. I part my lips and engulf the air like a person drowning. Each time I place my right foot on the floor I suck in another breath, on the left step I breathe out deeply. Seven, a lucky number for some, but for me it's the number of steps it takes for me to reach the door that has my father on the other side.

Deklan raises his hand and knocks on the wooden door. It's loud, like the thump you feel vibrating in your chest when you fear a shadow is something more than just a shadow. Light footsteps approach the door, there's a hushed commotion on the other side and definitely more than one voice. Oh God, what if my birth mother is there with him? I have foolishly deluded myself into forgetting her existence because it's easier than facing the truth. The door handle unlatches, I pull the cloak away from my face as the door begins to open. My heart stops and I grasp onto Deklan's arm to steady myself.

"I said I didn't want to be..." The man begins to say, but he comes up short as his eyes fall on Deklan.

"Theo, this is Adaline, your daughter," Deklan says.

"Hello," I say stupidly.

"I, um..." he mumbles. Disbelief is hard-pressed across his face.

"Who is it?" An annoyingly soft voice asks from behind him.

"Get out," he barks to a barely dressed young woman. She clutches her clothing close to her chest as she brushes past us, vanishing down the hall.

Aedan's eyes follow her form longer than necessary. I elbow his abdomen and he laughs uncomfortably pulling his gaze back to my father. Theo steps aside to allow us passage into his chambers. He's much younger than I had imagined, late twenties at the most.

His skin is warm and flushed. It's at this moment that I am able to take in his state of undress. His hair is a mess atop his head, the bottom half of his shirt is undone and there's a tightness in his breath.

"Where's the Queen?" Deklan asks, ignoring the elephant in the room.

"Traveling, like she always does this time of year," Theo replies. His eyes haven't left mine since we walked into the room. It makes me nervous. "You're all grown up," he says.

"You're young," I say. "I mean younger than I had imagined."

"Royal perks," he replies. "I thought the guards were going to escort you from the temple," he says.

"Complications. Somehow the vampire woman found us," Deklan says.

"Aedan isn't it?" Theo says.

"Yes, Your Majesty," Aedan says formally.

"Thank you for your service. I'll have my men compensate you before you leave tomorrow," he adds. Panic overwhelms me at the thought of being abandoned here.

"I would feel better to have him here until after the coronation, the others will arrive momentarily, besides Aedan is now the appointed leader of all four vampire clans so he will need to be present for the events to come," Deklan adds.

"Others?" Theo says raising his eyebrows.

"My friends," I clarify.

"Fae friends already? Well, any friend of yours is more than welcome. I'll have the attendants take you to your room, I'm sure you would like to change into something more comfortable," Theo says. He reaches forward to place his hands on each of my shoulders. He stares at me for a moment before pulling me into a hug. His shoulders are tense and it's too stiff to be anything more than awkward. "I'm glad you're finally home," he says with a broad smile.

"Me too," I reply. Am I?

It's possible that I had built up this moment too much in my head. I may have set my expectations too high because meeting my father for the first time is very underwhelming. I had imagined my father opening his arms lovingly and holding me like a small child. I had expected there to be an instant warmth between us. In my dreams he would shed a few tears, then again, he was also older and had a beard. Sadly, there's nothing even slightly parental about him. He's just a man. My abilities were no help either, I couldn't sense anything from him. No love or joy, no fear. It was like looking into a void or a cruel throwback to the days before I could see past someone's façade, the days when I was human and had to take people at face value.

Deklan is called away as beautifully dressed attendants with elaborately painted markings across their skin arrive to collect us. They lead Aedan and me through the castle until we reach a smaller less extravagant door. One of the female attendants opens the door and offers the room to Aedan, she also emphasises how pleased she would be to assist him. I roll my eyes at her forwardness and for the second time today I smack him for his wandering eyes and the flattered smile leaves his face.

"Thank you, but I'll be accompanying the lady to her chambers," Aedan says formally.

The attendant looks displeased, even more so as her eyes wander over my less than impressive form. When we arrive at my room I'm amazed at the beauty within.

The roof is draped with layers of sheer fabrics and lace, tiny lights twinkle behind them looking like the stars in the night's sky. The walls are adorned in the same kind of fabric fusion, minus the lights. The bed is a carved-out tree with branches that weave intricately around the cloth canopy. There are fresh blossoms in a vase that perfumes the room with a scent that closely resembles wild lilies.

"It's beautiful," I tell the attendant.

"It's one of the Queen's creations, she will be pleased you like it," she says sweetly.

"Thank you," Aedan says shuffling the attendants outside. "Are you okay?"

"I feel kind of dirty actually, do you think they would be offended if I asked for a different room?" I say.

"Possibly, it's also possible she decorated all the rooms," Aedan replies.

"Do you think they are going to lock me away in this tower until the coronation?" I ask.

"I imagine your father will make an announcement of your return and send out the appropriate invitations to all the Seelie clan leaders and he will need to invite the Unseelie King as well. Both sides must agree when a new ruler is going to be named," Aedan says.

"You make it sound like a party," I scoff.

"Afraid not. There will be a number of hurdles you will need to jump before the throne changes hands, but don't stress we will be here to help you through it," he says with a smile.

"As if I haven't been tested enough," I reply.

There's a loud knock at the door, Aedan is already opening it before I have time to turn around. I hear Deklan's voice and my tense muscles relax, but the presence of someone behind him eases me more.

-58-

SETH

The guards take their time ushering us into the castle, waiting on orders, they claimed. I know different, they are keeping us out in the open intentionally. That way they have the advantage if an attack should ensue. I'm on my last nerve when Deklan pops his bulbous head out from behind the guard's barricade. He vouches for us and the guards lower the blades they have been clutching since they 'welcomed' us inside the gates. As our group begins filing through the doors, one of the guards grabs me by the scruff of my shirt.

"This one is human." The vile creature practically spits on my face as it speaks.

"He's an exception. Don't make me tell the King you disobeyed his request," Deklan says.

"What's your name?" I ask the guard.

"Sampson," he says politely, but his eyes say he's eager for a challenge.

"I'll remember that," I tell him confidently and inscribe his name immediately on my mental hit list.

"Do you always have to make things difficult?" Deklan whispers to me.

"The prick started it," I tell him.

"Just try not to start a war while we are here," he pleads.

I roll my eyes at him, I would be more worried about the clans accepting Adaline than the actions of a meagre human. We follow Deklan into the lower levels of the castle where he opens a modest door that must have been beautiful back in its day. Behind the door is a dorm room. Multiple beds are lined up side by side against the wall with uniformed covers and minimal furnishings. If I didn't have firsthand knowledge of how bad the dungeons are I would swear this room is one. Shay scoffs as we walk the length of the room while Jason jumps eagerly into the nearest bed. Deklan apologises for housing us in the training barracks, but the other rooms will be needed for the clan leaders. I never thought I would miss the feminine rooms Aedan and I had been given in previous visits, I wonder if he will be willing to share this time.

"I want to see Adaline and my brother," I ask Deklan.

"I figured. The rest of you stay here, I'll arrange dinner shortly. Hob, I suggest you keep as low a profile as you can manage," he says to Beetok.

Deklan leads me up a number of hallways and staircases, I make a mental note of the exits and the number of guards and attendants as we pass, it never hurts to have an exit strategy. We finally arrive at an oversized door in the north wing. Deklan knocks firmly, as his hand reaches to knock a second time Aedan swings the door open. I can see Adaline behind him standing by the window. Her back is to us, but my heart still does a little flip, and as she begins to turn the little flip changes into boisterous somersaults. I had worried I would still be angry when I looked at her, but I'm not. At first, her expression looks displeased, then it quickly shifts into a smile when her eyes fall on me. Aedan and Deklan excuse themselves to allow us some much-needed privacy. I linger in the doorway, unsure how to proceed.

"Do you want to come in?" She asks. I cross the threshold tentatively, pushing the door closed behind me. Things feel different between us, not worse, just different. It feels like we are starting over again, like the first time I was alone with her, it's the uncertainty that hangs in the air. "I'm glad you came back," she says rubbing her arm awkwardly.

"I had sex with Shay," I blurt out. The shock in her eyes matches the shock in my own voice, I can't believe what I just said. Her face changes from shocked to pained and I try to correct my mistake. "I didn't mean, it was before you and me, it was after..." I stumble on my words.

"I already knew, only recently, but I knew," she says. "It just hurts to hear you say it."

"I'm sorry, I meant we both have made some choices we shouldn't be held accountable for," I whisper.

"And I'm sorry for my own transgression," she says. "I need you to understand what I did, I never would have done if, for a second, I thought you were alive. I love you, pigheadedness and all and I'm sorry I hurt you."

I don't say anything, bringing her lips to mine is the only words we need. She kisses me back forcefully, I can taste the saltiness of the tears that have run down her cheeks and coated her lips. She leans into me pushing me back onto the bed. My hands slip under her shirt to caress her lower back. I move my lips across her neck and shoulders, she leans back pulling her shirt over her head, as she fumbles with her shirt I see the moonlight catch in the pigments of scarlet in her hair and it makes me smile. The small flames that light the room brightens as she leans down to kiss me with an intensity stronger than any flame, I run my fingers along the edge of her bra until it slips under the clasp.

"Your fathers requesting..." Aedan says swinging open the bedroom door. "Oh, sorry," he yelps and stumbles into the door frame in his haste to escape.

Adaline's face and chest turn into a shade of red that's brighter than any rose and she gathers her shirt in inhuman speed. She continually recites 'oh god, oh god' until she is fully dressed and even applies a second layer of clothes. She sits on the edge of the bed with her head in her hands trying to shake off her embarrassment.

"I'm mortified, how am I going to look him in the eye again?" She mutters nervously. She raises her head and looks to me for reassurance.

"If it makes you feel any better he's already seen you naked," I say, recalling how her clothes had burnt away from her body at Bristeal Mountain.

A smile breaks onto my lips and she furrows her brow, which only makes me laugh louder at her horrified expression. Her eyes squint, annoyance burning on her face, then she hits me with an overstuffed pillow. I catch her wrist as she tries to hit me a second time and pull her back to me, placing a swift kiss on her lips.

"He's waiting outside isn't he?" She whispers.

"I'M NOT LISTENING!" Aedan shouts from the other side of the door.

"Just come in," she yells. "You've already seen it all anyway," she mutters under her breath.

Aedan finishes what he was saying when he so rudely interrupted us. Adaline's father has insisted all of us join him for dinner, so he can thank us personally. Aedan has to pry me away from Adaline's side, so we can dress for dinner. Sadly, any event with the Seelie King is a formal affair and my jeans and t-shirt don't exactly cut it.

-59-
Adaline

I've washed myself briskly by the time one of the attendants returns to my room with an assortment of dresses draped over her tiny arms. Her hair is shaved on one side with an intricate ruby coloured tattoo decorating the empty space. Her ears are elongated with pointed tips, not as defined as I have seen in movies, but the difference between us is noticeable. She catches me staring, thankfully she asks if I like the gold jewellery dripping from her pointed tip down to her earlobe. She places the dresses down on the bed and vanishes in a white blur that swirls around me. I draw in a single intake of breath and before I've exhaled I realise I'm wearing a sheer white camisole and nothing else. I release a panicked cry and the white blur slows and her tiny frame becomes visible once more.

"Have you not had helper elves before my lady?" She asks puzzled.

"No," I reply quickly, as I try to cover up the intimate parts of me she hasn't already seen.

"Oh, my lady. Forgive me I have mistaken, I'll send myself to the flogger. How many lashings?" She asks. I laugh thinking she's kidding until I see the quiver of her lip and the frightened tremor that runs over her tanned skin.

"Oh God no, there's no need for that. Maybe just don't take my clothes away without me asking you to," I tell her.

"Thank you, my lady," she replies with a bow and her doll-like eyes beam brightly.

"What's your name?" I ask.

"Eldar, my lady. I've been assigned to you, anything you need please just ask," she says.

"Since I'm already in this maybe you could help put one of those dresses on… Just leave my underwear alone though," I ask.

She laughs wildly, and I quickly realise why. What I thought was multiple dresses is actually one. By the time she has added the decorative layer over the functional three, I feel like I'm carrying the weight of two people around my hips. Eldar pulls in the lacing of the corset until I can hardly breathe, then she stands aside so I can admire her handy work. I walk towards the elaborate freestanding mirror and I catch my breath. I look like a medieval princess that has fallen through the looking glass into Wonderland. The emerald green brings out the red in my hair and it brightens my eyes, which is good since they are looking so tired lately. The long sheer sleeves sway as I turn, their jewelled embroidery glistens under the fires light giving it an ethereal glow to it. It's stunning, except for one thing.

"Are you sure about this?" I ask gesturing to the abundance of cleavage. My father doesn't need to know I'm that womanly, I think. She cocks a quizzical eyebrow at my question. I look at her barely-there frock and the low cut that's exposing more skin than my own and I figure modesty isn't something the fae worry about. "Never mind," I add.

I spin once more, making certain I can hold myself upright with the excess weight, a soft knock at the door interrupts my beautiful daydream. Eldar opens the door and before I can even ask who it is I see Deklan towering over Eldar's petite frame, like a mountain shadowing an ant hill.

Seth is finding his own struggle to peer around the broadness of Deklan's shoulders. Seth's eyes meet mine and I can feel lust ignite in his chest and other parts.

I feel myself turning as red as the lipstick I'm wearing. Why do I feel so exposed whenever he's looking at me? I'm wearing a million layers of clothing and somehow, I feel more naked now than I did two hours ago, when his hands were all over my uncovered skin.

"Shall we go, princess?" Deklan asks formally, keeping his eyes upright.

"Only if you cut out the princess crap," I say, and he rolls his eyes making me laugh.

Seth takes my arm leading me down the extravagant hallways. The outside of the castle is built of thick sandstone blocks, but inside it's another thing entirely. The walls are lined with various shaped crystals and glass that gleam under the light of the fire orbs. As the fire floats weightlessly, it reflects the coloured glass and stones, casting rainbows across the floor. Every so often a tree appears, sprouting out of the floor as easily as if it were sprouting from the soil. Small sprites and pixies flit around the branches that decorate the ceiling. I stare in wonder at the beauty the castle beholds, a small voice reminds me not to judge by first appearances, especially after the concerning comment Eldar had made. We arrive at a large entrance that reminds me of the ballroom at the stronghold. I clench Seth's hand tighter to steady my nerves. This is it, I'm finally going to see the world that's destined to be mine.

-60-
Deklan

Eighteen years I have waited for this moment, and I still can't believe I was able to keep my promise. Adaline is safe, she survived her change and now she's finally home. No matter how many boxes I check I still feel like my work isn't done. I open dining hall doors and announce Adaline's arrival. Only a small table is set up for tonight's festivities. Theo is sitting at the head in his usual place, the Queen's seat is empty, and the rest of our friends fill the other seats surrounding the table. I lead Seth and Adaline to the head of the table, Theo gestures for Adaline to sit beside him in the Queen's chair. She smiles nervously and releases her hold on Seth, so she can take her place by her father's side. I sit across from Adaline on the other side of Theo while Seth wanders down to sit beside his brother in the empty seat. A collective breath is held amongst us, all waiting for someone to speak.

"I would like to personally thank each of you for your hand in returning my daughter to me. I will make sure each of you is compensated for your efforts. Deklan has advised me that some of you may wish to remain at court with the princess, I am happy to accommodate this for a time," Theo says regally, but I hear his emphasis on the word 'time', especially as his eyes fall on Beetok.

One of the attendants announces dinner is being served and we are flooded with light-fingered wait staff delivering plates as secretly as ghosts drifting through the night air.

I can see Adaline's rosy cheeks burning brighter as time ticks on, Theo speaks to her softly asking her about her life in the mortal realm.

He seems fascinated with her survival of the plane crash, quizzing her on the secret of her endurance. I can see tears forming in the corners of her eyes as she politely answers his questions about Sarah and Jerry. I know he doesn't mean it, but his questions are upsetting her.

"Perhaps Adaline has had enough talk of the past for one evening," I say boldly, eyeing my friend hoping he will understand my tone and back off.

"Oh, of course, forgive me dear girl, I've just missed so much," he says to Adaline.

"I understand," she says softly, shooting me a grateful glance and warm smile.

"Perhaps we should discuss what is going to happen now. I imagine the Queen has been contacted about Adaline's return," I hint.

"Yes, in a sense. I have sent out riders to all the clan leaders, and all efforts are being made to locate my wife. It will take a few weeks for the leaders to assemble for the inauguration," Theo says gallantly.

"Are you sure this is a good idea? Don't you think I should spend some time… I don't know, with the people or something?" Adaline asks.

"It's your birthright, everything we have done, everything we have sacrificed to keep you safe, is all for this," Theo beams.
Adaline smiles politely at his words before looking down at her meal. She's the epitome of refinement for the rest of the evening, but I know her well enough to recognise the hint of panic in her eyes and the way she's pushing the food around on her plate has me worried. Seth notices too, I can feel his eyes fixated on her with worry more intense than my own. I guess I had convinced myself that once Adaline was here everything would fall into place. I search her stricken face once more looking for a glint of hope, if there is any it's definitely hidden from me.

I'm glad to see that Wren has recovered from his injuries and is overseeing the royal guard until I can resume my duties. His second Jackson is also doing well, but I'm afraid Florence was hurt worse than I had thought and is still recovering in her home. Wrens guards will watch over Adaline tonight and in the morning Aedan, Jason and I will take over, rotating on eight-hour shifts. Now that her identity has been announced and the Queen's location is still unknown, Adaline's safety is still in question. Shay and Beetok have taken it upon themselves to familiarise themselves with everyone at court, as well as the fae in the surrounding villages. Tripp is still struggling with nightmares from his time as a captive and watching him during dinner I know there are other things worrying his mind. It doesn't take a father to recognise the yearning in his eyes every time Adaline enters a room or the trodden expression that washes over him when he sees her eyes searching for someone else. My son isn't in the right frame of mind for this, and the best place for him to be right now is at home.

-61-
Tripp

Adaline looked beautiful tonight, she sat by her father's side with the grace and beauty befitting a princess, her grim expression, however, told a different story. Her and my father were too far away for me to hear their conversations with the King, but I could see my father's intensity growing stronger as the night wore on. Everyone else talked comfortably, swapping tales of battle and normal fae pleasantries, but I wasn't able to force it. I excused myself from dinner early, I can't be sure if the feelings stirring within me are from my recent ordeals or the look on Adaline's face when she entered the room on Seth's arm. She looked into his eyes and I could see how much she loves him. I have always considered it a childish notion to have every waking moment consumed by thoughts of another, but here I am. When I was very small, my mother and father were that way, always connected, even by the slightest touch. I remember my mother brushing back my father's hair with her delicate fingers, such a simple gesture, but it always seemed so intimate. I see the same devotion between Adaline and Seth when they are together. Touches lingering longer than they need to, their eyes always falling back to one another. It hurts, I'd be lying if I said it didn't. What I need is to find a way to move past my feelings for her, but I'm struggling.

As I was leaving dinner my father had suggested I return to my childhood home to rest for a while, time to collect my thoughts or something like that, but I know what he meant. Time away from Adaline, time to let my feelings fade. I pack the few belongings I have with me and make the ugly bed in the dorm room, I make sure to pull the sheets in tightly just like they taught us at the academy.

The others have gone to celebrate with mulled wine and some off-key singing at a pub in town. The door behind me creaks and a gust of frosty air howls into the night. I turn to find Seth standing gawkily in the doorway. He glances at the bag on my bed and back to me, he looks like he wants to say something, but is having difficulty choosing his words.

"I'm going home for a while, I will be just outside the village if I'm needed. Say goodbye to the others for me," I say.

"What about Adaline?" he asks still blocking the exit.

"Say goodbye to her too," I snap, I don't intend to be harsh, but the way he says her name with such reverence wounds me.

"I would be happy for you to slip away into the night and never return, trust me I'm not by any means a decent guy, but I think Adaline would be hurt if you didn't tell her you are leaving," he says.

"It almost killed you to say that didn't it?" I reply.

"Look, I'm not great at the selfless stuff and if she never laid eyes on you again I would be okay with it, but as much as I hate it, she cares about you. She cares about everyone, even people not worthy of her. She deserves for those people to do right by her, you and I included," he says running a hand through his messy hair.

"I'll go say goodbye," I tell him, and he steps aside so I can leave.

As I walk through the doorway and into the hall I hear Seth release a breath I hadn't noticed he'd been holding. I suppose if I can't be the one to love her, I'm glad she can have someone who despite all his flaws can still put her needs first.

One of the helper elves is all too happy to escort me to Adaline's chambers. Word of her return is spreading through the castle-like wildfire and everyone wants to have a piece of her. I hear the elves whispering in the hall about the travesty of a human being welcomed at court. Obviously, no one has told the King about Seth's new status and honestly, I can't blame them, who would want to be the bearer of that news.

The elfin woman leads me through the winding castle halls into one of the royal wings. The halls have a distinctiveness about them, they are more opulent than the rest of the castle that's hard to dismiss. We arrive at the end of the glowing rainbow where we face a wooden door with tiny golden embellishments on the hinges and handle. A single guard is watching her door, I ask the elf to leave and I raise my hand to knock as the guard eyes me cautiously. Before my knuckles tap the ornate wood, the door is thrust open making me jump with surprise.

"You're leaving," Adaline says with a grim expression on her lips. Her hair is disorganised, her nightgown is a simple fabric that looks built for comfort, but she still manages to take my breath away.

"Did my father tell you?" I ask casting my eyes to my feet. I feel myself turning red thinking of the beauty that's under her simple apparel.

"You broadcast loudly when you're upset, it was impossible for me not to sense you through the door. Do you want to come inside?" She asks.

"No, I'll lose my nerve if I do. I just wanted to say goodbye," I tell her. I can see the glistening of water forming in her lower lids and my stomach churns.

"Asking you to stay would be selfish. Can I ask you to come back when you're ready instead?" She asks.

"I'll be back, I promise," I reply, she pulls me in close, and I can smell the sweetness of her hair and the saltiness of her tears. "I have to go," I whisper into the top of her head.

She releases her hold on me and forces a smile for my benefit. I reach out my hand and wipe a stray tear from her cheek with my thumb. I can feel her eyes watching me as I walk the length of the hall, even when I turn the corner I can still feel her gaze prickling along my back.

-62-
Adaline

Sleep came easily enough after Tripp left, crying will do that to you. I wake in the early hours feeling sick and exhausted despite my undisturbed sleep. I draw one of the curtains and can see the sun is hiding behind the peak of the mountain and the air still has the briskness of night. I splash my face with the cold water Eldar left for me. It smells strongly of rose petals and lavender, I remove my nightgown and give myself a brisk wash with the cool water and a cloth. I consider warming it with magic, but the chilliness of it helps wake me from my half sleep. I dress in some of the clothing Phedora had given me for the journey, a simple tunic in bright colours and a pair of pants I would almost call leggings if they weren't so sheer. I run my fingers through my hair, catching a knot every so often. Once satisfied I secure it back with a ribbon that has been left unattended.

I open the bedroom door silently, expecting to find guards on the other side, but the hall is empty and still. I step into the hall, my bare feet shiver as they touch the stone floor. The jewelled walls aren't glowing this morning and the fire orbs have burned themselves out. It's chilly without all the colours and warmth dancing off the walls. I turn a corner and try to remember the path I had travelled last night, but it all looks different in this light. I wander the halls until I find a familiar object, it's the door to my father's chambers. A guard stands sleepily leaning against the wall, I'm tempted to approach, but something stops me. If I'm being completely honest with myself it's the fear of rejection. Last night during dinner it was becoming clear that I'm not the child my father was expecting and eventually he's going to see it too.

I disregard seeing my father's door and instead explore the rest of the castle. It doesn't take long for me to get lost through the twisting stairways and never-ending halls. I stumble across a room unlike the others, it's busy with sound and excited chatter. There's the distinct sound of metal pans clinking together as they are hastily thrown from one shelf to another and I can't ignore the heavenly aroma wafting out of the kitchen. I sneak up to the door hoping to open it just enough to see inside, unfortunately, it's one of those doors that's split across the middle, and the top half is open and secured against the wall. A loud bang makes me jump, in the soundless shock I hear a familiar voice cursing in French from inside the kitchen.

"BACH!" I shout, pushing through the half door. He drops the tray he's holding when he sees me, I take it as a cue to hug him. He seems worn since we last saw one another, his face has a strain to it, but I'm glad to see he's still pleasantly plump with a whisper of pink in his cheeks.

"Oh miss, I'm so glad you're safe," he says squeezing his arms around me. A harsh cough from behind us forces me to loosen my grip. As I look around the large kitchen I see a mix of men and women who could easily be related to Bach, each unique in their own way, but they have the same build and colouring.

"I'm sorry for interrupting," I say. Bach squeezes my hand affectionately.

"Don't apologise my dear, but the kitchen is no place for you," he says.

"Can I stay for a little while, I promise I'll keep out of the way, I can even help. I can chop or something," I ramble. Bach glances around at his kitchen hands who stare blankly back at him. "Please," I beg.

"Of course Princess," he replies.

The others don't seem thrilled about my presence and continue with their work in silence. Bach sets me up at a workstation with a small stool.

I make myself comfortable and hook my bare feet through the legs of the seat to stop myself fidgeting. Bach hands me some curious looking fruits and quickly notices that I have no idea what they are, so he instructs me on how best to slice them. The other workers move back and forth with impressive speed, weaving around one another like they share a single mind. They have stopped the cheery chatter I heard from the hall. It's strange having people behave so anxiously around me, treating me like I have horns growing out of my temples. Bach ignores their glares and asks me questions about our time apart, nothing specific, but enough that the conversation makes me feel human. Suddenly I wonder if humans the right word to still describe me. I know I'm not human, not physically, but inside I still feel human. I feel the heart beating inside my chest and the rush of blood through my veins. Everyone in the fae world seems to think of being human as less than, to me it feels like so much more.

"Hungry?" Bach asks loudly, my mind must have wandered because he looks concerned.

"A little," I reply. He hands me a bowl containing some of the fruits I had just cut and some other items I have never seen before. I bite cautiously into the fruit, its sickly sweet and the juice runs down my throat like a waterfall. I finish all the fruit and move onto a strange cake like ball, as the moist food touches my tongue I feel instantly sick. I spit it out as politely as possible if there even is such a thing.

"I'm sorry," I say to Bach.

"Don't worry they are an acquired taste, your father loves them," he says with a little laugh and hands me more fruit.

Eventually, the other cooks relax and begin chatting with one another, no one talks directly to me but that's okay, progress is progress. I feel better sitting amongst the steady chaos of the kitchen. It reminds me of when I was a child, and I would sit and watch mum and Jerry cooking on one of our visits, they were always dancing and singing off-key.

The fact that the noise helps drown out all my worries is an added bonus. One of the female cooks with a button nose and greying hair hands me a glass of lilac coloured liquid, it smells sweetly of violets and has a mild fizz.

"Thank you," I say with a broad smile, she smiles back if only for a minute. A moment is all I need to sense the sadness escape her firm façade. I move without thinking, I catch her hand before she reaches the stove. "Should you be here?" I ask keeping my voice low. She exhales deeply, allowing her shoulders to fall. A single tear tips over her lid, trickling down her cheek. The small stone woman breathes in deeply to strengthen herself. "Go home," I say.

"I can't, the King will be displeased," she begins to say, but I raise a hand and stop her.

"He can take it up with me if there's an issue. Go home and take the time you need," I tell her. She looks around like I'm hosting a prank show and she's waiting for someone to jump out and catch her off guard. I squeeze my hand on her shoulder reassuringly until she removes her apron and heads home.

"That was decent of you miss," Bach whispers as a dozen wide-mouthed cooks throw themselves back into work.

"Did you know?" I ask.

"Yes, her daughter has been ill for a while. I believe she was given the news last evening," he says with a grimace.

"My lady," A booming voice calls from the hall. I look around the raised pots and pans to see a large being leering over the doorway. "What is that?" I whisper.

"He's an Owlma, Tyro I believe is his name. One of the royal guards," Bach tells me.

"I think I'm in trouble," I say to him.

When I'm close enough to see Tyro properly I can understand why Bach called him an Owlma. He has owl-like features, large eyes and a tiny nose that points into a beak. He doesn't have skin, well if he does its hiding under the thin layer of shiny feathers. His feathers are a mottled mix of browns and golds with flickers of white, but he doesn't have wings which surprises me, and he has large hands sprouting from his feathered arms that are coated in a white baby bird kind of fluff.

"The King was concerned to find you absent from your quarters. I'll escort you back," Tyro says boldly. He begins his one-man stampede vanishing around a corner before I can retort his instructions. I wave goodbye to Bach and hurry after birdman.

-63-
Deklan

I should have been concerned the second I heard the knock at the door at this early hour. Theo rarely rises before the sun, but here he is, hours before dawn wrapped tightly in his jewelled robe. I stand aside allowing him passage. I close the door behind him, leaving his guard outside.

"She was found in the kitchen, with the help," he spouts. "THE HELP!" He shouts. I raise an eyebrow clearly missing the concern. "She was working with them, a princess shouldn't be consorting with the help," he adds.

"You and your brother played with me as a child, and I wasn't from one of the noble families," I remind him.

"Yes, we were all blind to the necessities of society back then. Besides your father was hand to the King, just like you are now. His position held status, unlike the kitchen staff," he replies.

"Adaline isn't going to sit in a tower while people wait on her hand and foot. She isn't that kind of girl. You should be proud, she's kind and loyal and fiercely independent," I tell him. "Exactly what we need in a princess."

"She sent one of the cook's home," he adds.

"If that's the case I would trust her decision," I say honestly.

"You have so much faith in her, I'm afraid all I have are doubts," he says weakly. "Maybe we made a mistake sending her to be raised among the humans."

"It wasn't a mistake, you've known her for less than a day. Trust me, you will easily find the same faith I have in her," I say. He pats me on the back as he takes his leave, I worry for him. I know too well what it's like to question your actions as a parent and Theo hasn't had the fast education one receives from raising a child. I still see him as a boy in so many ways.

It's impossible to get any more sleep now that I'm awake and I'm not the only one. Aedan and Seth are outside my door when I open it, neither of them looks pleased. It turns out the King doesn't look kindly upon Seth's human form and has requested he return to the mortal realm immediately. To say Seth is pissed is an understatement. I feel like a punching bag between the two brothers, each one placing a blow like I'm the one who has offended them. I promise to rectify the situation as soon as possible until then I advise both of them to make themselves scarce. Aedan sets his jaw firmly and tries to leave, but Seth isn't budging. Aedan links his arm around Seth's shoulders and practically drags him away from my door. I never thought things would be so difficult once we were safe inside the Vale, and I sure as hell never thought I'd be playing Dr Phil for Theo and the brothers.

-64-
Adaline

The guard interrogated me the whole way back to my room, his booming voice didn't give me the impression there was an option to lie so I answered honestly. He looked physically repulsed by my explanation as to why I had sent the poor cook woman home. When we arrived at my door, Theo was waiting for me with an exhausted expression on his face. He rubbed the furrow of his brow until his skin turned red and he finally asked if I was okay. I had lied and told him I was fine, but in truth, I felt like a prisoner being sent back to a pair of shackles in her gilded cage.

Not long after I returned to my prison I heard a ruckus at my door, the anger of the man on the other side burnt through hotter than any fire. I pressed my ear to the door, despite its thickness I was able to hear the reason for the commotion. Seth has been forbidden to see me, I heard the guard mutter something hateful under his breath and I tried opening the door. To my surprise, it was locked. I tried looking for something to jar it open with, but I quickly realised there wasn't even a lock in place, the door had been sealed by an enchantment. I kicked and screamed like a child until I lost my steam and it was clear the door would remain stationary.

Time ticks by at a snail's pace until my bedroom door swings open. I stand to greet Seth, hoping he has finally been given the tick of approval, but instead I see Theo standing before me. He's dressed in beautiful pale blues with intricate stitching's, I notice a large golden ring with an impressive stone on his left hand that shines under the suns rays streaming through my window.

It's a mottled mix of blue, green, red and yellow. Somehow all the colours blend together in a purple balance, when he moves the light strikes the stone in a different spot and the individual colours can be seen.

"I thought perhaps we could spend some time together. It's a beautiful day, we could take a walk through the gardens," he asks. My anger flares violently, and heavy rain starts descending from the heavens, the electric thunder of the sudden storm matches my outrage. "We could take a tour of the castle instead," he offers eyeing the storm.

"I've been trying to be polite, but I am so done with this... You need to apologise for keeping me prisoner and stopping my friends from seeing me," I say confidently.

"I'm sorry the guard took my instructions too literal, Deklan has explained the human situation and I've decided he can stay for a short time, but when the clans convene he will need to leave for his own safety. He is welcome to return to court when he is one of us again," he says.

"You handed me over to be raised by a human, a human that I believe you genuinely cared for, why do you have such contempt for them?" I ask.

"The short answer is humans threaten our kind, they destroy us without hesitation and drawing a line between us is what keeps us safe. Sarah was an exception, and it was different, I was in her world, she wasn't in mine. You're new to this life, you're still learning the dangers within it. If you give it some time I think you will see segregation is essential for our wellbeing." He steps aside from the door holding out a hand to guide me.

I fold my arms across my chest and walk past him. The anger is still bubbling beneath the surface, but I hold it back.

I follow my father as he shows me the layout of the castle, my favourite part is the enormous library, it's not as big as the one I coveted in beauty and the beast as a child, but it's still pretty spectacular. By the time we reach the gardens the rain has stopped, and the sun is making a small appearance. The private grounds are beautiful, high trees draped in coloured vines with fragrant flowers dripping from their branches. I see a number of tiny creatures flying from one tree to another, many of them too small to see from a distance.

"The sprites and pixies live in the royal garden, they help tend and care for it. Over here is where the Tarrax live. There aren't many left so the flock lives at court under our protection," he says fondly.

"Where's Cinder?" I ask remembering the majestic creature that came to the temple.

"Lost I'm afraid, never returned with your arrival plans. I hope in time Cinder finds their way back to us," he says.

"Why didn't you just kill the Queen?" I blurt out. He's clearly shocked, but it's a thought that's constantly on my mind. "Not that killing is something I approve of, but if she did try to kill me then why is she still around?" I ask.

"There was a binding tradition used in fae wedding ceremonies a long time ago. It was archaic and something we steered away from in modern times. When my first wife died the council insisted on bringing back the tradition, I suppose they thought it would solidify both our positions," he says.

"So, what does the binding do?" I ask curiously.

"Just that, it binds my life to hers. If she dies, I die. When you take the throne, it will sever our binding and I'll be free of my connection to her," he replies.
"Is that why I'm here now? So that I can free you?" I ask.

"No, you're here because this is your home and you belong with me," he says.

I try not to feel too hurt that he didn't say I'm here because he loves me, love doesn't come as easily for some, but I still wish he had said it. I look up at the entwined tree above us, its tops reach out creating a protective umbrella with a million places for the birds to hide. The wisteria that's grown around its trunk has crept into the canopy, its flowers drip low like violet bunches of grapes gently swaying in the breeze. If I look closely I can make out a few sets of beady eyes curiously peering through the leaves. Theo tries changing the morose subject of his wife and talks about his childhood. He's making an effort which I'm grateful for, but I'm still struggling to form the connection I dreamed of. Perhaps in time, we will both be able to find the bond we are craving.

-65-

SETH

I knew Adaline wasn't in her room when I approached, the lack of guards sends a pretty clear vacant sign. The room smells of her, not the same headiness I would be able to taste in the air if I was still a vampire, but her sweetness clings to my senses all the same. A gust of wind sends the redundant wall fabrics into a twirling frenzy, I reach forward to pull the shutters closed, hoping to seal in her scent a little longer. In the thicket of the gardens I can make out Adaline's form standing by her father's side, the black blobs lingering a few meters behind them must be the asshole guards who refused my entrance this morning. I watch in silence as they return to the castle, even from this distance I can see the nervous tension that surrounds her. From the moment I met her, she has had a self-assurance that I envy, but since coming to court all I sense are her doubts.

"Who are you?" A familiar voice asks.

I turn expecting to see King Theodore standing behind me, his commanding voice is impossible to mistake. I look down at the garden below and see him still by Adaline's side. I step around the floating silks and see a man the spitting image of Theodore in the doorway. They share the same eyes, same colouring and the identical upturn at the end of their nose, but this man is at least twenty years older. King Addison.

"I'm Seth, Your Majesty. I didn't know you had arrived already," I say. My time with Addison has been limited, the last time I saw him was just before Adaline's birth. He was younger then, looking the same age as his twin brother looks today.

"Ported in this morning. You're Tom's friend, aren't you? And you have a brother, Aedan," he says.

"Yes, Your Majesty," I reply.

"May I ask what you're doing in my niece's room?" He asks.

"My brother and I escorted her to court, I'm just waiting for her to return from her walk with the King," I say casually.

"I doubt my brother would find a vampire in his daughter's room very pleasing," he says.

"Oh, he's probably going to be more pissed since he found out this morning that I'm human," I laugh.

"Human… How is that possible?" He asks taking a step closer to look at me.

"That's not exactly clear," I lie. The last thing our people need is to think that Adaline's going to begin rendering them mortal.

"Fair enough. I will visit my niece another time. Would you please see she gets this?" He asks handing me a small stone carved box.

It's widely known how different the King brothers are, but no one had mentioned Addison's choice to relinquish his immortality. In the past, each royal has ruled in unchanged youth until the next heir is eligible for the throne, once the succession changes the previous rulers start to age, but Addison seems to have matured at human speed. I slip the carved box into the pocket of my jeans for safe keeping and go in search of lunch. Feeding this mortal body seems a never-ending job.

When I return to Adaline's chambers the guards have taken root outside her door. Aedan should be watching over her now but I'm guessing after our display this morning the King feels better having his own men watch over Adaline.

I had promised Aedan I would keep my cool, but looking at the guard's smug faces I can see I'm going to find keeping my promise rather difficult.

"Can you stand aside?" I ask. The bigger of the two scoffs before opening the door and announces my entrance. "Thanks, bug eyes," I say as I pass. Adaline's sitting on a cushion by the window, the silken fabrics dance around her harmoniously. As she stands the breeze changes allowing the fabric to fall back against the walls. My breath catches as she walks towards me, her cheeks turn bright with blush and her smile makes me quiver.

"Stop looking at me like that," she says through a laugh.

"Like what?" I ask.

"Like your undressing me with your eyes," she replies.

"Could you blame me if I was?" I joke. She smacks my shoulder, but she can't keep the grin off her face.

"What's that?" She asks pointing at the box I have removed from my pocket.

"A gift from your uncle," I say. Her face turns pale and the smile leaves her lips. "Theo's twin," I clarify.

Her fingers brush against mine as she retrieves the box, I don't need vampire abilities to know her heart skipped a beat when I mentioned her uncle. She sits down on the bed to open the delicate box. I move beside her to better see the gift. Inside is a ring and not just any ring. It's one of the royal stones.

When the fates built the boundaries centuries ago they also created two precious stones infused with powerful magic. One stone was gifted to the Talbot King who had dominion over the Seelie and the Blackwood King who ruled the Unseelie.

The stones create a powerful protective barrier to guard the wearer against spells or enchantments, they are also the source of the royal's immortality. When the last Blackwood King abdicated the throne sixteen years ago and having no children of his own he named Addison his successor and passed the ring onto him.

"It's very pretty, Theo was wearing something like this," she says admiring the jewel between her fingers. She places the ring back in the box and covers her mouth as an impressive yawn threatens to escape. "Sorry, I'm just so tired."

"Why don't you have a rest?" I offer.

"Not likely with those jerks hanging around the door. It feels weird like I can't properly relax," she says. I look past her beauty and flawless skin until I see the hint of grey that skirts her lower lids and the exerted force she's putting into her smile. She's exhausted.

"Lay down and I'll stay with you," I say.

She doesn't protest, she yawns once more and climbs under the thick covers, she tosses to her left and right until she's finally comfortable. When she appears content, I lay carefully beside her, she closes her eyes and I hear the subtle shift in her breathing. I lean forward and kiss her forehead, she crinkles her brow and a disgruntled expression slips across her lips, but only for a second before she falls into a deep slumber. I roll on my side and stare at the lines on her face, a small freckle on the right side of her cheek burns itself into my memory as I drift off to sleep.

-66-
Tripp

It's been years since I was home, the door has dust and cobwebs collecting in the jamb and sill. I'm surprised dad didn't hire a cleaner while he was gone, then again, he didn't like anyone touching my mother's things after her passing. As I turn the copper handle the door creeks the same way it did when I was a boy and the roses in the front garden still fragrance the air in the same heavenly scent. The small cottage is just as I had left it four years ago. I hang my jacket on the hook by one of my father's heavy coats, beside it is my mother's shawl. Apparently, it's the one she wore all the time, but I have trouble remembering that detail.

Surprisingly my room is almost dust free. The night I ran away to join the guard, I recall making the bed and putting everything in its place after I finished packing my bag. I had left a letter on the bed and it's the only thing missing from the memory of my room and the current state it's in. I wonder what my father did with the letter. I remember the hurtful words I had written, I had intentionally tried to inflict as much suffering on him as possible, I was so angry at the time I wrote it. The room feels different now, all the hostility and disappointment I had allowed to grow over its walls has long since evaporated.

The house is hauntingly still, even under the fall of night it makes no groans. I cook myself some of the venison my father had sent home with me and wash it down with a stale beer from the cellar, it's not five-star dining by any standards, but it's comforting none the less. Just like a hundred times before, I test the handle to my parent's room.

After my mother's funeral, my father locked the door and moved into the spare room downstairs. To my horror, the handle cracks under my grip and opens ever so slightly. The smell of dust and mildew escape the entombed room. I push the door open a little wider, some dust particles make their way up my nose and I sneeze loudly. The sudden burst of sound makes the room shake and the door creeps open when I release my hold of the handle to wipe my nose. Soft moonlight seeps through the scum coated window pane, years of neglect have allowed the grime to claim ownership of the pale pink glass in the frame. Their bed looks smaller than I remember and is still unmade. The closet door hangs open with a thick coating of dust along it. Glass pots and jars with strange coloured liquids that have turned thick with age line the top of my mother's wooden dressing table. I open one of the pots and smell the contents. The sourness makes me cough and I drop the lid, I climb onto my knees in search of the lost lid, I'm just about to give up my search until a piece of yellowed paper that has fallen behind the dresser catches my eye.

It's become fragile with age, I open the note slowly, careful not to damage it. As I unfold the note I can see the strong indents that only a quill leaves behind and the ink has faded. I squint my eyes until I can make it out.

I need to see you tonight. N.

Who the hell is N? A sickening thought crosses my mind, was my mother having an affair? I start pulling apart the draws of the dresser, clouds of dust take over the room and my lungs struggle to breathe. I turn my search toward the closet hoping to encounter less dust and more answers. I run my hand along the top shelf pulling out items of clothing and discarding them to the floor with neglect. I can't understand why I'm so worked up, is it because I want to find something or because I hope to find nothing.

My finger brushes against a cold metal box in the back of the closet. I climb up a shelf and retrieve it. It's an old tin I remember stealing cookies from as a child, I crack the seal and a hint of chocolate tickles my nose, but I can't be certain if it's real or just my memory playing tricks.

I take a breath and ask myself if I really want to know what's inside this box. Am I ready to change the image I have of my mother? I decide the unknown is worse, as I retrieve the contents I realise my fears are justified. The box is filled with love letters, some short and others long. Both are written back and forth between a single pair of lovers. One half is signed with the same intricate 'N' and the others are signed with a simple 'Yours Always'. My heart races in my chest, I hate the letters, I hate what they stand for. My mother was a good and loving woman, she wasn't disloyal. A voice in the back of my mind reminds me how little I actually knew of my mother. The things I do know are a short collection of the things people say when someone has passed. Nice stories and pleasant anecdotes, no one speaks ill of the dead. I wonder if my father knew. I instantly discard the notion, there's no way he could have suspected, not with how deeply he loves her still.

I secure the box under my arm and carefully refold the clothing and return them to their rightful place. I move the closet door back to the position I had found it and check the dresser is left in the same fashion. I seal the bedroom door once more and take the letters with me, my father should never have to see these, and it's within my power to spare him this heartache.

-67-
Adaline

When I wake I'm sad to find Seth isn't by my side. For the last few weeks, I have found myself in a routine. I explore a new part of the castle or the village in my limited free time, I spend an hour or so with Theo and a few more hours with tutors. It's hard to find time to be with my friends and I'm on the verge of exhaustion almost every day. Some days I wonder if my body is suffering prolonged jetlag from skipping between realms.

Just like every day before, there are two stupid goons positioned outside my door, it's not the same men who stalked me yesterday or the day before, but I doubt it matters, different men same orders. I wash and change briskly, it's hard to deny how much I miss human bathrooms. One of the town's people is working on the attached bath chamber for my personal use and I'll be happy when it's finished. There's a timid knock at the door, too gentle for Deklan, and Theo usually just strolls in at his leisure and there's typically some type of commotion outside when Seth arrives. I open the door and see one of the oldest men I've seen since coming to court. He looks like he's in his early fifties if I was to guess in mortal years. There's something familiar about him, but I can't immediately place it.

"Can I help you?" I ask while he stares at me uncomfortably.

"Forgive my manners, you look so much like your mother and I haven't seen you since you were a baby," he says, the deep set of his voice helps me place him at once.

"You're Theo's brother," I say.

"Yes, you can call me uncle or Addison if you wish. I was named after my great, great, great grandfather. I think your parents put a spin on his ancestry when they named you," he says offering a hand. I take it gingerly in mine and feel the roughness of hard work etched into his palm. There's no barrier between him and I, like with Theo. His emotions are warm and welcoming, he feels like family. In fact, I think of one person in particular that he reminds me of which makes me smile. "I'm so happy you finally made it back to us. Word of your survival is spreading quickly across the Vale and it didn't take long for it to reach me in Vargo, both kingdoms are rejoicing your return," he says sweetly.

"Well I'm certainly happy to be alive," I say cumbersomely. He laughs at my nervousness, but his laugh is genuine without any mockery to be found.

"Did your friend give you my present? I had meant to come back that day, but I had matters to attend to that couldn't wait." He asks.

"Oh yes, he did. It's beautiful thank you. Seth had told me it belonged to the Unseelie," I say.

"Yes, but I thought you could use the protection more than me. I only wore the ring for a year after receiving the crown, immortality didn't suit," he says looking at the wrinkles and age spots on his hands. He smiles fondly as he admires them like he's looking at a badge of honour.

"I think you and I have the same reservations about immortality," I say.

"Speaking of immortality, your friend Seth is an interesting character, I don't recall anyone ever transitioning back before. It might be wise if he keeps that type of thing private," he says. I understand his undertone, he has the same concerns about Seth's humanity as my father. "Anyways I had best be off, I'll see you at tonight's festivities. I believe my brother is going all out in your honour," he adds.

I roll my eyes at his comment which makes him laugh. He startles me by pulling me into a quick embrace, he's warm to the touch and there's a gentleness to him that I find comforting. I guess I had imagined the ruler of the dark fae to be a more menacing presence, I'm glad to find I'm pleasantly surprised.

-68-
Deklan

I spot Addison as he's leaving Adaline's chambers, the guards straighten themselves as they see me approaching. I haven't seen Addison in person for years, during treaty renewals he usually sends his second, but with Adaline's return, he will have to face his responsibilities at court in person. He averts his gaze when he sees me approaching and moves to the other side of the hall. I raise an eyebrow and step directly in his path.

"Addison, you got old," I say firmly.

"Deklan, it's good to see you. How have you been?" He asks politely.

"Busy," I respond.

"Yeah my brother does prefer others to do his dirty work," he scoffs.

"I'll never understand how the two of you let it come to this. You were always different, but you never hated one another. I can't believe you let this family fall apart because he changed our relationship with the humans and with good reason," I scold. When Addison left it was a big deal, the family lines hadn't wavered since the beginning and I hate to admit it, but it hurt. I felt like Addison was as much my brother as he is Theo's and losing him changed us.

"It was never that simple Dek," He replies. "Look I'll be here until Adaline takes the throne as mandated in the treaty, but I'll leave once it's done and I won't cause any problems before then, you have my word," he says.

"Does your word still mean what it used to?" I ask.

"I never lied about the man that I am Deklan, I just chose a life more fitting," he says

It's strange to have them both under the same roof again. When we were children the three of us lived in these halls. Always sneaking around court playing human hunters and pulling practical jokes on the guards. When we were in our teens we would steal wine from the cellars and meet up with girls in the village. When we came into our powers we would play fight in the forest until one of us got injured or someone conceded. My time with them were some of the happiest days of my young life, it's a shame that things have to change. If we had made different choices I wonder if our lives would be less complicated now.

-69-
SETH

Aedan is sitting across from me with a mulled wine warming his hand. I can smell the fragrance of oranges and cinnamon, and there's something hidden beneath its sweetness, I can't exactly smell the blood, but I know it's there. Aedan continues rubbing his thumb back and forth over the lip of his glass, taking his time considering the offer I have made him. I don't know what's more annoying the stroking sound or the maddening semi-suppressed sigh held in his breath.

"Just give me an answer, you have been sitting there for fifteen minutes, your drinks probably cold by now," I snap.

"It's a tricky situation I'm in, you have to understand that," he replies.

"It's not tricky at all, you have refused to help me, and this is the only way I can see a compromise," I press.

"Okay, I agree," he says.

"Seriously?" I ask in disbelief.

"Yes, if that's the circumstances we find ourselves in and you refuse to see reason, then I'll change you, but I have a condition I would like to add," he says.

"What is it?" I ask.

"You will consult with the fates about this first. If there is any indication that my actions will cause your eternal death I won't do it," he says firmly. "I cannot be the reason you die, Seth, I'm sorry."

"Agreed," I tell him.

Adaline has been kept busy with her studies, so our time together has been limited. I understand though, there's so much for her to learn before she takes the throne and I'm trying not to be a hindrance on her duties. Each night when the guards change shift, her evening watcher allows me to sneak into her room, he requires a large fee of course, but I happily pay. I can imagine what the guards think we are getting up to behind closed doors and trust me I wish we were but between her mental fatigue and the proximity of the guards we haven't had ideal circumstances for passion. Most nights we talk, specifically she talks and asks questions while I answer, and eventually, she falls asleep in my arms.

Aedan and I have been out in the village picking up some formal attire for tonight's celebration. With the majority of the clan leaders already at the castle the King has arranged for a ball to introduce Adaline to her people, he has even opened the doors to commoners in the surrounding villages. I'm not excited for the event, but once Adaline is known to the public it will solidify her hold on the kingdom and that's something we desperately need to keep her safe. If it's even possible, I believe Adaline is dreading the blessed event more than I am. Her sleep is never long enough and when she does finally get some rest she tosses and turns throughout the night. Last night she didn't settle until the early hours of the morning and I'm struggling to find a way to comfort her and at least once a day I offer her the option to run. Sometimes there's a glint in her eyes that makes me think she is considering taking me up on the offer, but she's not the kind of girl to take the easy way out.

Between Deklan, Aedan and I, our main concern has been focused on locating the Queen. No one has heard from her since Adaline's return was made public, which hardly surprises me, if I was in her shoes I wouldn't be game enough to return either. The King has been making a sceptical of himself, sending out search parties for the Queen, and it's clear that the clan leaders are becoming suspicious of the Queen's absence, which puts Adaline in precarious circumstances.

Aedan wants me to tell Adaline about the deal we have struck, but I'm not sure it's wise. I don't want it to influence her decision, maybe I will tell her afterwards. It's going to be hard enough to get the council to get on board with our relationship, that's if the King doesn't kill me first, but at least there's hope.

Its early evening and Adaline should be finished with her studies, no doubt she is being bombarded with handmaid's trying to get her ready for the festivities. As I arrive at her door I hear less commotion than I had expected and there are no guards to be seen. I rap on the door lightly, but even my gentle force is enough to swing the door open. There's a soft light escaping from behind the door, at first, I think the moon has risen earlier than expected and is casting its radiance upon the tower, but I can smell the familiar warmth of flames and the singe of a burning wick. Tall candelabras stand like soldiers encircling the room, they remind me of the ones back home, but I'm happy to find there's no sign of electricity running through their veins. A feather touch breeze lifts the room's drapery into the path of the open flames, I reach out to stop them catching alight.

"They won't burn," her musical voice calls from the shadows. I watch as the fabric wraps its self around an invisible force that keeps it safe from the flames. "My powers are so much stronger, I don't have to concentrate to keep a sphere of air around the flame," Adaline whispers.

"Why are you hiding in the dark?" I ask, approaching her carefully. I feel like a predator trying not to frighten a rabbit that's been backed into a corner.

"I needed to be alone," she replies. "You wouldn't believe what I had to do to make the guards leave."

"I can leave if you want," I offer, granted we both know it's the last thing I desire.

"Would you really run away with me?" She asks, taking me back a moment.

"In an instant," I say honestly.

"I have thought about it. I can see the romance of it all, just the two of us travelling the world, searching for a place to call our own, it's tempting. Then I think about having to hide and lie for the rest of my life. I remember all the time's mum and I moved when I was a child, at the time it didn't worry me, but now I wonder how much I missed out on. Most importantly I think about you," she says, but I feel like she's talking more to herself than me. I crouch down before her, so I can see the delicate features of her face in the dim light, she looks tortured. She turns her eyes to me and a glistening tear rolls down her cheek, and over her lips, that fight to form a smile. "It would be treason, both sides wouldn't rest until they found us and the thought of losing you is too much to bear," she says.

"What's brought all this on?" I ask.

"Today I learned all the laws, not just the main ones. I know what happens to traitors of the crown," she sniffles. There are several rules that all fae learn in their early years. Both sides agreed to the decrees long ago and the rules have remained unchallenged since their creation. Failure to abide by the laws results in unspeakable suffering to the offenders. I believe treachery to the crown is third on the list, not as bad as if you kill one of the fates, but it's not by any means less pleasant.

"Those laws haven't been invoked in decades and only a King or Queen can enforce them," I assure her.
"My father isn't exactly your biggest fan, even getting him to allow you to stay tonight was a challenge," she says sadly. "This life is never what I wanted for myself. I hadn't planned on claiming dominion over others, but it's the only way I can keep the people I care about safe," she says.

"Firstly, your father is going to fall in love with me eventually, let's face it, I'm adorable. Secondly, don't do this for me, don't do it for anyone else. I want you to be happy and if you refuse this life that's okay and you will always have me," I promise her.

She touches her still shaking hand to my cheek, it feels so soft against the coarseness of my stubble. She has reason to worry about my place in this world, but it shouldn't be her concern. Adaline is far too kind for this life, but I won't trouble her with my worries, she carries enough for us both. I do the only thing I can do, I bring my lips to hers.

-70-
Adaline

I miss privacy. I miss the stillness that washes over you when the world gives the impression it's unoccupied. When I was younger I thought I had privacy, looking back I realise I was never often alone. My mother kept me close, there were only a handful of times over the years when I was utterly alone. The privacy I had were the nights I stayed awake long after my mother had gone to bed, watching television or reading in my room. There were a few moments that I stole for myself between classes or lunch. Even the odd occasions where mum was running late to get me from school because her shift had run ten minutes over. In my life, there has always been someone around, but this is different, its constant and unyielding, an endless observation that's making me feel paranoid. I had to threaten the guards with brutality just to make them wait one hall away. Even now as Seth presses his lips to mine I hear the delicate shuffle of Eldar's feet as she arrives to burst our bubble. I'm beginning to think there are watchful eyes in the walls. Seth ignores Eldar's disapproving glare and kisses my forehead before he leaves. He's not worried about the secrecy of our relationship these days, but I'm starting to think I should be.

I have become fond of Eldar, even though she has voiced her concerns about the relationships I keep. I know it's only because she worries for me and I believe she too knows the struggle of heartache, though she tries to keep herself guarded in my presence. The gown she has chosen is more intricate and beautiful than the last, it also shows far more flesh. The pale blue fabric lightens my skin and the open back and low-cut neckline makes me feel exposed.

"Are you sure this is the look you're going for?" I ask Eldar.

"It makes you look older and there's no harm in making you look desirable to the clan leaders. You're still something of a novelty, and you didn't grow up among your people which will cause the council to have their doubts," she insists.

"Thanks for the confidence boost," I say.

"Forgive me, I just want this to go well for you. I would be pleased to be able to call you my Queen," she beams.

"You're too kind," I tell her.

"And you're beautiful," she says stepping aside so I can see myself in the mirror. Eldar was right about one thing I definitely look older, almost dignified. "About the human, perhaps you should keep your distance, at least while the council is here. It's best that attention isn't drawn to him," she adds.

"I'll keep that in mind, thank you," I tell her.

I want to scold her, I know where my loyalties reside, but I also know that Seth's mortality will bring about a lot of questions and after being educated in our laws, I understand the danger that our relationship poses for the both of us. My father had explained the prearrangement part of both his marriages, apparently, it's the way it has been done for every firstborn since our family took control of the Seelie. He also not so subtly hinted that I would be expected to do the same. He is going to be in for a rude awakening when I tell him otherwise. I didn't have the heart to tell Seth about my real concerns. No matter how I look at the scenario if I want to be able to decide my own fate and keep my loved ones safe there's only one choice.

Theodore arrives to escort me to the ball, he ignores Eldar's presence focusing only on me, which irritates me. I offer her a kind smile to apologise for his behaviour, and I promise myself it's something I will try to work on with him.

I want to believe that it's simply because of how he was brought up, but then I remember the kindness that encompasses Addison. The brothers were raised alongside one another, similar in every way but they don't share the same arrogance. I lock my hand around Theo's extended arm and pick up the hem of my dress.

It's a long march to the great hall, my stomach flutters wildly as we turn each corner. I tighten my grip on my father's arm as we reach the closed doors. I can hear enthralled music playing loudly on the other side. The music is nothing compared to the excitement I can feel coming from the guests, I can sense all their emotions piercing through the doorway. Their collective hearts beat in anticipation, some have traces of fear and loathing, others consumed with joy. One thing they all share is their focus on me, it's a peculiar thing to sense yourself in the thoughts of others. I'm sure everyone has had that moment when they walk into a room and think someone was just talking about them, it's another thing entirely to know it for certain. Theo release my iron grip and kisses my hand. He strokes an unblemished finger against my cheek and smiles warmly. Before I open my eyes, he's gone, vanished behind the threshold. I'm alone, waiting in a dimly lit hallway with nothing to comfort me except my own fear, and sadly Tripp isn't going to step in and save me this time.

The two guards positioned by the door look like statutes, unmoving, unbreathing statues. I watch them both anxiously praying for a sign of life. My heart thumps dangerously in my chest, my breath quickens fighting desperately for the extra oxygen that my anxious body needs. I turn from the door in a panic, the urge to run into the deserted hallway is overwhelming. I lift the hem of my skirt and ready my feet to make the great escape, I lift my right heel.

It hovers a moment above the floor before I place the delicate heel back to the ground as I'm flooded with light. In my panic, I didn't even hear them announce my name. I stand frozen with my back to the open door, too scared to see the mass of people behind me.

I hear hushed inhalations as they wait for me to turn. I feel a presence approaching from behind, the small hairs on the back of my neck rise and I allow my abilities to recognise the person approaching me. He's sad for me, guilty almost, but there's a calmness to him.

"My brother forgets this type of thing isn't easy for everyone, I'll lead you in if you like?" He asks. I turn to see my uncle Addison standing before me. His arm outstretched just like my father had done, but unlike him, I know he won't leave me alone to face this. I take his arm appreciatively and whisper him my thanks. He smiles, and the crinkles of his eyes pull together showing his age. "I think we can forgive my nieces nerves, seeing so many beautiful faces in one place is overwhelming for anyone," he says boldly to the crowd.

They laugh wildly at his flattery and soon their attentive gaze dissuades from me as they fall into comfortable groupings where they can drink and chatter freely. The few friends I have here are keeping to the fringes of the party, I understand their discomfort. The council members stick out from the other guests and I can sense the uncertainty pouring out of them. As I look around the glittering room it's clear that high school cafeteria seating exists here too and the longer I feel the council members motives, the more I see that they're too arrogant for their own good. Addison hands me a second glass of wine and I thrust it back as quickly as the first, the invisible barrier that's between me and everyone else is beginning to shrink. I can't be sure if it's because the servers are sending out too much wine or because the others are letting down their guard. It might sound conceited, but I had expected to be flocked by people with greetings and questions, what I hadn't prepared myself for was to be ignored. I look over to see my father talking enthusiastically with a group of ladies, some of whom only come up to his knees, he looks comfortable being the centre of attention.

"Do you want to dance? People tend to relax when they dance," uncle Addison asks.

"No one else is dancing," I reply.

"Then we won't have any competition," he says pulling me forward.

"So what kind of music do you listen to?" He asks as he leads me into a gentle sway. "Our family has always been musically inclined, I myself play the harp, and Theo has a wonderful voice if you haven't noticed."

"He certainly knows how to use it to charm people…" Addison laughs at that comment. "I like a mix of things I suppose. Mum and I always listened to a lot of stuff from the eighties and nineties, granted I haven't had much time for pop culture lately," I reply.

"Understandable, Justin Bieber has been knocking it out of the park lately. One of my witches can spell a music player for you if you would like one," he says with full sincerity.

"I can't believe you have Bieber fever," I laugh. "I would love a music player. Don't get me wrong I love how low tech it is in the Vale, but I miss Spotify and Netflix," I tell him.

"Done, we can call it a late birthday present," he says.

He spins me around the dancefloor for another song and I admit I do feel more relaxed. Feeling confident enough to leave his company I wander over to my father's side. He's talking to two gentlemen? I guess you could call them. One has a long-pointed nose resembling a beak with high pointed ears. The other man looks like a larger, scarier male version of Eldar.

My father's smile beams as I approach, and he takes my hand drawing me to his side. He introduces me to the men and a few more flock toward us like seagulls fighting over the last chip on the beach. I find it hard to focus after that. The night turns into a blur of strange faces and vivid coloured gowns. Some people stick out more than others, it's their sentiments I focused on rather than their faces, which are often very different things. I smile and shake one hand after another until the corners of my cheeks begin to ache, and I struggle to suppress my yawns.

As things begin winding down, the music has softened to a gentle hum of violins and flutes. I noticed early on that the musicians have an enate ability to sense the type of sound the crowd needs. The people from the villages are the first to call it a night, they appeared overcome with the decadence of the evening. The few characters that are left I vaguely recognise and most of them are clan leaders and their inner circle. My own inner circle has thinned out leaving only Aedan, Seth and a tall dark-skinned man I have never met. I pull away from my father's side and make my way over to them. The beak-nosed man who hasn't left my father's side casts a wave of disapproval, but I ignore it.

"Beautiful as always," Aedan says as I approach.

"Thank you, Aedan," I reply. "Seth," I say addressing him with a curt nod.

"Princess," he replies formally, but to me, it feels intimate. "This is Samuel," he adds. Now that I'm closer I can tell his skin isn't as dark as I had first thought, like Shay his chocolate colouring has a glimmer of pearl to it. It's nothing that would make me take a second glance if I didn't know any better.

"You're the other vampire leader. It's a pleasure to meet you, I've heard good things," I say reaching out my hand. He surprises me and reaches forward for an embrace and kisses me warmly on each cheek.

"It's an honour, Princess. I am very sorry your involvement with our kind has been so troubled," he says in a thick accent.

"One bad person hasn't affected my opinion of an entire race, besides. These guys have made up for anything she can dish out. Are you from Canada?" I ask.

"Yes, I was born and raised there until my twenties when I followed a striking beauty across the world. Spent years traipsing after her, until I found my fate. After my rebirth I felt the need to return home, I reside there still," he says.

268

"And what of your striking beauty, is she here tonight?" I ask.

"I'm afraid I lost her a long time ago," he says mournfully.

I take his hand in mine to comfort the sadness that's washed over him. I close my eyes as his thoughts bleed into me, I see the pretty girl he speaks of. She was indeed striking, fair-haired with snow-white skin and pale eyes. He loved her so deeply, I feel his heartbreaking still. I open my eyes to see a gleam of liquid circling his iris. I touch my hand to his cheek and smile warmly.

"She was beautiful indeed. That kind of love is rare, you're lucky to have had it for as long as you did. I'm sorry it had to end," I tell him.

"A friend once asked me if it would have been easier to never have loved her in the first place," he says, eyeing Seth.

"And what did you tell him?" I ask Samuel.

"It might have been easier, but I would rather have shared her love for an instant than lived an eternity without it," he replies.

"Excuse me, gentlemen," My father intrudes. "It's time to call it an evening, Adaline I'll accompany you back to your chambers," he adds.

"Good night, gentlemen. Samuel, it was a pleasure meeting someone so wise," I say and follow my father out of the ballroom.

"The majority of the council have been won over by your charm, a few have even begun discussing potential suitors, it's very good news," he beams.

He continues to chatter excitedly, but I can hardly focus on the fact he mentioned suitors because I can feel someone watching me. I look over my shoulder in the direction of the pained energy, but there's no one there.

Whoever is watching me has a great deal going on, their emotions are a chaotic mess, the sense of longing and rage are deafeningly loud, but love and heartache swirl around the pained emotions like a tornado ripping up everything in its path. By the time we reach my chambers the hairs on my forearms are standing boldly upright and a shiver trails across my exposed shoulders. Theo kisses my cheek fondly before excusing himself, I hang in the doorway a moment longer while the guard posted at my door eyes me curiously. I try to fixate on the inconsistent emotions, but before I can decipher whose shell is carrying them the sentiments fade. I search once more, but the stone walls of the castle are void of life.

The feelings stay with me the whole time I undress, the anguish they felt was palpable and I'm having a rough time shaking it. My own distress is probably drawing at the negative emotions like a moth seeking the allure of a warm flame, and there's little I can do to change the moth's course. I lay down on top of the velvety covers while I wait for Seth to join me as he does every night. I'm trying not to admit it to myself, but I can't find a sense of security within the castle walls and having him by my side has become something of a necessity. The hours tick by and it's evident I'll be sleeping alone tonight, perhaps this guard couldn't be bribed. I close my eyes making deliberate breaths, long even inhalations and deep exhalations that try to ease my tense body.

My limbs become lighter as I feel myself drifting off, the scent of lavender fills my nostrils and a warm breeze brushes across my lips. I open my eyes to see the golden woman resting just inches from my face. She looks more solid than the last time I saw her, more real. As I rise she floats back giving me space, the moonlight that's breaking through the window touches her skin exposing its luminous transparency.

"You're back," I say.

"I'm never really gone, always watching. What else do I have to do after all," she replies.

"Can you see everything?" I ask. Instantly worried about the few intimate moments I have experienced in my life.

"Yes, but I don't watch everything, although I find myself wanting to watch more frequently lately. It's hard not being able to speak to you whenever I want," she says as she strokes my hair.

"I wasn't an angel, was I?" I ask her.

"No. Are the memory's returning?" She asks.

"Some, not enough to be helpful. Phedora knows more than she was willing to tell me though, maybe I could contact her again," I say.
"I've always liked that girl... Try not to force things this body is frail, it will all come in time," she says.

"I guess I don't need any more bombshells right now, I have enough drama to contend with," I say absentmindedly. "How come no one else speaks of you? I have been learning the fae histories and there's no mention of the architect," I ask.

"Oh darling, I didn't create the fae, or the humans for that matter," she says removing her fingers from the curls of her hair and walks towards the window, she gazes out across the vastness of the gardens and mountains that surround us. "Do you see all of this?" She asks. I stand to follow her gaze. "All of this is mine. Each blade of grass, the scent of the night sky, the sweetness of the earth. This is what I built," she says proudly.

"So, was it evolution, you created the building blocks and from it, humans and fae grew over time?" I ask.

"Mankind has evolved, but not in the ways that matter. You're different than the mortals. I created you a long time ago and just like the earth around us you were perfect," she says brushing my hair back from my face.

"Are you saying I'm not perfect anymore because I chose a mortal existence?" I ask.

"Absolutely not, you are still just as perfect, it just seems our opinions about your life were different, that's all," she says. I feel a sadness overwhelm me, what have I given up? "Please don't be sad, that's the last thing I wanted. Every day I watch you grow stronger and it brings me such joy," she adds.

"I don't feel strong," I admit.

The sun begins rising in the distance threatening to chase away the stars, she hugs me tightly as she vanishes with the night. When I wake I'm in the same position on the bed as when I closed my eyes. The sky is still dark with night, but I can feel the dawn approaching. It's a new day I remind myself.

-71-
Tripp

Every morning when I wake my breath catches in my chest, I look at the familiar surroundings of my room and I feel like I'm several years younger. As I begin to breathe, a thumping sound echo's around me, it's not my heart beating like I had thought the first time it happened, it's the haunted beating of the box I've hidden under my bed. The secrets my mother kept from my father, the secret that's now mine to keep. As much as I despise the box and the horrors it holds I find myself almost thankful for it. I have very little left of my mother and even though these letters show a side of her I wish I didn't know, it's still a connection.

I've found myself in old routines, waking at the same hour each morning, bathing and dressing mechanically. I make the breakfast of my childhood each morning, warmed oats with honey and fresh cream, it's possibly the only thing my father knew how to make back then, but it's comforting. My nights are still filled with broken screams and the pain that was inflicted into the earth, I worry the memories are something I'll never be rid of. I wonder how Neema is coping, for my nightmares are her reality. The thought of seeing her wounded body still makes me feel sick to my stomach, I try to imagine better times. I remember meeting her at the front gate of the stronghold, she looked so regal amongst the rich greens and pale frost that settled across the countryside. Back then she seemed content with her life among Aedan's clan, I wonder if she still feels the same sense of security.

I've packed a small bag with a few rations before I even know where I'm going. I pull the handle of my bedroom door, as it creaks I pause, and my eyes travel toward the black nothingness under my bed.

273

No one can see the box, it's securely tucked away at the back of my bed, but I still know it's there. I lower myself to the floor and stretch my fingers out into the darkness. My hands know exactly where they will find the box, I feel a ripple through my skin as I wrap my fingers around the cold tin. I shove it into my bag before I can think too much about its contents. I know my father wouldn't come here looking for it, but it feels too precious to leave unattended.

Travelling alone I can take the main roads as safety is no longer a concern, it will half the time it took us to get to court but travelling on foot will make the journey slow going. I reach Loora village which is a small working town built on the outskirts of Loora Lake, not far from my home. I can see the water through the trees and the sunlight blinds me as it reflects off the pastel pink surface. The lake's surface is unnervingly still, no boats or swimmers dare break through its crystal surface, the Seelie know better than to temp the maiden of this particular lake. When I was sixteen some friends and I had drunk too much and ended up at the lake. I can't be sure who started the game of truth or dare, but we all took turns approaching the lake, none of us had the stomach to touch the cool waters, at least until Jon had his seventh drink. I watched the water rise to his ankles, then his knees, by the time the water reached his thighs the others had stopped laughing. Panic filled my chest as he splashed the waters playfully. I wanted to go in and pull him from the lake, but the need for self-preservation was too strong and then suddenly, it was too late. Jon was pulled under in an instant, my friends and I waited for him to come back up, but he never did, the maiden of the lake had him. As I pass the lake I can almost hear the gurgled scream Jon let out all those years ago. I still keep a piece of cork from one of the bottles we drank from that night. I carry it with me as a reminder of what happens when you give up your mind to alcohol.

The village feels smaller than I remember, maybe it's because things always seem larger than life when you're a child. I can smell the tang of metal being heated and moulded over an open fire, the blacksmiths making new shoes for the horse that's tied to the wooden post outside his shop.

I can hear the ruckus of men drinking in the pub, it's early morning, but judging by the volume of sound escaping the pub it's possible they have been drinking since the night before. I make my way through the town until I come to the general store, granted it's not like any store in the mortal realm. The witch who runs it is big on trades. When I left for the academy as a youth I gave her a weeks' worth of my magic in exchange for passage out of the Vale, I just hope she's still in the trade business. A bird whistles an obnoxious tune as I enter the dilapidated store. The windows have a thick black paint coating their glass so minimal light is able to break through. As I stumble through the dimness, I bump into several things that slink and spit slime, my skin crawls when I knock a wind chime made of a dead child's bones. Witches, they are powerful creatures, but honestly, their practices make me sick.

"What will ya have today boy? Another ride into the human world?" Her shrill voice crackles through the darkness.

"Not this time, I wanted to hire a horse. I will have it back to you in two days' time, three at the most," I tell her.

"Very well, but it's my last one, won't come cheap," she says.

"Figures, how much?" I ask.

The old woman makes her way through the mess of hanging trinkets and jarred limbs, it's a wonder she can find her way through this disorganisation, especially since her opaque eyes have minimal vision left. The woman sniffs loudly taking in the scents around her, her attention to my direction makes me thankful I bathed this morning.

"You have a box of secrets, that's the cost," she says.

"You can't have them," I reply.

"Then, there's no trade," she crows.

275

"What purpose would they serve you?" I ask her.

"Secrets are power. I'll tell you what, when you return the horse I'll return the box," she offers.

I pull the box out of my bag and cradle it in my arms like a child. I weigh its significance, they are just letters. Leaving the box with the witch would alleviate some of the burdens I'm carrying, and my mother's secrets would still be kept safe from my father. I hand over the box, the relief I feel is immediate. I arch my shoulders together enjoying the physical relief of no longer being weighted down with worry. The witch leads me through the back of her shop and out through a half hanging wooden door. Maybe I should have asked to check the horse before I agreed to the trade.

The woman opens the gate to a small attached shed and leads me into the darkness. The smell of damp hay and horse droppings fills my nose, the smell is overwhelming, but not entirely unpleasant. The horse is dark in colour, a rich russet kind of brown with sparing white flecks across its flank. I'm happy to find the horse is in better health than his owner or her store. I saddle him quickly and make sure he's fed and watered. The sun is already set high as its approaching midday, I straddle the horse and begin the trek back to the temple.

=72=
Deklan

Court has been in a disarray since the arrival of the clan leaders, people lurking in the shadows, listening to every word whispered in the halls. It makes security difficult, the guards are less concerned with maintaining their posts when beautiful sirens and elfin women waltz down every corridor, hypersexual women barely clothed and loose legged, I can hardly blame them. The last time there was this many fae living under the castles roof was the night of the ball. I say it like it's the only one and that's because it was. The celebration of Adaline's birth was supposed to take place on the first full moon of the year, but the night before was when the attack on Adaline's life was made. The joyous event turned out to be a night of great tragedy, for the King, the kingdom and me.

This morning Theo finally received word from the Queen who I'm told is making her way back to court as we speak. He decided to begin preparations for the inauguration, that way as soon as the Queen returns, the council can approve the exchange and the binding between him and the Queen will be broken. If Theo and Leonora are no longer linked and Adaline has the power to imprison the Queen, then we can right all the wrongs of the past. The plan is all good in theory, but I still have trepidations. I have assigned Wren and Jackson to watch over Adaline from now until the council's vote in a few days' time. I wrestled with whether I should ask Tripp to return to court to help guard Adaline. I struggled more as a parent than an officer, do I spare my son's emotions and risk leaving Adaline unprotected or do I set aside his feelings to ensure her safety? In the end, it didn't matter what decision I made because Theo requested his presence.

I collect a quill and a piece of parchment and begin writing. I address the letter formally, being sure to write my son's full name and rank since Theo has kept his word and declared him a member of the royal guard. I use the code of the guards to keep the sensitive information safe from prying eyes and begin melting a stick of wax over an open flame. When the wax turns liquid, I dollop a large drop on the back of the parchment and press my seal into it. The wax dries leaving a clear imprint of my houses sigil, the wolf silhouette is hidden beneath the intricate carving of a hand. It was created when my father first became hand to Theo's father and he passed it on to me. My son doesn't suffer the same wolfen affliction as me, but in time I'll pass the sigil on to him and, when he has children of his own it will become theirs in turn.

I slip the letter into my pocket and blow out the candle. I worry the garden will be overflowing with the court's guests, but I'm pleasantly surprised to find it empty. The birds are singing high in the trees, by the time I look up the only evidence I can see of them is a shadow vanishing into the trees. I hear the crackle of leaves and grass, as serpents skulk across the field chasing the warmth of the sun. I reach the Tarrax tree, it's usually a hive of screeching chaos, but today it's tranquil. I walk around the uniquely grown branches and raise out my arm and whistle to signal a Tarrax down. I wait, none answer my call. I walk further into their guarded home lifting branches above my head as I go. Behind a large bunch of stone bramble, I hear a familiar song, I reach into the leaves and find Cinder huddled in a ball. The poor thing is injured. Cinder's usual white colouring is tainted, the tips of its wings are black. Cinder must have only just changed back into their docile state. One leg has a deep laceration in it and there are deep wrinkles under its eyes, the poor things dehydrated. I scoop Cinder into my jacket and rush back to the castle in search of the gamekeeper.

The elderly gamekeeper is able to heal Cinder's leg and once the bird has drunken its weight in sweet juice the gamekeeper is happy to release Cinder back into the garden. I'm surprised whoever took the bird didn't have it roasting over a fire by now, it's foolish to let a Tarrax go, they have an exceptional memory after all.

I've been racking my brain trying to understand how Maura is getting her information, for a time I thought someone had corrupted Cinder. Now, the only possibility that makes sense is that someone within the castle is helping her. My money is on one of the clan leaders, the council has never seen eye to eye on all accounts and with the future of the fae in jeopardy, it makes sense that one of them would make an attempt for the crown. I just wish I knew who, hopefully, Cinder will be able to help with my investigation.

-73-
Adaline

I've decided I hate riddles. I'm too mentally drained for them, the mystical woman from my dreams is a big fan of riddles and nondescript seeds of suggestion. When I'm in her presence, not knowing what she's really saying isn't an issue. I feel too sheltered to care and not knowing everything doesn't seem like a big deal. Then I wake up, and the euphoric warmth she provided fades and I become irritated. I'm aggravated with the way she hints at something rather than just getting to the point. I'm annoyed that she has all the knowledge of my past, but she won't hand it over freely. It's like when you go to a fortune teller and they claim to know your past, present and future, but can't give you the nitty-gritty details. That's usually when people cotton on to the fact the fortune teller is a fraud. Maybe this is my 'ah ha' moment? Maybe the woman is lying, maybe she's a challenge sent to tempt and mislead me.

I lay back on the fluffy bedding and close my eyes. I squeeze them tightly until there's nothing, but an inky blackness, I squeeze tighter trying to remember something of my past. The absence of light deepens until small flecks of light flicker across my closed lids, perhaps I'm depriving my eye sockets of blood and the sparks are a warning signal. My skin begins to warm, I can feel a bead of sweat forming on my brow. I raise my hands to entice a cool breeze, the air obeys instantly supplying a steady flow of feather touch wind. I can hear the draped fabrics begin dancing in chorus with the draft. I pull the strength of the earth close to me, like a child searching for the embrace of a security blanket. The orb of fire I have glowing brightly in the corner picks up its ferocity as it inhales the extra air in the room, the smell of its ardent flames fills my nostrils making me shiver. I can hear the trickle of the water spilling over the edge of the pitcher as it fights eagerly to be a part of the moment.

I'm not sure where to focus, or what I should be focusing on, so I watch the lights moving in the darkness behind my closed lids. They swirl back and forth, like children playing red rover in the middle of the night. The lights pull together, joining into a single ball of energy like flecks of metal finding a magnet. The light turns into a burning white force as it extends itself chasing away any darkness. I open my eyes to the sheer brightness of it, but I'm no longer in my room. I'm not even formed. I'm aware of myself and my body, but there is no body, I'm pure light and electricity. I move forward chasing another ball of energy. I can feel another, but I cannot see it. We are racing, the three of us. One is further ahead, and I struggle to catch up, the other is close at my heels. I feel myself laughing joyfully without sound and the others laugh in unison, but no physical sound escapes in the place of lights, but I can feel the sounds as easily as I feel my own heartbeat. The word siblings' springs to mind. Yes, siblings, the word feels right as I roll it around my memory. These shapeless, indistinct collections of energy are my brothers, two of them, both older than me. I see no faces which makes it impossible to connect to the memory, but the affections and love between us is tangible. There's a larger energy in the distance, it has a golden aura. Mother.

The golden woman from my dreams, in this memory she hasn't got the lovely face and feathered hair I've come to know, like myself she's a glowing sphere of energy and light. The brother beside me gains speed and surpasses me, catching up with our eldest brother. Both of them race ahead until they reach our mother. I'm further back, but I can feel the warmth and love radiating from her presence. It reminds me of the security I felt when I was home with my mortal mother, unconditional love is something I have always known, but this is different. It has a taste to it, gently spiced and distinctly sweet, I feel its fullness all over my body. I push forward to reach my family and the senses overwhelm me.

My physical body begins to burn and the cool breeze I'm casting isn't enough to sauté the fire that's building within me. I open my eyes and let go of the memory.

As I come down from the intensity of the recollection I feel myself drop back into my body, it's that feeling of shock when you're on the edge of consciousness and you suddenly feel yourself falling. I snap myself back into this world and clutch my shaking hands to my overheated body. I try searching for something solid to hold on to. Heavy breaths catch in my chest as I regulate the air in the room, the air has turned into a whirlwind and the fire light has become swept up in it. The water pitcher has been lifted into the commotion and the water is no longer contained inside it. I swallow the energy in the room and break my connection to the magic. The pitcher falls loudly to the floor shattering into pieces, the drapes release themselves from their entanglements and the fire burns itself out. I can feel the grounding vitality of the earth as it pulls me back to my centre.

"Everything okay in there?" Wren calls from the hall. I can't answer at first, my voice is missing. He starts opening the bedroom door forcing me to pull a voice from nowhere.

"Fine," I choke. "I dropped the water pitcher."

He pulls back the door before he can see the disarray of the room. I lay back on the bed taking everything in. I can still feel the memory, its pale in this reality, I don't think the world is strong enough to hold its entirety. Brothers, the concept feels foreign but right. In another life I had siblings, it felt nice, it felt whole. If that strange and wonderful existence felt right, I wonder why I felt the need to leave. My body's weak and craving sugar. I wipe my face and chest with a cloth, trying to absorb some of the sweat, but I can't wipe the flush away from my cheeks or the gentle sheen my skin has taken. I open the door cautiously, slipping outside and closing it before the guards can see the state of the room.

"Are you well Princess?" Wren asks.

"I'm fine, just hungry, I'm going to the kitchen," I tell him.
"We can send for something," Jackson offers.

"No," I snap. "I'm sorry I didn't mean to be so curt. I'd just rather do it myself, I need the walk," I say.

They smile politely and let me lead the way to the kitchen. They walk close at my heels, but not near enough to trip me up, I would rather they walk beside me, maybe then we could talk. During our time on the island, we didn't chatter like girlfriends, but we spoke. We discussed the weather and general things about their lives, kind of like co-workers. It wasn't much, but it was nice, it was normal.

-74-
SETH

I didn't join Adaline last evening, when I'm with her I know she can unearth what is buried within me, no matter how hard I try to hide it, and dread is shadowing my thoughts. From the moment Aedan agreed to my terms I've been apprehensive, too scared to follow through with my decision. When the sun woke me this morning and I was in bed alone, any fear I had felt was gone. I felt empty not waking up with her lying beside me. For centuries I have lived a life of solitude, I had shared passionate moments with women, but never anything as intense as simply being with the person that makes you feel whole. Most people think being connected sexually with someone is the ultimate form of intimacy, but for me, that isn't the case and it's more than enjoying the warmth that radiates from another as they rest beside you. Real love is purer and simpler than that. It's the sanctuary that allows you to let your guard down, it's wanting to show someone every part of you and it doesn't always require words.

The night I decided I wanted to spend the rest of my life with Adaline there was nothing profound like a life or death situation that brought me to my decision. It was a moment, exquisitely ordinary like so many others. We were lying next to each other on her bed, on top of the covers and fully clothed. She turned to face me, her eyes were sealed tight with sleep, her lips parted, and she released a soft breath. Usually, the very thought of someone else breathing directly on me would make my skin crawl, but with her it was different. I felt safe enough to breathe in. I embraced the air that had filtered her lungs and sustained her life. At that moment I felt closer to her than I have ever felt to anyone. It was all I needed, a single breath, a simple moment and I knew she was undoubtedly the one.

The others are still asleep, except for Shay and Beetok who have been keeping themselves busy stalking the other clan leaders. I dress hurriedly and sneak out of court before the guards change shift. On the shadier side of the village, there's a tavern full of drunken men and women, all of whom seek the nymphs who are waiting to fulfil their every desire. The tavern just so happens to be run by an old friend of mine. The sex and wine trade has always been fruitful, but Harmon has an equally lucrative side business as well. When I reach the entrance to the tavern the echo of laughter and clinking glasses spills into the street. A smile pulls on my lips, it's not even time for breakfast and the fae are already deep in the embrace of debauchery. The tavern is thick with the scent of sin, a heady mix of salty sweat and booze. I inhale it, drinking it into my pores, I used to love this lifestyle, carefree with endless possibilities. I thought I would miss it more, but this kind of life doesn't give you the fullness that I now crave. A nymph with long pink hair snaps her doe eyes in my direction, and a coy smile forms on her glitter painted lips as she approaches me. I keep my eyes set high as she flaunts her barely clothed body toward me.

"Do you want a drink, or will you get straight down to me?" She asks boldly.

"Neither, where's Harmon?" I ask.

"Customer or friend?" She asks.

"Both," I reply.

She rolls her eyes and slithers through the brood of drunken fornicators, shaking her hips the entire way. I walk up to the bar and settle myself on a stool. A nip of ambrosia appears in front of me, I look up to the end of the bar and a busty werecat winks while she simultaneously polishes a glass and licks the silken fur on her forearm.

I nod my thanks and drink the ambrosia eagerly, no harm in a little liquid courage. As I slam the glass back down onto the bar, the pink haired woman returns hanging on Harmon's arm.

The sound of her shrill giggling pinches my ears, she laughs louder when Harmon gropes her backside before giving her a playful smack and sending her back to work.

"Well, look what the cat dragged in," Harmon says loudly.

"Oh, he came in on his own, don't you start blaming me." The bartender laughs.

"Watch the front Georgie, I'll see this bastard out back," he says with a wink. I follow him behind the bar into a lowly lit room, Harmon snaps his fingers and the fire orbs spring to life. "Rumour has it you and your brother are staying at court long-term, fancy business that is," he says.

"Yes, there's a lot going on," I tell him.

"I've heard, the princess has returned from the dead, the whole towns in a buzz about it. I'll admit business hasn't been this good since she died. Mourning and celebrations, it's my bread and butter," he says.

"Yes, it's very exciting," I reply.

"Still not much of a talker are you, that's okay tell me what you're after," He says.

"Last time I was in here you had something special, a ring," I say.

"That was years ago, I've had lots of rings pass through since then, what one did you have in mind?" He asks.

"Rose gold band with a painite stone. Do you still have it?" I ask.

"Boy, that's an expensive ring, one of the last ones in our world. Can you afford it?" He asks.

"Anything you want is yours," I assure him.

He offers me a calculating smile and snaps his fingers once more. This time a section of the wall shifts, and a metallic box floats out hovering between us. Harmon pulls a blade from his pockets and slices a nick into his finger, just deep enough to draw blood. A single drop of rich red blood lands on the box while he whispers an incantation. Invisible ribbons spring to life in vibrant colours and begin unravelling themselves. Once the box's lid springs open an array of rings emerges, each resting comfortably on a stone carved pillow. The stone I'm after glistens under the warm light, the flecks of scarlet buried within the burnish charcoal stone remind me of when the light catches in Adaline's hair.

"It's perfect, how much?" I ask.

"I want one of your guys," he says. I raise an eyebrow at his request. "Not for those reasons, I need one of your kind to work here. I have more than enough women, but some of my patrons want something a little darker and preferably male. Shall we say two years' service?"

"We don't slave trade, you know that," I respond. "How about two hundred units?" I offer.

"Three, that's a five-carrot stone," he counters.

"Done," I say. He snaps his fingers and a piece of parchment and a quill appears on the table. He dips the quill in his open wound and signs the parchment, I cut myself and do the same.

"You seem different, what's the ring for anyways?" He asks.

"A girl," I reply. He places the ring in my hand and pulls me into a tight embrace.

"I'm just happy you are finally settling down. Who's the lucky girl anyway?" He asks.

I smile and thank him, he's a friend, but I'm not sharing my involvement with Adaline with him. I slip the ring into its trinket box and place it in my pocket. I make my way through the sleaze of the tavern and emerge into the heated embrace of the sun. This is it, tonight I'm going to ask her to marry me.

-75-
Tripp

The temple doesn't have the same awe as the first time I saw it, but the flowered maze still calls to me with a soothing naïveté, I envy the purity of Mother Nature. Don't get me wrong nature has brutality, animals kill for survival or food, forest fires destroy everything in their path, but unlike people, nature isn't unnecessarily cruel. No attendants are walking the perimeter of the grounds which isn't completely unreasonable, but after the open attack on the temple, I had figured the place would be crawling with security. I slow the horse to a gentle trot, there's more bounce when travelling this slowly, but I need to pace myself, I need time to think.

I knew I needed to come here, but I hadn't given much thought as to why. I have to check on Neema, that much I know for certain. I feel an undeniable pull to be with her, it's not romantic in nature, more protective, like when a parent feels the urge to comfort an injured child. After her ordeal we left her behind, she was wounded and fragile, Adaline's safety took precedence, and we neglected what happened to Neema. The longer I think on it the more confident I am that this is what's been preventing me from sleep. The insomnia is from more than the guilt of my inactions when we were held captive, it's the lack of support I gave Neema afterwards. I had apologised for being unable to help her, and she had accepted, but there must have been more that I could have done for her, more that all of us could have done for her.

I climb down from the horse and lead him through the gates on foot. I tie his reins above the water trough and he begins drinking eagerly before I finish securing him.

I climb the few steps to the temple door, the red stone the building is made of still glistens under the sunlight like a home for the gods. I raise a hand to knock, but it feels uncomfortable, I've bled in this temple and I grieved in it in more ways than one. I reach for the handle, but the door swings open like it's being drawn to a magnet. Mikael is on the other side with a wide toothy grin, I don't mean to, but my body shivers nervously at the sight of him. He must see the apprehension on my face because his smile weakens.

"Hello," Mikael says.

"Hey, is Neema around?" I ask.

"Present," she says appearing behind him. She looks well, she has more colour than the last time I saw her, her gentle olive colouring has returned, and her cheeks have a mild blush. More importantly, there is a genuine smile on her lips. She places her hand on Mikael's bulging bicep, he smiles back at her and steps aside. She gives him a reassuring nod and he vanishes into one of the back rooms. Neema walks towards the sitting room and I take the queue to follow her. "I didn't think I would see you back here so soon," she says.

"I didn't expect to be back either," I reply. She settles into one of the raised cushions on the floor. I pick a seat across from her and sit down in a painful position, my bodies too tall to sit comfortably on the tiny cushions. "Honestly I came back to check on you and to say I'm sorry."

"We discussed this already. It wasn't your fault," she says dismissively.

"I know, I'm talking about leaving you here alone. All of us left you, and we shouldn't have," I say.

"I wasn't alone," she says. "But thank you."

We both smile, and I feel some of the weight lifting from my heart. We talk about her time here and the events that are going on at court.

The discussion is easy and doesn't require as much work as I had thought, she talks of Mikael fondly and raves about his support in her recovery. She's a better person than me, just the thought of his heritage makes me doubt his intentions. In the battle there hadn't been time to think, I let her go with him willingly. I know he's the reason Neema made it out alive and I'm grateful, but it's hard for someone to deny their true nature.

"Please don't," she says.

"Don't what?" I reply.

"Your face grimaces every time I mention his name, he's not like the others," she insists.

"I'm sorry," I say.

The air turns stale, an uneasy tension sits between the two of us. The light catches on Neema's necklace, its Adaline's. The jade pendant has a golden tinge to it that I don't remember, but I'm certain it's hers. There's one time in particular when it was the only thing that Adaline was wearing, I remember how it sat at the nape of her neck when I kissed along her collarbone.

"How is she?" Neema asks. I feel myself blush like she can read my thoughts.

"I haven't seen her. I didn't stay long, I had some business for the King I needed to deal with." I lie.

"Neema, perhaps you should tell the boy, he should know," Phedora pipes in, appearing in the doorway like an angel from a dream. Her blue hair is hanging in loose braids with purple flowers that have been weaved in between the strands and her feet are bare and coated with a light dusting of dirt.

"Tell me what?" I ask.

A knowing look passes between Phedora and Neema, a whisper without words. Both sets of eyes fall on me and there's a hint of secrecy in the air. Phedora strolls forward and collects three pale green glasses from the shelf and a bottle of shimmering green liquid. She fills the three glasses with the alluring liquid, the scent of alcohol fills the room. Phedora hands a glass to Neema and positions another for herself, she considers the third glass and fills it higher than the rest until its resting level to the brim.

"Firstly, I'm so excited and I want to say congratulations," Phedora says raising her glass. I lift my own glass mirroring her movements and sip back the drink. I feel the scorch of the liquid as it trickles down my throat. "Babies are such joyous news," Phedora screams excitedly as she wipes the moisture off her lips. The drink catches halfway down my throat, I cough trying to force out the droplets that found their way into my lungs.

"Baby?" I choke.

-76-
Adaline

The kitchen isn't the busy mess it was the last time I was here, and Bach is nowhere to be seen. A few of the staff are hectically cleaning up copious piles of dishes from the decadent lunch I didn't attend, and in the corner is the woman I sent home a few weeks ago. I can sense her sadness as it filters through the other bodies in the room, creating an invisible wave of grief. I cross the threshold and the guards begin to follow, I wave my hand using the air to close the door between us. The last thing I want is them hovering over me while I eat. The kitchen staff glide effortlessly out of my path as I approach the woman. Her eyes are red and a little glassy, there's a flush in her cheeks and I can tell she has been crying. A small smile forms on her lips when she sees me.

"My lady," she says with a curtsy.

"Forgive me, I didn't get your name before," I say to her.

"Martha, my lady," she replies.

"Call me Adaline. How is your daughter?" I ask.

"She passed. We laid her to rest two nights ago, I had wanted to thank you, but I wasn't permitted an audience," she says.

"I'm sorry for that, it wasn't my decision, I'll be sure to have a word with the guards. I'm very sorry for your loss if there is anything you need please ask." I offer.

"You allowed me to be present for her final days, I can never thank you enough," she says. I reach down and give her a hug, it's quick but warm and I feel her heart lighten because of it. "Can I get you something to eat?" She asks as she wipes a stray tear from her eye.

I don't get a chance to answer because she begins busying herself with plates and knives and a wondrously smelling loaf of bread. In a few moments, she has an extravagant sandwich placed before me complete with thick lashings of butter, cheese and cured meats. My mouth starts watering as I lift it to take a bite. If this meal is anything to go by, Martha definitely isn't the kind of woman who counts calories and I couldn't be more thankful. She hands me some of the rich fruits I had helped Bach with last time and I eat them eagerly. My stomachs overfilled by the time I'm finished, and I feel too bloated to move. The fullness doesn't stop me from slipping three pieces of fruit into the crook of my arm or the enormous slice of cheese I carry between my lips. The kitchen door opens with a helpful gust of wind, Wren and Jackson straighten themselves and once again allow me to lead the way.

Juggling my fruit while I polish off the piece of cheese I hardly register the man waiting outside of my chambers. When I see the dark pair of jeans my heart flutters wildly and the lump of cheese has trouble sliding down my suddenly dry throat. As I get closer the fluttering subsides as I see it's not Seth, but Aedan standing at my door. He turns and smiles broadly as I approach. He takes the fruit from my hands and nods his head for Wren and Jackson to give us a moment alone. We enter my room and I close the door behind us sealing the world away.

"Where would you like these?" He asks holding up the fruit. I grab them off of him and place them where my water pitcher usually sits.

"Haven't seen you in a while, or Shay, or Jason or Beetok for that matter," I tell him. My tone isn't scolding, but there's a hint of disappointment in it.

"I'm sorry we have been kept busy with all the leaders at court. Is everything okay?" He asks.

"I suppose, it's been lonely. They like keeping me in my room unless there's a function they want to show me off at. I haven't heard from Seth since yesterday either, have you seen him?" I ask.

"I have, he's actually the reason I'm here. He asked me to give you this," he says pulling a crumpled piece of parchment from his trousers.

My heart sinks, the letters I have received in the past haven't exactly contained good news and between Seth's absence, and the fact he had his brother hand deliver the letter is worrisome. I try to suppress my fears and force a smile for Aedan's benefit. I close the door behind him and place the letter on the end of the bed. Suddenly I'm back in my bedroom at my uncle's house and the same feeling of dread washes over me. It can't be that bad I try to tell myself, and Seth wouldn't leave me in a letter. I decide not knowing is worse than anything he could have written down, and I break the seal on the back of the parchment.

Meet me at midnight in the garden under the Tarrax Tree.

Yours always Seth

One sentence is all the letter contains. I re-read it over and over again, trying desperately to turn fourteen words into a thousand. How does he expect me to sneak away with guards watching my every move? I can't begin to imagine what he was thinking when he wrote this, but I'm no longer feeling dismayed. If anything, I'm excited at the prospects this letter holds, a romantic night under the stars with Seth might be exactly the thing I need to lift my spirits. There's just one problem, how am I going to get out?

-77-
SETH

I feel like the ring is burning a hole in my pocket, its weight rubbing against my leg reminding me of its presence. I tap my hand against my pocket where the ring is hiding, the movement is more to settle my expanding nerves than to check its security. I climb the steps to a small building that sits on the corner of the main road as you exit court. This is the Vale's form of a post office, unlike the mortal realm we don't have computers and machines to send our communications. Instead, this building houses a number of messenger birds and two riders with their horses to handle all incoming and outgoing messages for the local village. An elderly sprite hovers over the order desk, her blue hue has dulled with age. She shifts into a human-like form as I approach and offers a welcoming smile. Her hair is a crisp white and the wrinkles on her face soften her features making her appear sincere.

"I'd like to send a message to the vampire stronghold in Ireland," I say.

"Bird or rider?" She asks.

"Rider," I respond.

As much as I like the secrecy of birds I also know they don't always travel well between the boundary and I have to ensure my message gets home. I scribble my instructions to Roland who is in charge in my brother's absence. I give him the authorisation to release three hundred units of blood to be shipped to Harmon over the coming months.

While I'm paying off my debts and making arrangements for the future an image of an elderly couple holding hands at the dinner table jumps to the forefront of my mind. The couple naively gave me the money to find my way home and I haven't returned it. The two thousand they gave me is a miniscule amount, but for them, it was a lot to give out on a whim. I make a note for someone to make sure they receive fifty thousand dollars with my kindest regards, it's a small repayment for their kindness. I add in Thomas's payment and seal the letter with a blob of melted wax and stamp it closed with the postal sigil. I slip the rider an extra payment to ensure his devotion to his job is unwavering and I pay the woman at the counter. The second the money is secured in her makeshift till the sprite returns to her natural form and hovers back toward the ceiling.

For the first time in a long time, I feel good about myself and I can't help but be enamoured in the wholesome feeling. I arrive back at court and set about my plan. Aedan is in the garden waiting for me when I arrive and has already set to work bending the flora and fauna to his will. His abilities aren't connected directly to animals, but when you can control the environment they live in its amazing what you can bring out of the woodwork. The Tarrax Tree has always been a thing of beauty, but Aedan has transformed it into something otherworldly. He has scattered a number of night-blooming flowers across the earth, ranging from scented orchids to evening primrose and there are even tropical water lilies that are bursting with colour on the top of the pond. He's even covered the bare branches of trees with a wild jasmine that tickles my nose with its sweetness.

"What do you think?" Aedan asks.

"Exceptional, I think you're in the wrong industry, it's a shame vampires don't have much need for florists... Thank you for everything brother," I say and pull him into a firm hug.

"That's not all," he says.

I step back to get a better understanding, he whistles a high-pitched sound that fills the silent night sky with melody, at first nothing happens, and then I see it. Small lights floating down from high in the treetops. Some pink and blue, even a few scatterings of white. "The pixies owe me a favour, they are yours for the night," he says proudly. "I know, I'm amazing and you want me to be your best man, I already accept."

I listen intently as the pixies begin to sing their song, the sound is hauntingly beautiful and brings the garden to life. The branches sway with the rhythm of the melody and the flowers turn their faces trying to follow the alluring sound. It's perfect. Aedan gives me another excited hug and walks me back to the castle with his arm secured tightly around my shoulder. As we reach the door he excuses himself to arrange travel for me in the morning.

After tonight if Adaline agrees to marry me, I'll be going to Vargo to seek out Fallon, the fate of the future. Aedan had agreed to change me back into a vampire, but only if I could get proof that accepting the bite wouldn't mean the end of me. If Fallon can assure me that I will be able to survive the change a second time, and we can convince the council to agree I will be able to spend the rest of my days with Adaline as my wife.

I collect my clothing and decide to soak myself in the hot springs in the guest chambers. The warm water soothes my skin and reminds me of the fire that used to flow through my veins. I lay back and drink in the weightlessness of the water. As I float I can hear the rushing sound of the water as it moves beneath the surface. There's a distinct pressure that I can feel forcing the flow of the current into the stone pool and back out the other side. It's strong, but steady, kind of like life. I find myself coming back to the thought of death more often lately, it's a thought that has been a frequent visitor in my mind since becoming human. Perhaps death is something that is always present in the minds of mortals, a thread of a thought, that each day could be their last.

It's a strange sensation, I've even had fleeting moments where I had pondered the afterlife. I push the notion from my mind, death will no longer be a concern soon enough. I close my eyes and continue to float. As death leaves the room I think about life, specifically the life I'm going to build with Adaline if she will have me. I hurry out of the pool and dry myself, dressing quickly. She's going to say yes. I tell myself as I comb my unruly hair. I hurry to the garden to greet Adaline, of all the nights to be late it can't be this one.

-78-
Adaline

I've watched the old windup clock tick away slowly on the shelf all afternoon. The clock has a disgruntled appearance to it, perhaps it isn't pleased with the replacement water pitcher Eldar supplied me with an hour earlier. The last pitcher was made of a terracotta-coloured stone that didn't handle itself well when I dropped it from the sky, Eldar has been diligent and replaced it with a sturdy metal one. I call to the water in the pitcher until it begins to slosh around in its restraints, I float mouthful sized balls of water across the room until they hover above my head. I push them back and forth with my mind moving them in a dance, I line them up in a row and one by one I march them into my mouth, swallowing them whole. The freshness of the water fills my body, giving me strength and nourishment. I need all the strength I can get with my nerves growing wilder by the minute.

The silent room is shocked by the sudden burst of sound from the striking clock, its deep-set chime pauses the beating of my heart. It's finally midnight, I had spent all day thinking about the best way to ditch the guards and meet Seth in the garden. When I was running short of ideas, the thought of climbing out the window popped into my mind. I laughed at first, what a silly notion to even consider, but then the thought took root and didn't seem so silly after all. I'm wearing a lightweight white dress with delicate sleeves that fall off my shoulders, it looked angelic on the hanger when Eldar brought it in. She had to help me put it on because the intricate ribbons and beading on the back were too difficult to handle solo. The whole time she assisted me I could feel her curiosity growing, but she kept her queries to herself and I'm glad because I would have found it hard to come up with a believable lie.

I look out the window at the garden below, the royal gardens are always a beautiful sight, but when the soft moonlight glistens on the garden it brings it to life. I often feel the magic awaken in the evening and hear gentle songs being sung amongst the trees, it's absolutely breathtaking. I pull the ends of my dress into a bunch and tuck them under my arm, with my free hand I pull myself up onto the ledge. I can feel the coolness of the stone on the back of my thighs as I sit myself precariously on the edge, my feet dangle weightlessly drifting back and forth in the breeze. It's now or never, I draw the air toward the tower building a powerful force beneath me. I suck in my breath and push myself off the ledge. My stomach lurches as I fall, a moment of regret flashes as I descend. Swiftly I'm cradled lovingly into the embrace of the air, it's icy against my skin and my dress flails around me, like a paper bag caught in a draft.

My feet touch the ground lightly until the air releases its hold. When all of my weight returns I feel heavier, like when you have been floating in water for a long time and then you step out and the world feels weighted. In the dark, it's hard to find my way through the grounds and I don't dare create a flame or it will draw attention. Instead, I close my eyes and kick off my slippers. My feet welcome the softness of the grass and the wetness of the dew. I ask the earth for guidance and it responds. Small mushrooms sprout either side of me creating a path, the mushrooms have a pink neon glow. The lights too dull to alert the people inside the castle but it's more than sufficient enough to lead me to the tree.

The smell catches my attention first, it's heady and sweet, jasmine, but I can't remember there being any in this area of the garden. I reach the small pond that has water sprites dancing on the ripples during the day, at night the water is still with glowing flowers resting atop its glassy sheen. As I approach the tree I can see an abundance of flowers that have wrapped around it like lightly sealed gift wrap.

Jasmin has grown in between the wisteria hanging from the branches like a curtain. I slip my fingers between two jasmine vines and pull the curtain apart to enter. There's candles floating in the empty spaces, no, not candles, pixies of all colours and sizes creating a heavenly glow with their light. There's a blanket atop the grass at the base of the tree, and there's a picnic basket beside it. It's just like the day we spent at the lake, my heart swells remembering the fondness of the memory. It's one of the few times I was truly happy after the accident and there haven't been many other days since. It's perfect, the only thing missing is Seth. The pixies begin to sing their heavenly song and the tree sways along with them.

"You're glorious," Seth's voice calls from behind me. I turn to see his sparkling eyes staring at me from across the divide. The jasmine falls back, closing the curtain and separating us from the rest of the world.

"Did you do all this?" I ask.

"I think we both know I had some help, but generally it was my idea," he replies.

"It's beautiful," I say feeling my heart stop in my chest. His gaze is so fixated on me I'm frozen.

"You're beautiful," he says and leans down to kiss me.

The electricity and fire builds between us just like every time before, just because the magic has left Seth's body doesn't mean it's lessened the passion between us. I throw my arms around his shoulders as he lifts me into his embrace. He kisses along the exposed skin on my neck and shoulders and I'm thankful for the scarceness of the dress. The pixies song shifts into an excited tone and I'm suddenly aware we have an audience. I pull myself back from him with great difficulty.

"We aren't alone," I whisper. Seth whistles into the sky and the flickering lights float away into the treetops until their glow is nothing more than a distant memory.

"I wanted to ask you something," Seth says as he smooths my hair behind my ear.

"Right now, I don't really want to talk," I tell him.

I slip the straps of my dress completely off my shoulders and turn my back to him. I loop my finger around the ribbon and begin pulling it loose. I'm nervous and my fingers tremble as they get caught in the intricate ties. Seth moves closer and kisses the back of my neck. My skin rises in tiny bumps, shivering in pleasure. His hand expertly removes the knotted ties and the dress falls off my body and lands on the grass. I summon all of my courage and turn to face him, wearing nothing except the lace undergarments that are stunning to look at, but incredibly uncomfortable. I breathe in deeply as his eyes wash over me. He wastes no time and scoops me into his arms kissing me feverishly. I relax into his body, I feel empowered under his gaze. As we sink into one another I feel whole, we fit together Seth and me, nothing else has ever felt so right. I can feel the passion explode inside him as he runs his hands along my nakedness and I drink in his pleasure as I release my own. The earth erupts around us, the day flowers burst open, and the air warms in elation. Small surges of flames light up around us as I let go of my control and my magic is unleashed. The water in the pond rushes in waves until my breathing settles and the world turns still.

We lay silently under the shadows of nature, our bodies wrapped up in one another as we listen to the steadiness of each other's breathing. We had both been waiting for this moment for what felt like an eternity and I'm glad to say I wasn't disappointed. It was better than I could have fantasised and I'm a little sad it's over. My stomach who can't appreciate the splendour of the moment makes an annoyingly loud rumbling sound destroying the blissful silence.

"Hungry?" Seth asks.

"Always it seems, magic takes a great deal of fuelling," I joke. I shiver feeling the coolness of the night's air for the first time.

Seth slips on his trousers and pulls a second blanket from under the basket and drapes it over me. He fusses through the basket looking for something in particular, he finds what he's after and hands me a basket of strawberries. "You wanted to ask me something... You know before," I say.

"Ah, yes I did," He replies running his fingers through his hair nervously. He taps a hand against his pocket and looks around like he's confused.

"Is something wrong?" I ask.

"I just had it planned differently," he says. He takes an exaggerated breath and kneels beside me. I sit up straight wrapping the blanket tighter around my chest. He seems so serious all of a sudden, I feel like I should be wearing clothes. "I love you, Adaline. Each day I wake thinking the feelings I have for you will have faded because its crazy to think that anyone can love someone that deeply. Yet, every morning when I wake my feelings have grown stronger... You are kind and brave and every day there's something you do that makes me love you more and I can't imagine my life without you... No one will support us and it's going to be near impossible, but there's nothing else that makes sense except my feelings for you." He rambles.

"What are you asking me?" I ask.
"I'm asking you to marry me," he blurts out removing a ring from his pocket.

"I, I, I..." I stumble is what I do.

"I want to wake up next to you every day for the rest of eternity," he says.

"I love you Seth and marrying you is insane and I would do it in a heartbeat... But," I stammer.
"But?" He asks.

"But, I cannot live for an eternity," I tell him.

"Aedan has agreed to change me if you accept my proposal. The council would never agree in my current state, but they will be more likely to accept me once I'm back in the fold," he rambles.

"And once you become Queen you will be immortal too," he says confused. I can see him trying to rationalise my words.

"I don't think you understand. I will not live forever. I don't want to and when I become Queen I will renounce my claim to immortality, just as my uncle did," I say. I can feel the warmness of tears streaming down my face, I know this isn't what he wants to hear but I won't lie to him. I can see the realisation flash across his eyes. His hand closes over the ring that's lingering between us. I can feel the fear bleeding out of him, he tries to hide it, but his wall is weak.

"But we can have forever Adaline?" He echoes.

"For me, I think it comes down to quality over quantity. There are only two real things I want Seth. I want to die an old woman, with grey hair and wrinkles, with my husband by my side and more than anything I want that husband to be you, but can you stay mortal for me?" I ask.
"I'm sorry but I can't live in a world if there's a chance that one day you won't be a part of it." He kisses my forehead once, it's soft and void of the passion we share. I feel his heartbreak as he steps behind the curtain of flowers and vanishes into the night.

-79-

SETH

She's just scared, she can't seriously want to live a mortal existence. I'm sure she's just worried about me dying if the bite doesn't take, but if I can get the proof from Fallon she will change her mind, just as Aedan did. Once she sees the immortal future we can have together she will accept her inheritance and I can be by her side as a vampire. I feel it in my bones, she just needs to feel it too. As I open the door to the back entrance of the castle two guards are blocking the other side.

"The King would like an audience." The larger of the two says. I leave my dress shirt and jacket on the seat by the door and try to straighten myself. The beasts have probably been watching us the whole time, the Kings going to have my head mounted outside the castle walls before dawn even approaches.

"I can see His Majesty first thing in the morning if you like, I wouldn't want to interrupt his sleep," I answer.

"The King will see you now." The other guard says as he approaches me from the side.

I don't get a chance to respond. The guard places a tight grip on my shoulder and I know he could break it into pieces without hesitation. The two of them lead me down a hall I haven't walked before, but I'm getting a sense of where it leads. I lock myself into muted silence as the men take me to the King.

The guard digs his clawed fingers deeper than necessary into my skin, I bite down on my tongue to keep myself in check. The castle is quiet at this late hour and the only sound to fill the silence is the steady stomping of metallic shoes on the stone floors. The coppery taste of blood tickles the back of my throat as my teeth sink deeper into my tongue. The guard who's not holding me as aggressively opens the door to the dungeon, the other pushes me through with enough force to knock the wind from my chest. I fall in on myself until I can lift my head and the air returns to my lungs.

This dungeon is separate from the main ones the guards use, this is where unspoken problems are dealt with. Through the darkness of the damp smelling room, I can see the King standing before me. He's leaning casually against a partially rotted table that has seen better days. I don't need my vampire senses to know there's freshly spilled blood on the table that hasn't yet had time to dry, the glossy blackish sheen is all the evidence I need.

"Finally, we can have a proper chat," King Theo says.

"How can I be of service Your Majesty?" I ask.

"Well, I believe there are a few things you could explain. Deklan has been rather cryptic about you which is odd, he's usually so forthcoming. Let's start with the most pressing issue, how did you become human?" He asks. My circle knows that I'm alive because of Adaline, but none of us knows exactly what she did. Deklan decided its best that no one else knows how powerful Adaline really is.

"Unsure how it happened Your Majesty. The last thing I remember is being stabbed through the chest and the world fell away. I had been in the ground for a few days before I woke," I say.

"Did my daughter have something to do with it?" He asks.

"Can't see how, she and the others were long gone by then," I reply.

"What's your relationship with Adaline?" He asks.

"We are friends," I lie, the guards can probably still smell her scent on me. "If there's something you want to know just ask," I bluff boldly.

"I know everything I need to. I think its best that you leave the Vale tonight. The council is starting to talk and it's best that there are no distractions while Adaline's position is still in question. You understand I'm sure," he says with a smile, but the hostility in his undertone starts to curdle the blood on the table.

"If that's what you feel is best of course. I'll go pack and be out within the hour," I begin to say.

"No need, the guards will accompany you to the portal immediately," he says with the wave of a hand. "It will be safest."

The forceful guard jumps at the chance and he sinks his fingers deeper into the marks he has already made in the meaty part of my inner arm. He squeezes tighter and pushes me back the way we came. As we approach the common area of the castle, the guards veer off and open a passageway behind a hanging tapestry. The larger of the two has to hunch over to fit through the doorway and the other shoves me forward until I smack into the back of the giant. My teeth clink together as my face hits his metal brace. The passageway is narrow and dark, I can hardly see one foot in front of the other as we walk. If I was still a vampire I could navigate through the passage with one eye closed whilst jumping hurdles. The further we get, the more I'm beginning to believe that I won't be leaving the Vale alive. The King could have killed me in the dungeon, but I'm guessing he wants to claim innocence when Adaline discovers my demise. If I was tasked with this kind of disposal, I would take the intended victim a reasonable distance from the castle and then get rid of him. That way, the incident can be justified as an unavoidable tragedy and the murder blamed on bandits or vagrants. Being a human and alone in the Vale, it won't be hard for Adaline or my brother to believe whatever tale the King and his men tell.

-80-

Deklan

Last evening Theo told me to take the next two days off, so I could go home and escort Tripp back to court. I was hesitant to accept the much-needed break, but Theo has doubled the guards and between Seth and Aedan I know Adaline will be kept safe inside the walls. It's a little after one in the morning when I finally settle into bed. I replay my mental checklist as my body relaxes into the feathered mattress. I checked in with Aedan and informed him of my impending absence, I spoke with Wren and Jackson who were posted outside of Adaline's chambers. I didn't wake Adaline due to the late hour, but I will say goodbye in the morning before I leave. I sent a Tarrax ahead to tell Tripp I would arrive tomorrow evening. I have checked off everything on my list, but I have that niggling feeling that I have forgotten something.

I toss and turn as I go over the events that have happened since returning to court. I have done everything I had set out to do, but I still feel like it isn't enough. Adaline and Theo's relationship isn't as solid as I had hoped, and I find her still needing me around as a buffer. I don't want to overstep my position, but Theo is having trouble relating to Adaline and I find myself trying to compensate for it. I just want Adaline to be happy and I'm a fool if I try to make believe that she is. She sleeps on and off throughout the day, hardly leaving her room and skips regular meals with the council members. She attends festivities when her presence is requested, but I can see her heart isn't in it.

She seems happy enough with her handmaiden, the annoying little elven girl irritates me no end, but Adaline likes her. She appears to enjoy her lessons and training, although, with the level of power she has, I don't think she needs much help from us in the training department.

The guards inform me regularly that Adaline is spending more time with the support staff rather than with her peers, which doesn't surprise me. Theo believes the council is amenable with Adaline taking the crown and is making arrangements for the inauguration, but the council likes rulers who are involved, and I think they are being agreeable because they believe Adaline is going to be a pliable ruler. If any of them knew her like I do they would know how far from pliable she is.

My worries eventually move from Adaline to my son. Tripp is never very far from my thoughts and I'm glad he has sent messages often. Mostly the letters say he's okay, but I find it hard to believe. He's so much like his mother, he feels things deeply and a lot has happened to him in his young life. I'll be glad to spend some time alone with him before we return to court. I will have fewer worries with him and Adaline under the same roof where I can keep an eye on them both. I feel a sense of hope burning in my chest and it eases my restless legs. I look at the candle burning brightly on the table next to my bed, I release a small breath of air and extinguish the candles light. The scent of the cooling wick fills the emptiness and the plummet into darkness is wonderous.

-81-
Adaline

I sit under the tree until I don't have any more tears to cry, although I wish I did. The aroma of jasmine smells different in my sadness. It's overpowering and sickly, I cast up a breeze to banish the unwelcomed fragrance from under the tree. I collect my dress from the grass and slip it back on. I tie the back in a haphazard knot and pull on my underwear. I open the basket and pull out some of the food. I begin picking at a piece of bread and place the small pieces in my mouth thoughtlessly, the bread quietens the disgruntled sounds of my stomach, but it doesn't fill the ache in my chest.

The branches above begin to rustle and shake as a mysterious weight moves from one side to another. The crunching sound increases and more branches being to move. I get up onto my feet, unsure what to expect. Dozens of pure white Tarrax descend from the tree. They circle around me in a calm uniformed movement. I sit back down on the blanket and offer some of the broken pieces of bread to them. The birds eye me curiously, one of them is a bit larger than the others and has a small black streak at the top of its head, that runs down the centre of its back and ends in a single feather in its expansive tail. The bird moves forward and snatches the bread from the ground, the others follow in suit eating eagerly. The birds make happy noises to each other while they eat. The black streaked leader sits next to me laying its head on my lap, I take the hint and stroke its beautiful feathers that feel like silk paper beneath my fingers. The birds are comforting, and their company fills up the stillness of the night.

"Maybe I asked too much of him," I say aloud to the birds. "Most people would kill to be an immortal."

The bird offers little advice and the one on my lap just digs its head in closer, my fingers scratch the top of its long neck feeling the firmness of its feathered roots. As I hit its sweet spot the bird releases a pleasure filled screech that makes me laugh. The branches of the trees begin to creak once more with the sounds of weight, I look up expecting to see more Tarrax, but there's no white to be seen. The bird in my lap leaps up and the black streak expands across its body. The angelic birds all begin to shift into their charcoal black suits and their eyes turn a blistering red. The leader flocks toward the tree line and the others follow making screeching defensive sounds.

The tree begins to shake uncontrollably and the Tarrax start dropping from the heavens like flies hit with a swatter. Some of them have blood dripping from fresh wounds, others have traces of black gooey liquid dripping from their beaks. The black substance I remember well, gargoyles. I seal myself in a sphere of blue fire and start fumbling through the grounds.

"If you leave, he dies," a gruff voice calls halting me in place.

Seth? I can't see through the fiery protection and I'm forced to lower my guard. As the flames die down I can see a gargoyle floating above me, his impressive wings cast a powerful gust of wind that swirls around me making my eyes water. I can see movement behind the creature, but I'm more concerned with the person laying immobile in his arms. There's an awful gash down the side of his face and I can see blood dripping from his stomach as the gargoyle sinks his claws deeper into Aedan's rib cage.

"PUT HIM DOWN!" I form a ball of fire in my hand, but I can't guarantee Aedan's safety if I release it.

"I'll put him down if you agree to come with us." He pulls out a small vile from a woven bag strapped to his side and drops it on the grass in front of me. "Drink that and the vampire will live, well maybe, he's losing a lot of blood."

"What is it?" I ask.

"Don't worry it won't kill you, but it will ensure our safety," he replies.

"Place him down and I'll drink it," I reply.

The beast drops Aedan from the sky and his limp body hits the ground hard, I hear him wince and the shattering of a bone or two pierces my ears. I hope he hasn't lost too much blood. I open the vial, it smells mildly of flowers that I cannot place. I look at Aedan bleeding out on the grass, I ache as my feet absorb the energy of his blood as it sinks into the earth. I tip the vial back, pouring the liquid down my throat. My body warms instantly, and I feel myself falling, the beast scoops me into its cold arms as the numbness takes effect.

-82-
Tripp

We rode through the night, Neema, Mikael and me. The whole journey my head has been reeling. I'm going to be a parent, it's more common than not for fae to start families young and being almost twenty-three I'm older than most, but I'm still not ready for this. Neema's abilities make her acutely attuned to pregnancy. She can sense the exact moment of implantation which is kind of gross when I think about it and a little intrusive. When Adaline and I had sex the last thing on my mind was protection. Most fae girls have a blocking spell put on them when they start puberty so an unplanned pregnancy isn't really a concern. I was so stupid and now this has happened. Neema believes Adaline may not know she is pregnant yet, she will only be five weeks along, and there's the chance that the pregnancy may not even take since her body has been through so much since her change. I shudder at the thought, although unplanned the thought of my child coming to harm before it's even born makes me feel sick to my stomach.

Neema takes Mikael's hand as we enter the gates into court, gargoyles aren't welcome, but Mikael isn't like his brothers and I'm finding it hard not to like him. I watched him with Neema the whole time we were at the temple and he doted on her, even on our journey he was nothing, but attentive to her needs. It's strange to imagine the two of them together romantically. Neema's a striking beauty and Mikael's a sickly green, oversized monster with grotesque wings that tower over Neema's slight frame. I suddenly think of beauty and the beast, I wonder if Neema's love could change him into a handsome prince. I doubt it. One of the guards sends for my father while the others place us in a holding area awaiting his arrival.

We are waiting longer than usual, I doubt my father would still be sleeping, at this early hour. One of the guards makes a grunt towards Mikael and Neema as he eyes their tightly linked hands. Mikael makes an obscene gesture toward the guard who responds by pressing his sword to Mikael's neck. Neema exposes her fangs with a vicious hiss in his defence.

"Put your weapon down, you idiot!" My father yells as he approaches. His hair is dishevelled and he's wiping sleep free from his eyes. The guard looks disappointed but withdraws his weapon.

"Dad, I need to see Adaline, it's important," I tell him.

He doesn't respond or ask why. He excuses the guards and leads us through the castle toward Adaline's chambers. The castles workers stare outright when they see Mikael. Neema touches his shoulder reassuringly and glares at the unwelcomed onlookers. Wren and Jackson are standing watch outside her door when we arrive.

"Tripp your back," Jackson says with a smile and a manly embrace.

"We missed you around here."

"I missed you guys too," I lie. Honestly, I enjoyed the peace and quiet not being surrounded by people. "Is the Princess awake yet?"

"Hasn't made a sound since she went to bed last night," he replies.

I knock on the door and wait for her to reply. No response. I open the door and announce myself, but it only takes me a second to see the room is empty. Her bed is freshly made like it hasn't been slept in and there's a staleness lurking in the air. My father pushes past me in a panic, he sniffs the air and makes his way to the window following the scent.

"She's hasn't been here since last night, her scents too weak," Deklan mumbles.

"How would she have left?" I ask.

"She went out the window. ALL GUARDS TO THE GARDEN!" Deklan screams.

The royal garden is crawling with guards by the time we get down there. King Theodore is standing in the courtyard pacing anxiously with the Unseelie King by his side looking equally as grim. I haven't seen Addison since I was a child. When the brothers went their separate ways, Addison was no longer welcomed at court until he became King of the Unseelie. Addison was always kind, if a little foolish and I'm surprised to see he's aged. I had heard rumours that he had given up his immortality, but it's bizarre to see it firsthand. Addison looks more like Theo's father than his twin and the worry in his eyes makes him look older still.

One of the guard's hollers from deep in the centre of the garden. The earth shivers and tells me it's had blood spilt on it recently, my stomach sinks. The guard emerges with Aedan hanging weakly in his arms. He places him on the stone courtyard and Neema kneels beside him. She reaches for my hand and I give it freely. She sinks her teeth into my wrist and I press my hand to his lips. At first, he doesn't respond, then his eyes turn black and he tightens his mouth around my wrist sucking fiercely. I can hear the guard's revolted scoffs as I let the vampire drink my blood, but I don't care, I owe this to him. Aedan releases my hand and the gash on his face begins to knit itself back together.

"Gargoyles took her, there were too many and it happened so fast," Aedan says. I can hear the brokenness in his voice, he blames himself.

My father begins barking orders at the guards, and in a matter of minutes, large parties are flooding through the front gates and into the streets. Shay, Jason and Beetok are at Aedan's side and wait as he downs another cup of blood.

"They won't find her, Maura is too smart for them," Shay says.

"Where would she take her? You worked for her, you must know what she would do," I ask.

"She's sadistic. She would want to inflict as much pain as possible before she killed her, maybe she took her to the island where she killed her uncle..." She guesses.

"No, she's taken her home," Aedan chimes in.

"Home?" Mikael asks.

"He's right, Adaline had me make sure someone looked after her uncle's home, she wouldn't let us sell it or rent it out. It's the place that would hold the most pain for her," Deklan says as he enters the room. "Let's go, there's a porter in town I know who can get us there quickly."

"Where's Seth?" I ask. I find it hard to believe he isn't here with the rest of us looking for Adaline.

"No one's seen him since yesterday... maybe he's..." Shay says.

"He's not dead. I believe he left last night, I found his belongings gone when I checked in on him before I went to bed," Aedan says.

"He just abandoned her?" Shay says.

"All he does is think about her safety and what he can do to maintain it, he hasn't abandoned her," Aedan snaps at her.

"ENOUGH!" My father yells.

We make our way into town and with the guards knocking down every door, no one offers our mixed party a second glance. My father leads us into a dubious looking pub and snaps his fingers at the man behind the bar. My father pulls the man aside and whispers into his ear.

317

The man nods and beckons two scantily dressed women to his side. He whispers to them and they giggle, he smacks both of their behinds in an overt manner and sends them toward us. The girl with bright orange hair smiles boldly at me and her eyes wander towards my crutch, I feel uncomfortable like she's undressing me without my consent.
"So, you guys want a ride to Texas?" The other girl asks.

"Yes, a small town a few hours from Dallas," Deklan says.

"We can have all of you there within no time at all, it will take a few stops though with so many of you along for the ride." The orange haired girl adds.

"Done, let's get a move on," I say.

The girls make each of us drink two glasses of nauseating sweet juice before they agree to port us, apparently, the smell of vomit isn't good for their line of work. The sugar helps non-porters be able to stomach the jumps. I down my second glass and link arms with the orange haired girl who snuggles in closer than necessary.

"Okay handsome, hold tight," She coos. My stomach lurches, maybe I should have asked for a third glass of juice.

-83-
SETH

The guards appear to be acting as I had predicted they would. They are leading me toward Bristeal Mountain which is in the opposite direction to the nearest boundary. I've been the model prisoner for the entire walk, I'm being cunning, not compliant. I need to conserve my strength and wait for the right moment to make my move. Both guards are stronger and faster than me, the aggressive one is a Minotaur and could easily chase me down. The other is a Mothman, granted not as physically formidable as the Minotaur, but he can fly. Even if I did manage to get the upper hand on one, I'll still have to contend with the other. The only chance I will have is if I'm quick enough to surprise them and kill them both before they realise I'm a threat.

The Minotaur shoves his hairy fist into my back sending me soaring to the ground. I hear the graze of his blade as he pulls it through the leather scabbard. Looks like this will have to be my moment. I arch my back ready to move, the guard brings down his sword to stab me in the back like the coward he is. I roll to my side as his blade pierces the earth, narrowly missing my ribs. I use his shock to my advantage and kick him in the throat. He releases his hold on the sword as he falls back. I grab the blade and free it from the earth. Mothman is stunned and I thrust the blade into his stomach just below his breastplate. His eyes widen in surprise as he looks down at the gaping wound in his stomach. I withdraw the blade sideways slicing off the lower half of his wing in the process. I feel hot droplets of blood splatter across my face and his musty scent fills my nostrils. He falls to the ground, and a final spilling of blood escapes his lips as he takes his final breath.

The stupid bull regains his composure, but he's too late to save his partner. He snorts an animalistic snarl and scuffs his hoofed feet, as he kicks up a cloud of dust that settles around him like a shield. My body is human, but I have a lot of experience in battles with enemies greater than this. He's big, which means he's slower than I am. I close my eyes as the dirt cloud obscures my vision. I hear a single scrape as his hoof scratches into the earth, a second scrape, his other foot kicks back the dirt as he presses his weight forward. He's charging. I crouch low and spin with the sword extended in one strong swift motion, the blade slices cleanly through the meaty flesh of his calf. He lets out a blood-curdling scream as he tumbles to the ground. I stand over him as he begins thrashing around in pain. The old me would put a cut into his lower spine, that way he would have to suffer the torture of immobility from the waist down while he slowly bleeds out. As I look down at his anguish I feel sorry for him, I deliver a swift injection of the silver blade directly into his heart. The thrust puts an instant end to his suffering. I killed him compassionately, personal growth goals achieved for today, I think to myself proudly.

I take the guards garments as well as a helmet. Once I'm dressed, if no one looks too closely I can pass as one of the guards. I tighten the scabbard around my waist and slip the sword into its casing. I wipe the blood off my cheeks and try to ignore the vile taste as some of it touches my tongue. I can't return to the castle, not now, not until I'm fae again. The only hope I have is to go to Vargo and follow through on the plan I had in place. Getting the King's acceptance is going to be a bigger challenge than I thought.

-84-
Adaline

My heads foggy, I'm not awake, but I'm not asleep either. Everything around me feels light, not like sunshine, like weightlessness. I'm back in the memory, the one where I'm chasing my brothers. This time the memories not as difficult to grasp and the balls of energy are taking on shape. My older brother's light fades to reveal his true face. It's not unlike my mothers, his hair is golden and feathered just like hers and his smile radiates warmth. My other brother has a chocolate red coloured hair, much like my current form. He and I are close, closer than our older brother who is always stuck to our mother's side. His name forms, it's a sound and a feeling more than words. Ezekiel is the closest word I can find to name my eldest brother and it's still not quite right. I think harder as I look upon my other brother, his name is on the tip of my tongue.

"Stop it, Julius," Ezekiel cries. Julius, of course how could I forget. "Mother he's doing it again."

"Let your brother's creations be," Mother scolds.

I turn to see what Julius is doing, he's knocking down Ezekiel's toys. No sooner has my eldest brother built them, Julius laughs and has pushed over another one of Zek's winged creatures. I watch as the creature vanishes through the ethereal boundary and into the world below.

The boundary that separates our home is flowing like a current, it's gloriously white with a velvety texture.

I grab Julius by the hand and pull him away, I collect a scoop of the light and form a creature of my own. It resembles something almost like a horse, only the lines aren't as clean or smooth and the colouring isn't quite right. Julius applauds my ghastly creation like it's the most beautiful thing he has ever seen. I laugh wildly as the creature tries to walk. The light changes, it's dark and I'm alone. I feel overheated and the air in my lungs hurts, I open my eyes and I'm in my uncle's dining room tied to a chair.

I can see some light peeking through the closed curtains, it's daytime, but maybe late afternoon because the dining room is usually warmer earlier in the day. The room smells different than I remember, it's fresher. It reminds me of the time mum and I came to visit, and we arrived a day early. My uncle wasn't home, luckily, he had hired a cleaner to ready the house before our visit and the elderly woman let us in. I look around at the cabinets and see there's no sign of dust collecting, I guess Deklan kept his word about keeping the house in order for me.

I crane my neck until I can see the gun cabinet in the corner, it's still locked with all the guns in place. The house is eerily silent, I'm certain I could hear a pin drop on the carpet upstairs if I listened hard enough. Why would Maura bring me back here and where the hell is she? I twist the rope that's binding me to the chair and it pinches my wrists. My fingers are stiff from the suppression of blood flow and a tingling sensation is starting to gnaw at my fingertips. I try to influence the elements, but I'm not getting the usual pushback from them. I focus on fire and try to encourage it to burn the ropes, a small spark flickers on the edge of the knots, but the heat isn't in it. The spark fades and so does my optimism, the drugs in the vial must have weakened the connection to my magic.

The hairs on the back of my neck stand up and a cold shiver creeps up my spine. I close my eyes and focus on the air around me, when I close off my other senses it's easier to see through the haze. I can feel someone watching me, I can feel their hatred and disgust trying to pour into me like a toxin.

"Come out Maura, I'm tired of your games," I say.

"Glad you're finally awake," she says as she glides out from the shadows. Her heady arrogance perfumes the room with a bitter, bile scent. Her golden hair catches in the light and I'm taken back by her beauty. It feels wrong that someone so physically blessed can be so viciously cruel. "Your magic should be out for another few hours," she says.

"Is that why you finally have the courage to face me? You think I'm no longer a challenge," I laugh. "Speaking of actual threats, where are all your minions?" I ask.

"They will come if called," she says politely, but I can tell I've struck a nerve. I wonder how many gargoyles she has left.

"That's very wicked witch of you, shame you couldn't get the flying monkeys," I joke. "Are you going to kill me or what?" I ask, and she cocks a thick black eyebrow. "Haven't you seen any movie ever? Every time the villain delves into a ridiculously long speech about their motives or messed up childhood they get killed and the hero gets away. Trust me someone will come crashing through that door to save me while you're still babbling on and on…" She slaps me, hard. My eyes water and I can feel the grazes from her long claws that have scratched my skin.

"I don't understand it," she says, taking a seat beside me.

"Don't understand what?" I ask.

"What the big deal is. Seth, Aedan and even Shaylin are giving up everything for you, it makes no sense," She hisses.

"Jealous?" I ask.

"Of you, never," she replies, but I can feel the envy inside her, its ripe and green.

"You never thought I was going to destroy the fae did you?" I ask.

"All of this has been for what, power?"

"Oh please, stupid fairy tales and prophecies. I was hired to complete a job and I always deliver," she says.

"Hired by who, the Queen?" I ask.

"Oh darling, it's not good business practices to share clientele secrets," she replies reaching forward and sinks her nails into the back of my hands. I bite down on my lip to stop myself from screaming, I feel the warmth of my blood as it trickles to the surface of the fresh wounds. I refuse to look down at it, I won't give her the satisfaction of my pain.

"You're pitiful, I can feel your insecurities weaving themselves around your body like a second skin. The truth is you're forsaken, and it terrifies you," I tell her. Her face tenses and I see a flash of a man with the same colouring as hers, he's carrying a satchel and she's begging him to stay. "Did daddy never love you, is that why you're such a bitch?" I snap.

She sucks in air like she's sucking on an invisible straw, her fingernails release their hold on my hands and she straightens her shoulders. I can feel her trying to build a wall between us, she doesn't like me seeing the skeletons that are hanging in her closet. She smiles broadly exposing her fangs and leaves the room.
I can hear her ascend the staircase, there's a creak in the floor that I know well from all the times I've stepped over it in my bedroom. I hate the thought of her touching my things, but I guess it's better than her having her hands on me. I push past the feeling of nausea that's stirring within me and turn my attention to the more important things like trying to break free of my restraints.

I try leaning forward to loosen the ropes with my teeth, but the binding across my chest is pulled too tightly and pins me in place. I can't move forward so I try pushing my weight backwards, the chair is old maybe I can break it. I begin tilting, I'm trying to angle the chair, so it hits the floor on its weakest point. I'm just about to fall when I hear a ringing upstairs and it isn't the house phone. I lean forward and stop wriggling, so I can listen. My abilities are weak, but not gone, I focus on the emotions overflowing from Maura's energy. She is frustrated. Whoever hired her is negating on their side of the deal, it's probably the only reason I'm alive right now. Maura shouts demands that I can hear without effort and she hangs the phone up exasperated. The person on the other end didn't give her an answer, and I can feel the indecisiveness struggling within her. She's going to hold off killing me until the person agrees to her new terms, I close off her emotions and put my concentration back into the chair.

-85-
Aedan

My brother wouldn't have left without saying goodbye, but if his proposal didn't go as planned there's no telling how he would have reacted, and Seth has always preferred to run from his problems, especially when they are the emotional kind. I wish he was here, I hate the feeling of dread that sits in the pit of my stomach when he's gone. After he died something in me shattered and it took all of my strength to keep myself from falling apart. I flipped a switch and cut myself off to the emotions, it was too painful pretending I was okay. Forcing myself day after day to ignore the fact that he was nothing more than a rotting corpse that was a million miles away was torture. Denial was the only way I could survive. When I saw him coming down that hill in Ireland I thought I had finally snapped, the grief had won its battle and sent me insane. He will be back, I'm sure of it. The second he knows Adaline's in danger he will come back for her, his bruised ego won't be able to stop him, not with how much she means to him.

The women have taken the first half of our party, porting can be a tricky business if you're not careful, the last thing we need is for someone to end up halfway through a wall, so multiple ports are necessary. The orange haired tramp comes back to collect me, she flutters her extended lashes and caresses her hand over my thigh. I'm repulsed by her approach, which I shouldn't be, I've had more than my fair share of paid services from women like her. Still, there's something about her that screams worthlessness and it isn't appealing. She picks up on the vibes I'm sending out and adjusts to a more professional embrace.

I see the erratic pulsation of the porter's skin as she releases her magic, the faint smell of sulfuric acid and heated plastic fills the air. Most fae wouldn't detect the scent and humans wouldn't stand a chance, but my heightened senses take in everything. I can hear the rush of her blood as it quickens with the surge of magic, I can feel the subtle change of temperature in the air around us and my eyes can see the tinge of pink that pools in her cheeks as she exerts herself.

In a flash, we arrive in the heart of Dallas, my stomach lurches, but thanks to the juice I don't feel the urge to vomit. Deklan, Tripp and Shay are waiting for us, each of them looking a little green around the edges. Neema is on the other side of the orange haired woman, looking as pristine as ever. Jason, Beetok and Mikael have been dropped closer to Adaline's home to scope out the area. The other woman returns and links arms with her sister. Both of them reach out for us to link arms, I place one hand in Shay's and the other in the porters. Everyone else does the same and before I know it the sick weightless feeling has returned, and I open my eyes to find myself in the woods behind Adaline's home. We are too far back to see the house, but I know the area well and can pinpoint the exact location of it behind the vastness of the trees.

"Good luck, be sure to call us if you make it back alive." The girls say, one of them kisses Tripp's cheek and his body shivers in response, I hope it's because he's repulsed. He was lucky enough to have someone as divine as Adaline and to slum it with anything less is disgraceful.
I send out ripples through the earth trying to pick up the locations of any enemies that might be lingering on the outskirts. The earth responds hesitantly, it isn't keen for the violence that's going to ensue. The earth finds no traces of the gargoyles resting in its rich soil, it's possible they are inside the house or even perched on top of it. The sun is starting to go down and I can smell the evening dew trying to settle on the grass and leaves surrounding us. The cloak of darkness is going to be the only advantage we have, gargoyles can see better in the dark, but their other senses aren't as strong as ours and their bulky bodies make them slow.

"Mikael said that most of the gargoyles abandoned Maura after the attack on the Island, the few that were absent from Bristeal Mountain total six. It's unlikely the three that survived the attack would have come back to support her," Neema says.

"There's eight of us against six of them, nine if you include Adaline," Shay adds.

"We don't know what kind of state she's in," I remind them.

I still haven't completely healed from the bloodletting I endured. I try to ignore the bitterness that's taking root inside of me. I should have kept Adaline safe, but I put my brother's desires above her safety and look where we are. I won't make that same mistake again. I divide our group into pairs, Neema and Shay will enter from the west, Deklan and Tripp will approach from the south. We are waiting for Mikael, Beetok and Jason to arrive at our meeting point with their surveillance of Adaline's house. Tripp is pacing back and forth, he's more anxious than the rest of us or maybe he's just not as good at hiding his emotions. Neema keeps looking at Tripp and when their eyes connect I can see something between them. There's something they aren't telling me.

"Tripp, I want a word," I say. I walk a small distance until we are just out of earshot, I hear Deklan's weight shift as he glances in our direction, but he stays at his post.

"What is it Aedan?" He asks, but I can feel his attentions elsewhere. "Don't give me attitude! You're lucky to still be breathing right now, if it wasn't for Adaline and your father I would have killed you long ago," I snap, I feel my fangs starting to slip. "What do you know about this?"

"I know nothing about this, I'm just concerned with Adaline's safety," he says. I can hear the fraction of a jump in his heartbeat, he's lying. I wrap my fingers around his throat and lift him up against a tree.

"Tell me what you're hiding," I hiss.

"It's… nothing," he chokes. I tighten my grip until his face turns bluer than a corpse. When he reaches his limit, I drop him to the ground.

"Tell me or I'll kill you here and now," I say without hesitation.

"I can't tell you, she doesn't even know yet," he mutters through gasping breaths.

"Adaline's pregnant," Neema says appearing behind us. Tripp's eyes turn wide, Neema isn't lying. "It's not just about Adaline for him, she's carrying his baby."

"How long have you known?" I ask Neema.

"I had an inkling when we arrived at the portal, but I knew for certain when she left for court. I don't think she knows yet, it's the reason Tripp and I came to court," she says.

"You should have said something, you know what happens to fae women when they are pregnant," I scold. Neema flinches at my rage, and the earth shakes. It's not often that I let my emotions get the better of me or my element, but my anger is explosive.

"Leave her alone, she had her own shit to deal with, this isn't her fault," Tripp retorts.
"Not another word about this, no one can know. Can I trust you both to do your jobs and not get sidetracked?" I ask. They both nod and Tripp seals his worried mouth into a firm line.

As we walk up the small hill I can hear the others have finally arrived. Jason watched the house, but it's closed up with heavy shutters and there's minimal movement inside. Mikael and Beetok spotted three gargoyles positioned on the roof of the house and they suspect the other three are in the air awaiting instructions. I send Jason and Mikael east and the others to their posts. Beetok and I will be entering through the front door, I have always favoured the direct approach in battle.

-86-
Tripp

"Everything alright?" My father asks as we traipse through the thick underbrush towards Adaline's house. The woodland trees are eager to aid our approach, but I keep the magic on the edges of my fingertips, so we can keep our cover.

"Fine," I reply.

"We will get her back son, don't worry," he assures me with a squeeze of my shoulder.

I can sense the other's as they brush past trees and shrubs as we encroach the house. The only person I cannot sense is Aedan, but I can feel the magic he's pulling from the earth, and with the level of power he's tapping into, his plan for him and Beetok to be the distractions is definitely going to work. We can see the back fence from the edge of the tree line, now that darkness is upon us I can see the unaccounted gargoyles hovering above the house. If I didn't know any better, I would think they were bats flying in the distance. Everyone should be in position, we are just waiting for the signal from Aedan. He didn't give us anything specific, but he was confident we would know when to attack. My father's head cranks to one side and his ears perk up, he hears something I don't. The magic in the trees calls out, they feel the tension building and so can I. This battle is going to annihilate everything in its path and it will threaten our secrecy.

There's an exploding commotion coming from the front of the house, I guess that's the signal. My father leaps over the high fence in a single bound.

Once he's inside I hear the others forcing their way through the protective layer of gargoyles and into the house. I scale the fence after them, the sounds of battle ricochet off the other houses in the street, I have to contain this. I use all of my magic and tap into every living plant surrounding us forcing them to spread and expand. The branches weave and interlock forming a solid dome over the house, when the branches reach the apex I seal the dome shutting it around us. No light penetrates the wooden dome, less air can filter through the thickness of the branches. I loosen the vines at the top of the dome, just enough to let the air through. I can hear the faint sounds of the gargoyles trying to break through the strong boughs, each time they break through I make another layer of foliage in its place.

I fall weakly into the dirt; a burst of light penetrates through the blackness. Someone has broken a window and the light from inside the house filters across the back porch into the yard. The light illuminates a path for me to follow if only I could stand. I try siphoning some of the energy from the trees, I take just enough to give my body the strength to move so the dome can be sustained. I kick up my feet and run towards the light. I enter a kitchen that runs off the back porch. Pieces of broken tables and chairs are left in shattered pieces across the house. There are two piles of crumbled stone on the floor and lashings of black blood spilled across the walls. The wall beside me bursts open, a clawed gargoyle collapses to the floor, and Neema is riding atop him like a cowboy training a bucking horse. Neema sinks her fangs into its already wounded neck, she spits the chunks of flesh to the floor and wipes the black blood off her lips with the back of her arm, she looks wilder and more dangerous than anything I have ever seen.

"You good?" She calls.

"Yeah just weak," I reply.

I follow her through the crumpled remains of a broken building that might have once resembled a happy home. We walk into a large room, I see Aedan, Deklan and Shay standing around Adaline.

331

Adaline looks weak, she's tied to a chair with bruises and abrasions on her face and arms. Maura is positioned behind Adaline with a glistening silver blade held against her throat. Beetok appears beside Aedan and the two of them lurch forward to attack, but they meet a solid force field that electrocutes them, their bodies collapse and crumple. My father shifts into his wolf state and attempts the same assault but is propelled into the next room. Maura laughs wildly like she's enjoying the show, she presses the blade deeper into Adaline's neck. Jason approaches from a back room. I see his eyes fall to Aedan and he stances himself to attack, Shay grabs his wrist stopping him from touching the force field.

"Pull back your magic and I won't hurt her," Maura orders. She looks like a cornered animal, thrashing out instinctively for survival. "You won't break the blood shield, only she and I can enter."

Aedan regains some of his strength and stands, his face is more vicious than I have ever seen him. The way he looks right now he scares me more than Seth ever could and that asshole almost burnt me alive. Neema looks from Adaline to me, I can see a thought cross her mind. Blood shield. To build a blood shield Maura would have had to use Adaline's blood as well as her own, but she doesn't know that Adaline has a piece of my blood coursing inside her. Neema unsheathes a blade from her belt and tosses it to me. I don't waste any time and charge through the barrier.

-87-
Adaline

My breath is stuck in my throat, if I breathe too deeply the blade Maura is holding against me will penetrate my skin. Aedan's body is convulsing on the floor not two meters in front of me, Deklan sheds his humanlike skin and hurdles himself at the invisible field. The shield shimmers a sparkling crimson before catapulting Deklan into the next room where I think I hear him land inside a wall. Maura is barking orders while my friends regroup themselves. Aedan is back on his feet and looks as savage as the memory I have from his human life. His eyes are pitch black with rage and his penetrating stare doesn't leave Maura's line of sight. I try desperately to force the magic into my hands to free myself, but it doesn't respond as it should.

There's a flash of movement on the other side of the room, Tripp's running towards us, he has a small sword in his hand and there's a look on his face I have never seen before. I brace myself to watch him recoil from the shield like Aedan and his father before him, but he doesn't crumble. Instead, the shield burns white hot and he pushes his way through, I can feel the shields unwillingness to let him past, but it hasn't got a choice. Maura throws me aside, crashing me into a wall.
The chair shatters enough that I can start freeing myself from my restraints, I'm finally free and ready to face Maura, but she has Tripp pressed tightly under her. He doesn't have the physical strength to fend her off, his blade has fallen to the floor and I reach out for it, but Maura is ready and sends me flying into the wall with a gentle thrust of her hand.

Tripp takes advantage of the distraction and flips Maura off his body and goes for the blade. I use the piece of rope that's hanging from my wrist and jump on Maura's back. I pull the rope tightly around her neck. Tripp lurches forward and stabs the blade into her chest just below her heart, she falters and begins to fall. On her way down, she pulls the blade from her chest and stabs the dagger directly into Tripp's heart, his eyes go wide, and I feel the shock of the blade as it pierces him.

Maura collapses to the ground and Tripp is dead before his body hits the floor. Deklan's howl pierces my ears making me release my grip on the rope. The shield falls around us as Maura begins bleeding out on the dining room carpet. I crawl toward Tripp, but I can hardly see through the tears. My senses pick up something, Aedan has crouched down behind me, but that's not what I'm feeling. Maura pushes herself forward with the blade still in her hand and it's aimed at Aedan's heart. I don't think, I jump forward and push Aedan out of the way, shielding him with my body. I lock eyes with Maura and the magic in me flares. Fire explodes from my fingers until her body is covered in flames. Her blood-curdling cries drown out all other sounds and her body spasms as the fire burns itself out on her skin.

When the flames dwindle, and her screams come to an end, I don't even need to look at her to know she's dead. Her once lustrous blonde hair is stained red with splatters of blood and blackened with char that is still smouldering. The smell of scorched hair mixed with the coppery scent of congealed blood makes my stomach lurch. I suppress the bile that rises and force it back down. I won't lie, Maura deserved this, she deserved worse, she was the vilest kind of person and her wickedness ran deep, but she was a life that I ended. This is different than the guilt and hatred I feel for myself when I think of the people who died because of me. Maura is dead because I wanted it. I killed her because I decided my life and the lives of my friends meant more to me than allowing her to live. I know if we were in a court of law they would pat my back and send me on my way. But I'm a killer, that's what she turned me into and that's something I'm going to have to live with for the rest of my life. I just hope it's a weight I'm strong enough to carry.

Deklan is crying over his son's body. Tripp's face looks almost peaceful as he's cradled in his father's arms, he looks like a small child. I'm gutted and distraught by Tripp's death, but Deklan's heartache cuts me deeper than any of my own feelings could. Parents shouldn't have to bury their children, it isn't fair. Deklan cries heavier and my body aches in response. My head begins to waver until my thoughts have trouble forming words in my mind. My shoulder starts to prickle, the numbing of pins and needles spread across my torso. I look to the right side of my chest; the blade Maura had aimed at Aedan is protruding from my skin. Strangely enough, there's no blood to be seen, just the steady flow of pale gold fluid dripping from my wound. How pretty, I think to myself looking at the liquid. I see Shay and Aedan's faces change to panic when they focus on the blade and the seeping stream of gold. I laugh out loud as I rub the tacky substance between my fingertips. It has the consistency of blood, slightly thick and a little sticky, and it begins to dry almost instantly between my fingers. It seems silly for them to be so concerned by something so stunning.

My knee's start to feel weak, but Aedan catches me before I fall. I feel intoxicated, the room spins and the insane urge to giggle keeps making its way to my lips. Perhaps the blade was coated in a hallucinogen, I reach my hand to pull the blade from my chest, but Aedan stops me. I fade into blackness where the world is quiet and peaceful, at least until I wake to the excruciating pain of someone pulling the blade from my chest. It's a sharp and sudden onslaught of white-hot pain that renders me unconscious.

The next time I open my eyes I find myself back in my room at court. There's a figure sitting next to my bed. I long to see Seth so I can apologise for the way we left things, as my eyes adjust I realise the figure belongs to someone else, Deklan, and what happened comes flooding back to me. He's wearing clean clothes, but I can still see some dark brown spots of blood that have dried on his neck and arms. I remember Tripp's body and the distressing way Deklan clung to it.

Tears begin to well, I try to sit up to offer him some comfort, but I'm held in place by a burning awareness in my chest.

I remember the sensation of the metal blade as it scratched my bones, splintering them ever so slightly. The blade hurt worse coming out than it did going in. I think the shock of being stabbed subdued the pain, but when they pulled it out I felt everything. I try to move my arm, but the tight wrapping of bandages pins it firmly to my chest.

"How do you feel?" Deklan asks.

"I'm so sorry Deklan," I start to tell him, but I find tears come more easily than words. He hugs me closely and we cry together until there's nothing left for us to give.

"My boys gone, but at least I still have you, my darling girl," he says and plants a loving kiss on my forehead. He tells me to rest and settles me back into my bed.

"Where's Seth?" I ask. "Is everyone else okay?" I plead.

"He's fine and so is everyone else, they are getting some much-needed rest. Just sleep Princess," he says.

There's a gentle knock at my door, I see Neema and Shay standing there. Both dressed exquisitely in flowing gowns and the only signs of battle are the thin wraps of cloth bandages on one arm or another, which I'm sure aren't even necessary thanks to their speedy healing. Deklan excuses himself and tells my friends they can't stay too long. Something flashes across Deklan's face, a knowing look that Shay nods to in response. I haven't the energy to focus on the meaning of their unspoken agreement, but I hope it's a sign that they are building a friendship. Neema sits formally in the chair where Deklan had sat, while Shay spreads out like a cat on the end of the bed.

"Are you okay my lady?" Neema asks.

"I'm fine," I reply, allowing the tears to fall from my eyes. Tripp's gone and I'm alive, it isn't right.

I feel sleep teetering in the corners of my eyes as they flutter open and closed, I also feel nausea start to rise in my stomach. I don't even have time to warn Shay to move before it makes its way to my mouth. Neema must have seen it coming on my face because she has a bowl under my chin before the first wave escapes my lips. Four times I continue to vomit and just when I think I'm going to die, the urge eases and Neema is wiping my face with a cold cloth. Shay looks more than mildly disgusted by my illness and has shifted to the other side of the bed.

"Forgive me," I tell them.

"I'm just glad we don't get illnesses like that anymore, it's disgusting," Shay mocks.

Neema looks at Shay with wide eyes. I think she's going to chaste Shay for her informalities, but she says nothing. Shay's eyes widen in response. An unspoken wave passes between the women and I admit I'm more than a little confused.

"What's wrong?" I ask.

"Adaline, do you remember when Neema told you about her work for the royal families?" Shay asks.

"Yes, you worked for the women and cared for their babies," I reply.

"It was more than that, all the women in Neema's family have a rather special talent. There is a reason she served every ruler in the Egyptian dynasty. She can sense certain things," Shay explains.

"Sense what?" I ask.

"Pregnancy, my lady," Neema whispers.

Usually, I like hearing stories of their past but right now I don't understand why this is relevant information for them to be telling me.

Then I look from her face to the bowl she has politely covered with a piece of cloth. A flashing calendar races through my mind trying to remember what day it is. Since the plane crash, my periods have been irregular and it wasn't unusual for me to skip a month or two. The first time I was late, I was still in the Dallas hospital and the Doctor assured me it was linked to stress and my body would right itself when it was ready. I have been on the pill since I was sixteen, but I haven't exactly remembered to keep my birth control current with everything that's been going on. My god how could I have been so stupid and let this happen, how pathetic can I be? The only silver lining is that I'm not fifteen and on MTV, fighting with my baby daddy over child support.

Looking back over the last few weeks with new insight I can see I have been having symptoms for a while. Constant tiredness and nausea, but I hadn't thought anything of it and put it all down to stress.

"Did he know?" I ask Neema.

Neema's eyes begin to swell with water and she replies with a nod. Tripp died saving my life and the life of his baby that's growing inside of me. I lower my head and touch my good hand to my stomach, I can't feel anything, just the rise and fall of my breathing. I know without a second thought what I'm going to have to do…

Coming 2019

The Final instalment of The Seelie Court Chronicles

Renewed

Adaline must decide who she wants to be if she has any chance of surviving the final battle and keeping her loved ones alive.

Murderer, Mother or Monarch?

Being all three seems an impossible burden to carry, sacrifices will have to be made.

Will this be the end of the fae or the beginning of a new era?

About the Author

Hailing from the suburbs of Sydney Australia Jessica grew up in testosterone-fuelled surroundings, overwhelmed with football, fighting and alpha male prowess. To escape the ferociously masculine world her five brothers created around her she turned to the far-off lands of books for salvation.

When Jessica's own creative thoughts could no longer be contained and the pages of the books she read didn't fulfil her needs she turned her vivid imaginings towards paper and pen. In writing she discovered a kind of freedom she had never known, the euphoria consumed her. Writing like a woman possessed she beckoned the world of her dreams from the deepest recesses of her mind and thrust them into reality.

Jessica has a unique perspective on the human condition that captivates her readers leaving them on the edge of their seats, begging for more. She brings a relatable down to earth quality to her characters that will make you laugh and cry. Her beguiling world of fantasy, betrayal, and love will have you completely hooked.

The SCC Soundtrack Two

1.   Breath- Taylor Swift feat Colbie Caillat
2.   Don't Look Back in Anger- Oasis
3.   Let Me Go- Hailee Steinfeld, Alesso, Florida Georgia Line, watt
4.   Without You- Avicii feat Sandro Cavazza
5.   Drive- Incubus
6.   Yellow- Coldplay
7.   You And Me- Lifehouse
8.   Somewhere Only We Know- Keane
9.   I'll Be- Edwin McCain
10.   Overbehind- Flor
11.   Too Much To Ask- Niall Horan
12.   Wolves- Selena Gomez and Marshmello
13.   Let You Down- NF
14.   All Falls Down- Alan Walker, Digital Farm Animals, Juliander, Noah Cyrus
15.   Here Comes The Sun- The Beatles
16.   Two Princes- Spin Doctors
17.   Bloodstone- Guy Sebastian
18.   Silence- Marshmellow and Khalid
19.   Life Goes On- E^ST
20.   Something- The Beatles
21.   Split Stones- Maggie Rogers
22.   Stargazing- Kygo, Justin Jesso
23.   Homemade Dynamite- Lorde, Khalid, Post Malone and SZA
24.   Distant Sun- Crowded House
25.   Scared To Be Lonely- Martin Garrix, Dua Lipa

26.   Lonely Together- Avicii, Rita Ora
27.   Rich Love- One Republic and Seeb
28.   Meant To Be- Bebe Rexa, Florida Georgia Line
29.   The Spectre- Alan Walker
30.   Highway To Hell- AC/DC
31.   Alive- Krewella (acoustic version)
32.   Him and I- G-Eazy and Halsey
33.   River- Eminem and Ed Sheeran
34.   Home- Machine Gun Kelly, Bebe Rexha and X Ambassadors
35.   Never Be The Same- Camila Cabello
36.   Dancing In The Moonlight- Toploader
37.   Lemon To A Knife Fight- The Wombats
38.   Only To Be With You-Roachford
39.   Coming Home- Sheppard
40.   Swing Left- Jeremy Neale
41.   Circle- Edie Brickell and New Bohemians
42.   Better- Mallrat
43.   Way Down We Go- Kaleo
44.   Colours- Emma Louise
45.   The Other Side- Jason Derulo
46.   Light Surrounding You- Evermore
47.   Tired- Alan Walker and Gavin James
48.   Colourful- Jukebox The Ghost
49.   Alone- Alan Walker
50.   Til The Casket Drops- ZZ Ward

Sexual Assault is NEVER okay

Sexual Assault is something that no one should ever experience, sadly that doesn't mean it isn't happening. In my writing I have touched on a confronting issue and I hope that this isn't a trigger for anyone reading this book. If you have been triggered by this topic, please speak to a professional and get the support you need.

Please be aware that this is NOT in any way for shock value, but to highlight another perspective in a traumatic ordeal.

Often when we talk about sexual assault we speak about the survivor's personal experiences, which is extremely important, but the focus in my book surrounds the impacts of witnessing a sexual assault, which is something many people tend to forget about.

There is help available. Recovery is not easy, it requires work, and it's often not fair, but it is possible to recover from experiencing or witnessing a sexual assault.

If you or someone you know has witnessed or experienced a sexual assault, please seek help with the following information or contact your local emergency services or doctor.

Be brave, be kind and be forgiving to yourself, because it isn't your fault and you are stronger than your worst experience.

Australia

If you have experienced or witnessed sexual assault or sexual harassment, please call 1800RESPECT (Phone: 1800 737 732) for support or information. Counselling can be provided 24-hours a day, 7 days a week. If you are feeling unsafe right now, call 000.

All other countries please contact your local support service or doctor. A service can be located by a quick internet search just type your 'location' and 'sexual assault support' into the search bar and you will find a service closest to you. Below are just a few broad links that you can look at for examples and advice.

https://www.plannedparenthood.org/
https://www.sass.org.au/
https://thercc.org/
https://crcvc.ca/for-victims/

www.ingramcontent.com/pod-product-compliance
Lightning Source LLC
Chambersburg PA
CBHW070310040726
47501CB00019B/1983